Gladio

We Can Neither Confirm Nor Deny...

Steve Chambers

Zymurgy Publishing

First published in Great Britain in 2013 by Zymurgy
Publishing, Newcastle upon Tyne UK

Copyright © 2013 Steve Chambers

The moral right of Steve Chambers to be identified as the
author of this work has been asserted in accordance with the
Copyright, Designs and Patents Act 1988.

All rights reserved. No part of this publication may be
reproduced or transmitted in any form or by any means,
electronic or mechanical, including photocopying, recording
or any information storage and retrieval system without
permission in writing from the publisher.

A CIP catalogue reference for this book is available from the
British Library.

ISBN 978-1-9035063-8-7

This book is a work of fiction. Names, characters, businesses,
organisations, places and events are either the product of the
author's imagination or used fictitiously. Any resemblance
to actual persons, living or dead, events or locales is entirely
coincidental.

Cover artwork Paul Goldsmith
Back cover concept We Are Shift
Front Cover layout Simon Hubbard
Front cover font New Press Eroded courtesy Galdino Otten
Printed and bound by CPI Group (UK) Ltd,
Croydon, CR0 4YY

Author Details

Steve Chambers was born and brought up in Nottingham. He read mathematics at Imperial College, London and now lives in the north-east of England where he writes and teaches scriptwriting. An established dramatist, he has written extensively for all the dramatic media. For TV, he has written episodes of 'Casualty' and 'Byker Grove' and his feature film 'Hold Back the Night', starring Sheila Hancock, opened Critics Week at Cannes '99. He has adapted 'Waterland', 'The Grapes of Wrath' and 'Robinson Crusoe' for BBC Radio 4's classic serial and he co-writes the long-running Radio 4 comedy 'Highlites'. 'GLADIO: We Can Neither Confirm Nor Deny' is his first novel.

Acknowledgements

I am grateful to the following for their help, support and general encouragement.

I'd like to thank Malcolm Wright who was there at the start, Northern Arts for giving me the opportunity to write the first draft and New Writing North for their generosity, advice and feedback.

Thanks are due to all those who read and responded to the manuscript drafts, in particular, Ross Irvine for his important strategic suggestions and Mike Mould for his detailed notes.

I'd like to thank Sean Hamil for a wonderful research trip to Northern Ireland, Dickie Hodgkiss for the introductions and financial research in Amsterdam and Kate Adie for giving up her time to talk to me.

Finally, I'm indebted to my publisher, Martin Ellis, for his hard work, persistence and determination.

PREFACE

'Gladio' is Latin for 'by the sword'; the sword in question being the murderous, two-edged, stabbing short sword that carved out the Roman Empire.

'Gladio' is also the code-name of a shadowy CIA operation set up in western Europe in the 1950s and 60s to wage a guerrilla war in case of a communist takeover. Secret, self-contained cells were recruited, trained, funded and armed. The personnel were a mixed bag; criminals, pardoned fascists, assorted weirdos and other anti-communists, but in the fevered atmosphere of 1950s anti-communism, their background was disregarded. The Gladio network provided a convenient 'deniable' network for covert operations against left-wing governments and organisations. Missions Gladio operatives trained for included espionage, bombings and assassinations. The CIA suspended their operations in 1969 but the Gladio structure survived. The Bologna station bombing is now believed to be the work of an Italian Gladio unit. British and American governments have always denied that Gladio cells were set up in Britain... but rumours persist.

Time watches from the shadow
And coughs when you would kiss

W. H. Auden

PART ONE
Italy 2004

ONE

Overcrowded, hot, wildly expensive, the towns of the French Riviera flaunt a stylish confidence. Yet just a few miles to the east, where the mountainous coast sweeps from France into Italy, the Italian towns of the Riviera suggest a distinctly faded glory. Despite the statuesque palms and purple bougainvillea in their grounds, the grand hotels close to the railway and the sea have an air of neglect about them. Even in the heat of summer, few arrive by train now and fewer still linger here. The autostrada runs high above the coastal towns, swooping over impossible bridges, diving into long fast tunnels so that summer visitors, driving their air-conditioned cockpits back from Tuscany, can only glimpse the beauty of the 'Riviera dei Fiori' as they hurtle towards the French border. For those who look north, away from the sea, the landscape flashing by is enigmatic: valleys, hills and distant snow-capped mountains, the hinterland of a forgotten paradise before the next tunnel obliterates it.

The steep green hills behind San Remo are part of this mystery. A warren of tiny roads and unrecorded tracks with impossible gradients, terrifying bends and missing crash barriers leading to farms and smallholdings which cling to the hillsides; jewels of fertility among the relentless brambles. A good place to get away from it all; that's why John chose to settle here.

When he bought his rustico, his ancient olive-gatherer's cottage, it had no water, no electricity, no road access and the loo was an old olive pot stuck in the ground. On the hillside below the 'one-up, one-down' with the faded statuette of the Madonna between the small windows, were five crumbling, scorpion-infested terraces and sixty-five olive trees in dire need of attention. The two redeeming features of John's mountain

9

retreat were the views and the fact that it was so far off the beaten track. He'd sold up, come to Italy to get away from everything. Where once he'd wanted to make a difference, now it was invisibility he craved. In six months, he'd connected a water pipe, cleared the terraces, made a rough terrazza, repaired some of the walls, built an outdoor shower and made his bedroom comfortable. The physical labour suited him, made him feel useful, fit, optimistic even. That's when he'd started running. Every evening he loped through the olive groves, listening to the crickets and smelling the woods. Afterwards he felt liberated and energised but then again, maybe he was just satisfying the need to stifle the unquiet echoes of his past.

After an initial hostility, his ageing neighbour Giuseppe became friendly. Communication was rudimentary, a mixture of John's self-taught Italian and operatic gestures, but when Guiseppe realised John was serious about living in the hills, the barrel-shaped Italian with the bandy legs showed him how to repair the terrace walls and prune the olive trees. Guiseppi lived in San Remo and journeyed up to his olives on his ancient Vespa two or three times a week. Apart from him, John met the occasional local on the road but strangers were a rarity. That's why the car made such an impression.

It was parked behind John's ancient Land Rover in the recess afforded by the hairpin bend near the bottom of the path down to the road. Tinted windows, Milan plates, a silver Mercedes; he wondered what it was doing there. Then again, he wasn't the first to discover the area's potential. He had a brief nightmarish image of the hillsides covered in expensive villas then forgot about it - John was preoccupied with his water supply. He'd installed an eleven hundred litre tank on the terrace above the house but the water had been off for days now and the tank was finally empty. Reluctantly, he'd followed the plastic pipe a hundred and fifty metres back up the overgrown, terraces, hacking his way through thickets to see if it was damaged, but it was fine. The brambles tore his clothes, drawing blood, and by the time he got to the water meter he was in a foul mood. Someone had taken it upon himself to turn his bloody water off. Why? He turned the tap back on and listened to the water hissing down the pipe. He took the long way back, down the dirt track made by the water company, which is when he saw the car.

Two days later, the Merc was back. At dusk, John was walking along the road looking for the tail light cover, which had fallen off his Land Rover. When he first spotted the silver car, he wasn't really bothered. After all, if some property company was looking for land to build on, why wouldn't it come back? The idea of future development was depressing but nothing more. But after he had fixed the tail light back on, he noticed the Mercedes' tyres; they were new and fat, the complex tread packed with dirty sand. That was when he remembered. He stood up and looked round as calmly as he could but his pulse quickened. He walked slowly to the bottom of the water company track and looked up. He couldn't think why he hadn't seen them when he walked down - running up the hill in the sand, twin tracks made by fat, new tyres with a complex tread.

He walked the hundred and fifty metres back up to the house trying to rationalise the problem without success. Maybe the tap had been turned off by accident? Maybe he was mistaken about the car, maybe another vehicle had driven up there? Why would anyone turn off his water? Why come back and park behind his vehicle? He struggled to recall exactly who knew he was here. It didn't help. He was certain the car was here for him. It was time; they'd found him. They'd turned the water off to draw him out. He considered throwing everything in the Land Rover and driving off into the night but he'd made a commitment to his new home. He wasn't about to run away.

As the light went, he removed a loose stone from the terrace wall and took out a plastic lunch box hidden within. He removed the lid, unwrapped some oilcloth, checked the fading passport and the dog-eared bundle of cash before inserting the magazine into the small automatic. He replaced the box, lit the hurricane lamp, turned it down and sat in his sun-lounger listening to the crickets. Sitting in the lounger at night was a great way to watch the stars. Away from the city, the Milky Way was amazing, a sequinned scarf thrown carelessly across the sky, only tonight he wasn't stargazing. For once, he didn't open a bottle and listen to a Dylan cassette. Instead, he sat silently in the darkness, wishing he had a bigger gun and a dog.

He came awake with a start, grasping the automatic in his lap. He listened; a cracking of twigs and a rustling coming up from the road. Footsteps, definitely. He slipped the safety catch off, trying to suppress his own breathing so he could listen better. The footsteps came on, nearer and nearer, then abruptly halted. John listened but the night was suddenly still as if the whole hillside were listening with him. He considered shouting out or going to investigate but some instinct made him stay put. If they wanted him, they could bloody well come and find him. He didn't sleep again and by dawn, he was cold and exhausted. As the sun rose above the hills, he dismantled the gun and put it back in the wall. Then he had a cold shower.

As he combed his hair afterwards, he decided to confront whoever it was, find out what they wanted. He started walking down to the road. He felt like shit – his right knee clicked walking down the steep, uneven terraces, causing him to waddle rather than stride. He was hungry and he really fancied soaking in a hot bath. Then he stopped in his tracks.

The car was gone.

He had been so pumped up for a confrontation that he felt let down. He looked up and down the road, checking for the car, then felt idiotic. He hadn't heard it go. So what? He fell asleep didn't he? What about the footsteps? Must have been wild boar again. He'd lost a night's sleep for nothing. Besides, why would anyone be interested in him? At fifty-one, the ex-soldier, ex-journalist, ex-teacher, ex everything was well past his sell-by date. And after going without a night's sleep, didn't he know it.

He decided to treat himself and drive down to San Romolo for breakfast. It was a lovely morning and he sat outside Silvano's bar enjoying the view as he waited for his croissant and cappuccino.

Silvano appeared looking perturbed. 'Signor John? There is a phone-call for you... una donna?'

John looked up, puzzled. 'For me?'

'Sì.'

TWO

'John, is that you?'

The voice, for so long only heard in his dreams, came out of the past, exploding into his present, memories colliding with feelings, which stampeded through him. Alarm and fear competed with wonder, excitement, arousal. '*Jesus.*'

'It's me, Jess.' That voice again, that gentle lilt. He thought he'd forgotten but it was the same interesting, textured, husky voice.

'*Christ, Christ, fucking Christ!*'

He'd been all right. He'd found himself, accepted his fate, who he was going to be. His horizon had shrunk, his dreams had died; he'd had his adventures. He would never be a great journalist, never write his major work, never ride off into the sunset but it was OK. He had understood something important, come to enjoy his quiet routine. He didn't want any surprises.

'Am I speaking to John Bradley?'

John took a deep breath. 'Yes, it's me.'

'For heaven's sake, why didn't you answer?'

'What do you want, Jess?'

'To see you of course. What d'you think?' He said nothing. 'John?'

'I don't know, it's been so long.' It was her turn to pause. When she spoke again, her voice was quieter and more urgent.

'I have to see you.'

'Where are you?' He half-hoped she was in America or China. Somewhere far away.

'San Remo. Can I see you? It's important. Please?'

In his head, the thoughts hammered over and over. '*Just say fucking no. Just do it and it'll be over! Say No! That's all you have to do! Say No!'*

'Please,' she repeated, elongating the word slightly so that it became sensual, suggestive.

'All right.'

'I'll be an hour.'

He hung up and ordered a large brandy. He was angry with himself for agreeing to see her, but what could he do? He couldn't stop her. She could come up and find him. What was he afraid of? But he knew the answer.

Silvano placed the brandy in front of John and shrugged apologetically. 'The English woman call two times yesterday, and once last week.'

'What did you say?'

'That you were not here.'

'Thanks.' Silvano nodded. 'Irish.' Silvano looked confused. 'The woman,' John explained, 'she's not English.' Silvano shrugged and headed back inside.

She ran straight to John, throwing her arms around his neck and kissing his cheek. Again he was flooded with sensation and emotion. Tastes, images, memories competed with the present and he was suddenly self-conscious about himself. If he'd known, he'd have made more of an effort. She stood back, looked him up and down and nodded.

'Not bad,' she said with a smile. 'Not bad at all, John.'

He'd recognised her immediately. The same slim figure with that slightly angular way she had of holding her head. She was still stunning but close up, he could see the age in her. Lines around the eyes and mouth had furrowed and sharpened. If anything, she was even thinner than she had been. Her hair was greyer and cut short but it suited her. She looked tanned and fit and her eyes were still that brilliant blue. She wore an off-white, loose-fitting linen jacket with a matching knee-length skirt. She looked at him, then slapped his midriff gently, 'Look at you.'

'Bit more of me than there used to be,' he grinned sheepishly.

She shook her head. 'Yes, it suits you,' She looked round at the tiny village. 'Is this where you live? It's lovely.'

'This is the nearest village; I've got a place in the hills.'

'Can I see it, John?' she asked eagerly. 'Oh please, I'd love to?' her head bobbed slightly in that familiar way but it wasn't the same. Her accent was lighter than he remembered.

'How did you find me?'

'You pay taxes, John. Trust you not to have a mobile.'

'You speak Italian?'

She shook her head. 'French.'

'What do you want?'

'I was in the area. I heard you'd ended up somewhere near here. I just wanted to see you.' She seemed genuinely pleased to see him but he didn't believe it.

'Let's have a drink. We should celebrate, shouldn't we?' she said, heading into the bar. She returned with two beers and put them on a table. As she picked up her glass, the skin on the back of her hand wrinkled and folded slightly, reminding him of his mother's hands.

'Cheers.'

'Cheers.' He sipped his beer and stared at the view. In the valley bottom he could just make out the spire of Isolabona church. The people down there would be going about their lives, shopping, chatting, the butcher's shop full to the door but no one in a hurry. He didn't speak. She watched him.

'How are you, John?' He glanced at her then looked back down the valley. 'You've changed.'

'People do, after twenty years.' She nodded but her quiet assurance nettled him. 'And you, Jess, have you changed?'

'Of course I have.'

'So tell me about your family,' he said coldly. 'I'd like to hear about your husband. What does he do? How many kids have you got?'

Her eyes hooded and the lines round her mouth became sad. 'Don't be a bastard, please?' She was suddenly vulnerable. He was pleased it mattered, pleased he could wound her, surprised at how pleased he was. And then, knowing he had the

15

power, he felt a pang of guilt. Christ, his insides were churning again.

'So what, now?'

'We go to your place. I'd like to go to bed with you.'

For a moment, he wasn't sure she'd said it but his cock stirred unexpectedly. He wasn't in control of anything. 'Well er... look... the thing is, Jess...'

She began to laugh. 'If you could see yourself, you're blushing.'

He got annoyed. 'That's beside the point.'

'You're not going to turn me down, are you? Is there someone else?'

'No. I just don't think it's a good idea.'

'Why shouldn't we do it, we used to all the time?'

'We were different people.'

'We were younger. You think we're too old?'

'We don't know each other anymore. And that's not why you came here.'

'You're right. It's a bad idea.'

He stared at her. 'Why say it then, to test me out? A joke?'

'Don't be angry.'

'What did you expect for Christ's sake?'

'I needed to find out if you were still interested.'

'By making a fool of me?'

'Can we go to your place? I have to talk to you, in private.'

He shook his head and stood up. 'No, Jess, I don't want to talk about anything. That stuff's over, finished. I have a new life here.'

Now she stood up, eyes blazing. 'For Christ's sake, John, you're not going to say no. If you'd meant it, you'd have done it when I phoned!'

Her unrestrained passion unleashed some of the Ulster dialect of her youth. Her energy surprised him. 'Take me up to your place. Hear me out. If you say no, I'll go. I promise.'

'Then you're gone.'

THREE

On the drive back up into the hills, John found the familiar clattering of the diesel comforting. Jess was lost in thought. Parking the Land Rover, he was pleased to see he had the hairpin to himself, the mysterious Mercedes absent.

They climbed up to the rustico. Jess was like a child in her excitement. She ran round inspecting the house and cooing over it. 'It's gorgeous! How did you find it? You're so clever.' He couldn't deny it pleased him to hear her enthusiasm.

An unspoken truce seemed to have been agreed between them, as if she'd decided to behave like a guest instead of a ghost. She was in the bedroom, staring at the view across the hills from one of the two small windows, when he took her a glass of sparkling wine.

'It's amazing, it could be Malaya.'

'Could it?'

'The house on that distant hill over there, the trees round it look like palms, could be jungle and there's some mist behind it.'

'Here, have some wine before it goes flat.' She turned but didn't take the wine. Instead she regarded him seriously, as if searching his countenance for something. He was about to speak when she kissed him, gently at first, then with more intensity. Still holding the glasses, it was difficult for him to respond until she took them from him and set them down. She pulled him towards her but he pushed her away.

'No, no.'

'What's wrong?'

'It's a bad idea, remember?'

She stood up, straightened her clothes, sighed and nodded in resignation. She went to walk past him but her hand brushed

17

against his in a delicate caress. He remembered her doing something similar before.

'Is there someone else?' she asked, her eyes searching his.

'No,' he smiled. 'You're my first guest.'

She picked up the glass, gulped down the wine and shrugged. 'Can't blame a girl for trying.'

'What do you want, Jess?'

'To see you. Is that so terrible?'

'No. I'm sorry, I'm not used to visitors.'

She nodded. 'You're right. It's been a long time.'

'Look, why don't you go and explore while I make some food?'

She thought for a moment, then smiled. 'OK.'

He watched her go, then busied himself with cooking. The familiar activity settled him down and he began to enjoy the novelty of cooking for two. It was good to have someone there. 'Maybe it's true. Maybe she just wanted to see me,' he muttered to himself.

'What?' She appeared in the doorway.

'Nothing. Talking to myself. Comes from living alone.'

They ate mostly in silence. Afterwards, they sat on the terrace sipping wine and watching the sun go down. The gathering dusk seemed to mirror their mood, a lengthening of shadow, a sharpening of focus.

'I need your help, John,' she said, apropos of nothing.

'No.' He replied.

'They've started again.'

He refused to exchange the happiness of the day for her paranoia. He said quietly but firmly, 'That's all old hat, the west is obsessed with al-Qaida now.'

'Who funds al-Qaida? Who set it up?'

He stared at her and shook his head. 'I don't want to hear this.'

'It's the same strategy as always. Set up arms-length organisations, wait for terrorist outrages to create instability, panic, confusion. Move in behind the inevitable backlash... it's already started for Christ's sake!'

'I don't care.'

'You used to. It's unfinished business.'

'We lost. That's why I'm living in the middle of nowhere like a fucking hermit.'

'We both lost, John.'

'What happened to you, Jess?'

'If you had the chance to win, wouldn't you want to take it?' He shook his head slowly. She leant forward. 'The moment I saw you I felt... the chemistry was back... between us. I thought you felt the same. You do, don't you?'

She was right of course, right and wrong. 'That's not the point, Jess.'

She shook her head. 'What's happened so far is just a taster. There's much, much worse to come.'

'I've had my go, it's someone else's turn.'

'What if there isn't anyone else?'

'There's always someone else.'

'But if you knew you could stop it before it really got going? Wouldn't that mean something?'

'Jess, I'm done with all that.'

'Are you done with Maria?'

Something snapped. He strode over to her and grabbed her. 'Are you!? Is that the real reason you came here?'

She winced. 'You're hurting me,' but he didn't loosen his grip.

'You walked out on me, Jess. You think you can just walk back after twenty years as if nothing's happened?'

She shook her head. 'No... no.' He let go. She staggered away, rubbing her wrists and angry now. She waved a hand at his olive grove. 'Are you so scared of losing all this?'

He took a step towards her and she flinched. He stopped, put his hands up in a gesture of surrender. 'I'm sorry, I didn't mean to...' Leaving the sentence unfinished, he turned and walked down to the terrace below and stood in the gathering dark, listening to the familiar sounds of the night and waiting for his anger to subside.

After a few minutes, she followed him. She put her hand on his shoulder, turned him round and kissed him. 'It's me that should be sorry,' she whispered.

'I've disappointed you.'

'No, no you haven't. You've been fantastic.'

He yawned unexpectedly. 'Sorry, it's been a hell of a day.'

'Didn't realise I'd tired you out.'

'It's not just you. I didn't get much sleep last night.'

They walked along among the olive trees in the dark without speaking. The warm sultry night brought out a riot of fireflies, pin-pricks of violent red looping and diving. The night air was full of scent.

'It's so fresh here.'

'Might be a storm later.' Across the valley, in the surrounding hills, the lights of distant settlements hung like tiny jewelled clusters.

'Why didn't you get much sleep last night?'

'Couple of days ago, no three, there was a strange car parked behind mine.'

'What kind of car?'

'Silver Mercedes with tinted windows. Yesterday it was back. I thought they'd turned off my water.'

She gasped involuntarily and shrank back into the shadows. 'They were here?'

'Now don't start that again.'

But her mind was elsewhere, her body tensed and frozen, listening into the darkness like a wild animal.

'Ssh! Listen!'

He listened. 'What? I can't hear anything...' Just as he said this, he heard it - a car coming up from the village. He craned his neck, caught sight of its lights; it was travelling fast, on full beam.

She tried to run but he held her to him. 'On its way to Baiardo. When it's gone past, we'll go to bed,' he said calmly, forcing her to stand and wait for it to pass, but it didn't go past. It skidded to a halt below them. Doors opened, they heard the sound of feet running across the gravel, then up the terraces towards them. Torchlights danced drunkenly below as whoever it was came on. He watched, fascinated, then he was running, pulling her behind him, along the terrace, away into the night.

FOUR

Running along in the dark, John was having trouble holding himself together. He hadn't slept in twenty-four hours and seeing Jess again had shredded his innards. He had a dodgy knee and had drunk too much but he was fitter and leaner than he'd been in years. He knew the terrain and he was angry.

Half-running, half-loping, ducking under branches, he was boiling with a rage that kept on growing. He was angry with himself for his weakness, for agreeing to see her, for listening to her, for going to bed with her. He was angry with her for turning up, for thinking she had the right to walk back into his life and turn him inside out, for lying to him, for coming here and liking the place and bringing apocalypse down on it. He was angry because if he'd thought just for a moment, he could have been prepared, had money, passport, his gun; at least his gun. And he was angry with them, the unseen thugs invading his land, and this rage was the most primitive, the most unquenchable. Until this moment, he hadn't realised how much his tiny house with its five terraces meant to him. His fury gave him energy and an unexpected clarity of thought. It propelled him along the terrace then up through the brush when he turned and started scrambling uphill. It was pitch black but his time on the land hadn't been wasted; he'd explored the hills round the rustico. Scrambling up the terrace walls in the dark was tough but Jess didn't complain. Her former loquacity had deserted her as if she knew that to speak might make him explode. They didn't hurry, there was no need to in the dark and he knew where he was making for. After five minutes clambering they stopped and looked down on the house below. Pencil beams of light picked out bits of the terrace. They heard shouts and some coughing. John counted the torches.

'Four, possibly five,' he said, breathing hard.

'I'm sorry.'

'What gives you the right to do this to me?'

'It's not my fault.'

'Those people were waiting for you!'

She shrugged helplessly. 'What do we do now?'

'Sit here and wait until they leave.'

'All night?'

'Got a better idea?' An angry silence returned. It would be uncomfortable waiting all night but what else could they do? On the other hand, they'd be easy to spot come daylight.

'Couldn't we circle round and get down to the Land Rover?'

'Too dangerous.' His fury rose in him again at his impotence. Below, one torch detached itself and began moving along the terrace in the direction they'd come.

She pointed, alarmed. 'They're following.'

'They're just looking. No one could follow us through that scrub.'

A bat fluttered close before veering away. John stared down at the torches milling around his house and tried to think. He wished he'd asked her more questions when he'd had the chance but he hadn't wanted to talk any more than she had. Ignorance had been bliss, now it felt like a curse. She interrupted his thoughts, tugging at his sleeve and pointing down the hill. He followed her gaze. The lone torch had turned up the hill and was following their path. Other torches were hurrying to join in.

'How the hell..?' he began, then stopped as he heard a distant, gagging choking. 'Jesus, they've got bloody dogs.' Jess tried to get a better look but he was already dragging her up. 'Come on!'

'What if they let them go?' She struggled after him.

'They won't,' he said without breaking stride.

'How can you be so damn sure?'

'They'll lose them if they do.'

The next hour nearly broke them. Brambles and thorns snagged and ripped at their skin. Creatures slithered and scurried in the undergrowth but they hurried on, sweating like pigs, which excited the growing band of insects that joined the pursuit. After twenty minutes, they stopped, snorting for breath. Jess was overcome by a coughing fit and fell to her knees.

'I'm so thirsty.'

'We can't stop here.'

'I've got to rest, just for a minute.'

He wasn't in great shape either. His mouth was dry, his knee was sore and his right hand was bleeding from a deep gouge. The hillside had flattened slightly and they had lost sight of their pursuers. After a few moments, the pencil beams of torches appeared on the skyline below them and they heard the dogs gagging straining on their leads. They took off again but despite pushing on hard, their speed began to slow. After another half hour, Jess had developed a painful blister and was limping badly. Then the moon came up. Compared with the pitch dark of before, it was like being lit up by a searchlight. John appealed to the heavens.

'Nice one, God. Fucking thanks.' They stopped again, hidden under a huge overhanging olive.

'I thought you were an atheist.'

'I am. Oh shit!'

'What?'

'They've let the fucking dogs off the lead.' They could hear the animals quite clearly now; their pursuers couldn't be more than sixty metres away. He turned back to Jess. 'Come on!' but she shook her head.

'I can't.' He stared at her, bent down and lifted her but it was an awkward hold and his strength failed after a few steps.

'Leave me here.' He tried again and this time, managed a few steps with her in his arms. Breathing heavily, sweat dripping from his brow, he put her down again.

'Save yourself,' she pleaded, pushing him away. 'Please, I've caused enough trouble.' She kissed him lightly him on the cheek then settled down at the base of the tree. Emotions crowded in again; anger, frustration – he felt his eyes welling up. He'd wanted to punish her, to hurt her but he couldn't leave her here like this.

23

The dogs were very close now. It was over. He'd run out of road. It wasn't that he didn't want to escape; he just knew he couldn't go without her. It wasn't heroics; it was selfishness. He knew he wasn't strong enough to survive the guilt of saving himself. The realisation drained the energy from his tired limbs. He sighed and leaned back against the tree.

'Stupid. Thinking we could take on a bunch of thugs at our age.'

'Were we stupid to take them on before!?' Without waiting for his answer, she spat, 'Well I don't think so!'

Angry shouting distracted them. The dogs were barking furiously and howling in an odd distracted way. The dog handler was screaming at them, 'Viene qui! Viene qui!' There was some swearing which John couldn't translate. Another man was shouting now and in the background was a new sound, a low rutting grunting.

Jess struggled to her feet and peered down the hill. 'Something's upsetting the dogs. They've veered off.' The torches were moving away to the right. Beyond them, he could just make out the dark, muscled backs of the dogs jostling and pushing but there were too many, eight, nine, maybe more. Then he understood. 'Cinghiali.'

'What?'

'Wild boar. The dogs have found a scent and gone after the boar instead.'

'I don't understand.'

'They must be cinghiale hounds, that's why they're so good on this terrain. Come on.'

'Are you sure? They'll come after us again.'

'We've got a chance, or don't you think it's worth trying at our age?'

'Fuck off.'

John started uphill again.

'Can't we go back down and find the road again?' He slowed his pace but didn't stop. She tried again. 'I hope you know where you're going.'

He was dog-tired and thirsty, but he knew they would be

waiting if they tried the road. This way, they might just have a chance.

FIVE

After an hour of going uphill, they stumbled across one of the mule tracks that criss-crossed the hills. One direction went steeply upwards; the other appeared relatively level, so they went that way. After the rigours of the chase, they walked at an easier pace and found a water pipe which allowed them to slake their thirst.

Exhausted, they rested frequently and spoke little. John replayed the events of the last few days. Everything about the day felt like a carefully planned emotional ambush. What if the whole thing was a set-up? The car, the pursuers, the flight, maybe it was all to make him think he had no alternative. After all, he'd never actually seen the pursuers. A car, torches and some dogs that conveniently stopped following; what did it add up to? But, if she had set up the whole thing, why was he so important? He didn't know what to believe so he kept his thoughts to himself and kept on walking.

As dawn broke, the path began to descend a ridge. Through a break in the trees, they caught sight of a village in the distance. John saw it first.

'Do you know where we are?'

' Perinaldo, I think.' On the edge of the village, they stopped by an old water fountain and cleaned themselves up. Jess's skirt was stained and ripped but with her jacket over her skirt, she looked surprisingly good. John had a few euros on him and 7.30 a.m. found them boarding the first bus into Ventimiglia.

The ride was uneventful. Leaving the bus, the bustling chaos of the Friday market engulfed them. African hawkers peddled watches and vivid handbags from illegal pavement pitches. People shouted greetings, street traders called the odds, motor scooters buzzed like irritated wasps and cars hooted their frustration. After the dappled shade and calm of the hills, hot, bright, noisy Ventimiglia made the events of the night seem a million miles away.

'Come on, I'm hungry,' he said.

'No, we'll get a hotel first,' she responded.

'How? All my credit cards, passport and stuff are at the house. And you left your bag there.'

She was unperturbed. 'I've got a credit card.' She reached into the hem of her skirt. 'Emergency one, sewn into here.'

He was sick of her springing surprises on him. He was tired, hungry and pissed off. He gave her an angry glare, turned on his heel and marched away. Confused by his mood swing, she watched him stride away then hobbled after him. As she caught him up, she asked 'What's the matter? Where are you going?'

'The place where ordinary people go in situations like this, the police.'

'Are you mad? For God's sake! Can you slow down, my feet are damned sore.'

He stopped and faced her angrily. In the middle of the town, they looked out of place. He was dirty, unshaven, his shirt ripped. Her legs were scratched, her skirt filthy and she looked tired and bruised as if she'd been in an accident. A passing policeman glanced at them. Jess smiled at him then pulled John under the awning of a hardware shop.

'Italy is corrupt, run by the mafia.' Jess whispered. He shook his head and tried to pull away but she held him close. 'It began here. Have you forgotten?'

John stared into the shop window, at the odd mixture of machetes, hammers and drills displayed alongside stainless steel coffee machines and pasta makers. On another day, he would have wandered in. 'I have a life here, Jess.'

She wasn't finished: 'Provence, the French Riviera is one of their strongholds. D'you think it doesn't extend to here, of all places? For Christ's sake, they're running the place!'

Down the street, the African peddlers melted away as the policeman approached. Illegals, without papers or permits, controlled by brutal French gangmasters, they were bussed in for the day from Nice but always the next day, they were back.

'Suppose I go to the police?' he asked. 'What d'you think they're going to do? Take me outside and shoot me?'

'They'll come back later, when you aren't expecting it. You'll have an accident, disappear.'

'Why?' but he knew the answer.

'They think you're with me.' He sighed, fearing she was right. 'At least sleep on it?' she pleaded, sensing his doubt.

He stared down the street. The policeman had gone and the hawkers were creeping back to their pitches. He knew she was right. Everywhere has its shadowland, its underworld ruled by fear and violence. Italy was no different. Beneath its beautiful, passionate countenance, the truth was always veiled.

'John?' she asked, her face crinkled with concern. He took a deep breath and nodded in surrender.

SIX

With no papers, John suggested a truck drivers' dive near the autostrada for anonymity but she overruled him again. They weren't truck drivers and someone would talk. Instead, she chose a bright, beach-front hotel, marched up to reception and demanded a room, playing the annoyed tourist for all it was worth. They'd come for the day when some kid on a scooter had stolen her bag containing everything. Now they were stuck here with one credit card between them. Damn kid, damn country, damn police. The manager apologised for the police, the bambino, his country and offered them a room on the fifth floor .

The room had a small balcony and a sea view. In the midday haze, the mountains marking the border with France tumbled into a shimmering, pale blue sea. On the shingle beach below, the usual contingent of sun worshippers had claimed their sun-loungers and umbrellas. Tarzan, the life-guard, was lounging sideways in his high chair and talking animatedly into his mobile. The beach restaurants were starting to fill with lunchtime punters. An elderly man walked along the water's edge carrying a heavy bucket full of coconut pieces, uttering a mournful sing-song cry. 'Cocco bello, bello, cocco bello,' he lamented, as if calling the name of a dead child. No one bought any coconut.

After breakfast and a long, long shower, they closed the shutters and lay down on their beds, the room hot with the heat of the day. They groaned in unison, newly aware of their bruised and complaining limbs. John's legs twitched as if they were still walking. Jess fell asleep immediately but he lay, listening to the traffic and the screams of children playing on the beach. He kept trying to empty his mind but memories kept rearing up and galloping past. Finally he fell asleep.

It was dark when he woke. He looked up and saw Jess watching him. She'd slept badly, suffering dreadfully with night sweats in the stuffy room. He'd been dimly aware of her getting up and showering several times while he'd slept. He knew she must be exhausted - Christ knows, he was - but he found himself being cool and distant towards her. A plan had formed which didn't include her. The knowledge of his deception made him feel guilty, which made him grumpy and uncommunicative.

She sensed his mood and tried to talk. 'I'm sorry about all this, but you are still part of it. You made that decision after Maria.'

'I'm not interested in 'isms' anymore. Slay one dragon and another one appears in its place. It's the wrong target.'

'But if the dragon's right in front of you, you don't have a choice.'

'Wanting to slay the dragon is just another fantasy. We have to learn humility, to use less, to want less, to be less,' he said with a sigh. 'The oliveta is a start.'

She sat by him on his bed and touched his hand tenderly. 'We are on the same side. We always were.'

Her familiarity irritated him. 'No we bloody aren't. Besides, in twenty years, who's going to care?' Angry and hostile, he turned to face her. 'Well!?'

'We will.' She turned and went into the bathroom. He looked out into the night. The air was cooler now and a delicious breeze fanned the awning. Out to sea, a huge motor yacht, lit up like a gin palace, carried its cargo of souls slowly westward. In the darkness, the surf beat a funereal drum roll on the shingled beach below.

They had dinner in a deserted beach restaurant. The food was delicious but he didn't notice; he was too busy drinking. Back at the hotel, he had several more drinks so that oblivion was inevitable and discussion impossible. In his inebriated state, he fell asleep easily but although alcohol put him to sleep, it couldn't stop his dreams or his nightmares.

It was after eight when he woke and the sun was streaming into the room. Jess was still sleeping. He dressed quietly and left the room, closing the door gently behind him. Outside, the town was coming to life again. In the ornamental gardens by the river mouth, a group of people sat dejectedly among a pile of belongings in the shade of the palm trees. Swarthy men with moustaches glared fiercely at anyone who stared too long. The women wore baggy silk trousers and headscarves and shouted to their children in a strange tongue as they ran back and forth. Albanians, he guessed, wondering whether to stop or move on. As he walked towards the bus stop, he sympathised but he knew what he was going to do.

He got off the bus below San Romolo and took the mule track through the olive groves bypassing the village. Few people used the route these days and he saw nobody. It felt good to be back in the hills, smelling the wild thyme, eating tiny wild plums. It was such a beautiful day that the idea of plots and intrigues seemed ridiculous.

He'd made the decision in front of the hardware store. He knew all the arguments against going back but he had to be sure. She had no definite proof of anything and the idea of losing his little house had begun to hurt like a physical pain. He hated the thought of leaving it with his belongings scattered about. They'd probably gone by now. If everything was OK, he'd get what he needed and drive back in the Land Rover. If everything wasn't OK, well, he'd take his chances.

He'd discovered the mule track when the Land Rover had broken down and he'd had to walk. It had the advantage of allowing him to approach the house along the terraces, so if anyone was waiting, he'd see them first. When he first caught sight of his home through the trees, his heart missed a beat like a sweetheart seeing his love. He couldn't hear anything, but he decided to wait half an hour to see if anyone was moving. The terrace was quiet and peaceful. Insects buzzed about their business, a gentle breeze fanned tree branches. John checked his watch and whistled. There was no answering whistle, no shout of alarm. He crept nearer to the house and hid again. It looked deserted. The chairs on the piazza were on their side; the door was open. He picked up a rock and threw it. It hit the roof with a loud clatter and rolled off onto the piazza. Despite scaring himself, nothing happened. Finally he stood up and walked up to the piazza.

When his flat in Leeds had been burgled, they'd trashed the place and shat everywhere. He braced himself for the mess he knew was inevitable. What he found was an anticlimax. Everything was fine. No broken windows or smashed crockery. It was weird, as if he'd died and come back to find the new occupants enjoying his place, except they weren't there. Perhaps it was a set-up after all. They hadn't meant to hurt them, just to create an impression of fear. His papers and passport were missing and there was no sign of Jess's bag but the place was intact.

He tidied up methodically, stacked the chairs and put them in the cantina. He was carrying some rubbish down to the terrace below when he saw Guiseppe lying in the shade of one of his olive trees. He smiled. Guiseppe loved his siestas, they reminded him of his youth. He would lay out a cloth under a tree, share his lunch with John and drink his dreadful home-made cinzano. Then he would sleep for a couple of hours. Seeing Guiseppe made up his mind. Whatever happened, he was staying. This was his home.

Not wanting to wake the sleeping Italian, he tiptoed past with the rubbish. Then he noticed a machete lying on the ground beside Guiseppe. He looked again at the old Italian. He was lying very still and his face was livid and dark. He gulped air as the awful, obvious possibility formed. Trembling, he knelt down and felt the old man's pulse. He couldn't find one. They'd killed Guiseppe.

Time slowed, his limbs felt heavy and he thought he was going to faint. He turned round in a complete circle, unsure what to do. He went to the wall and took out the bundle containing the gun. Then he heard someone laughing. He froze as he tried to work out where the voice had come from. It came again, followed by voices talking on a terrace somewhere above. Then he heard a dog barking. They were still here, looking for them.

He began to panic. In a moment, they would find the house, realise that he'd been back, recently. He had the gun but how many would he shoot before they got him? Even if he won, he knew there would be others. Besides, a firefight would bring police, press, the whole circus down on him and his rustico. He had to get away. The house was between him and the way he'd come. He decided to go down and try for the Land Rover. He ran along the terrace into some undergrowth then began to slither down towards the road. It was hard going and he crashed through overgrown, untended terraces, ripping himself on the thorns and landing in a heap on the road. Picking himself up, he tiptoed down towards the bend.

The Mercedes was there again, parked behind the Land Rover. He couldn't see anyone. He heard excited shouts from above, they'd discovered that he'd been there. He ran a few paces towards the Land Rover then stopped dead; the tyres had been slashed. He looked round desperately and caught sight of Guiseppe's old scooter. The voices were getting louder; maybe they'd let the dogs go. He ran to the scooter, shoved it off its stand and began to freewheel down the road because he couldn't get the engine started. It probably saved his life. His pursuers didn't hear the scooter and didn't see the middle-aged English man struggling as he careered down the twisting mountain road at twelve miles an hour.

Finally, he managed to start the engine. He put on Guiseppe's ancient helmet, pulled down the visor and drove the elderly scooter away. About ten minutes later, he heard a squealing of brakes and a horn of a car coming down the road behind him. He was wondering what to do when it blasted past him, horn blaring. The noise was so loud he nearly drove off the road but they didn't recognise him. As far as they were concerned, he was just another peasant on an ageing scooter.

He rode the twenty miles to Ventimiglia in about an hour. He parked the scooter near the police station and walked along the sea-front, passing the park. The Albanians had disappeared, moved on he supposed.

Jess was checking out when he stumbled into the hotel reception, dishevelled, dirty and bleeding again. The manager stared at him with a puzzled frown; Jess had just told him that John had returned to France. She raised her eyebrows to the manager implying this was something she had to deal with a lot. Then she took John's arm and walked out into the street with him.

'Where have you been?'

'Guiseppe's dead.' She looked at him, confused, her mouth framing the unspoken question. 'My neighbour up in the hills. They killed him.' He paused. 'That's where I've been.'

'You fool. Why did you go back?'

'I wanted to tidy up.' She frowned, puzzled. 'I know it sounds crazy but I hated the thought of just leaving it. It's my home; well, it was.'

'I'm sorry, John. Come on, we've got to get out of here.'

He stared at her, angry, impotent. He was snared, press-ganged. What a fool he'd been. Her arrival had sealed his fate, ended his sojourn and caused Guiseppe's murder.

They bought some clothes from the street market, then a second-hand Citroen from a back-street garage he'd used in the past. Cash in hand, no documents, no questions asked. Jess insisted on the battered Citroen because it had French plates. It would blend in more easily where they were going.

Leaving Ventimiglia, they were held up behind a funeral. A horse-drawn hearse led the cortege followed by family and friends. A discordant band stumbled behind. Everyone wore black. It was like something out of a film but John was impatient to get away. The funeral felt like a trap and unsettled him. Finally they overtook the procession in a cloud of dust, speeding north towards the high Alps. After a couple of miles, the cliffs closed in, the road narrowed and began to climb.

'Where are we going?' he asked as the car slowed on the incline.

'North, the Low Countries.'

'What's there?'

She shook her head. 'You don't need to know that yet.'

'For fuck's sake, Jess,' but she put a finger to his lips and raised her eyebrows. 'It's for your own safety.' John grimaced.

The gun dug into his ribs and the money belt was a little tight but he was comforted by them. He'd learnt the hard way. Jess didn't need to know about them.

As the car groaned its way up the mountain road, leaving the Mediterranean behind, he wondered again how he had ended up here. Why him? Why now? But he already knew the answer. Maria had given it to him years before.

PART TWO

Yorkshire 1984

ONE

It was a time of flux, a time when the past stopped and the future began. A whole way of life was dying and, in the process, giving birth to the modern world. The 31-year-old John Bradley mirrored the confusion around him. Despite the daily battles of the miners' strike, his life seemed to be on hold as if he was waiting for something to happen. Still young, he had become disillusioned. He dissipated this feeling by drinking too much.

The night before everything changed, it rained heavily; a sumptuous, full-bodied August storm, a release after the heat of the previous few days. Cut off from the world by the dark and the torrent, those awake retreated into themselves to replay their hopes and fears. As always, in the darkness of the night it was their fears that dominated.

Something had woken Maria from her sleep. Looking out of her tent through the curtain of water, she could see strange lights at the base. Was something happening? She strained to see but couldn't be sure. There was a light which danced and bobbled violently. Lying next to her, Jess moaned and turned over. The sound comforted Maria and made her feel safe. She snuggled back into her sleeping bag and listened to the rain pounding on the flysheet.

Driving his brand new Ford Sierra up the motorway, Eric Guttridge peered through his windscreen as if trying to discern the future. He thought he caught a glimpse of a flashing blue light up ahead but, in the downpour, he couldn't be sure. He craned his neck, caught sight of its lights; it was travelling fast, on full beam. He held it together, slowing the car while his heart raced. As he passed over the motorway, he saw what he'd feared: down below, a police roadblock stopping every vehicle. He swore to himself, first in relief, then in anger. Fuck, he would have to travel by the back roads now.

The storm was hammering at the window when John woke. His brain was sluggish, his eyes sticky. He groaned, as he realised that he'd flaked out fully clothed on the settee again. The tiny coffee table next to him was covered with empty lager cans, the ashtray overflowing with fag ends and roaches. The smell made him gag, forcing him off the settee and onto his feet. The room spun violently, then settled. He stood swaying, staggered a few paces and threw open the sash window. Despite being in the heart of the city, the damp summer air which filled the room and his lungs was fresh and clean. He stared out into the impenetrable dark and wondered again what the future held.

The Nobel fucking drinking prize at this rate.

The turntable needle was still clicking on the end of 'John Wesley Hardin'. Christ, he couldn't even remember listening to Bob Dylan. He switched it off and carried the cans and ashtray into the tiny maisonette kitchen, depositing them in the overfull rubbish bin. The kitchen was in an even worse state than the living room. Instead of washing up, he'd used every piece of crockery and cutlery he had, until the sink, draining board and shelf were covered in used pans and plates. Some had been left so long that mould had begun to grow. He was going to have to sort himself out.

A loud banging on the front door interrupted his absorption. 'For fuck's sake, it can't be four-thirty!' he muttered to himself looking at his watch. He opened the front door complaining, 'Your watch is fucking ten minutes fast,' but Naz grabbed him and propelled him through the rain and into the waiting crew car.

'Are we all in?' Brian asked from the driving seat.

'He is,' laughed Naz. This was the signal for Brian to accelerate away. A huge man, his torso towered above the driver's headrest, his arms bent double as he grasped the tiny steering wheel, his face up close against the windscreen peering into the rain. For some reason he'd never disclosed, Brian had an aversion to windscreen wipers and so used them sparingly.

'You look like shit,' Naz said, handing John a flask of coffee and a handful of aspirins from the front passenger seat.

As John swallowed them down, he said, 'It's the strike, everyone's complexion's going.' Certain he was going to vomit, he wound the window down and stuck his head out. The cold sweat mixed with the rain and revived him. The nausea passed. Winding the window up, John slumped back in his seat. 'How much fucking longer?' he asked.

Brian replied with his usual mantra, 'Don't knock it,' then the three of them chorused, 'Think of the overtime.'

It was something they had in common with the police. 1984, the year Orwell's predictions came true. Two revolutionary armies locked in mortal combat. Scargill in Sheffield, Thatcher in Downing Street, cruise missiles in Britain, the enemy within; the end of democracy. The miners' strike was a war for the truth to the soundtrack of Frankie Goes to Hollywood. The world was collapsing about their ears but the overtime was great. As the car sped on, John dozed off again. The rain eased with the coming of the dawn.

TWO

Half an hour later, the rain stopped altogether. A grey dawn was breaking over the country lane, which was pitted with puddles. Multiple headlights drove at speed down the middle of the small road, forcing a battered Ford Escort van travelling in the opposite direction to swerve onto the grass verge. The armoured convoy - police Transit van, two battered coaches and another Transit, all with wire grilles - hurried past throwing a bow wave of water over the little vehicle. The van driver, Billy Hatton, swore under his breath, then relaxed and smiled to himself as the convoy disappeared. He drove a short way then stopped by the turning for a private road into the forest which bordered the lane. He checked that the road was clear, then made the sharp turn into the forest and drove for about a mile before stopping in a secluded glade. The closely planted conifers marched away in darkening ranks until light and perspective were lost. Mist steamed off the sodden undergrowth, rising through the trees obscuring the track. A dismal place, it deterred visitors, which was good. Hatton lit a cigarette and settled down to wait.

Sometime later, a red Ford Sierra appeared in the clearing, bumping over the rough ground like a young animal before skidding to a halt. Eric, a dumpy, balding figure of around forty, got out and removed a heavy holdall from his boot. Struggling through the mud, he carried the holdall over to the Escort. Sweating and uptight, he kept looking round nervously as he handed the bag over.

The same age as Eric, Hatton worked out and was muscled and fit. He began to examine the contents of the bag methodically.

'You're late,' Billy Hatton said in a controlled Liverpool accent.

'Car wouldn't start. All that rain last night...' Eric replied.

41

'New car, you want to complain about that,' Hatton replied with mock seriousness as he rummaged through the holdall.

Eric nodded, 'It's all there..'

'Just checking.'

'I had to come the long way round. Police roadblocks everywhere... Fucking strike.'

'It's good cover, Eric. Besides, I haven't heard you complaining about the money.' Hutton tutted. 'New car. People might wonder about you affording that, on your wages.'

Eric was scared. 'I'll be off then.'

'What's your hurry? The A-team's not on till tonight,' Hatton smirked. Eric didn't answer but stood, hopping from foot to foot. Hatton shook his head, 'You're a sad bastard.'

'Better sad than mad.' Billy Hatton didn't like being called mad. He took a pistol from the holdall and pointed it at Eric.

'I am the fucking A-team,' he said with a smile. Eric shook his head. Hatton's smile disappeared as he put the gun into his own mouth. Eric watched fascinated as Hatton pulled the trigger. The gun clicked but didn't go off - it wasn't loaded.

'For fuck's sake!' Eric said rattled, before he hurrying away to his Sierra. He badly wanted to get home, back to his bungalow and normality, but the car refused to start. Seized with panic, he kept trying the starter motor until the battery began to drain. Finally, when it seemed it was dead, the engine caught. Eric revved it furiously to make sure it didn't stall, then skidded away in a noxious cloud of exhaust smoke. Hatton watched him go and smiled.

THREE

Three miles away, an atmosphere of brooding anticipation hung over the deserted terraced street. A few battered Austin Allegros and rusting Avengers were parked amid the puddles. A dog began to bark furiously; another answered. Almost in slow motion, the first police Transit nosed into the street followed by the first coach and all hell broke out. The first thing to be heard was the cry, a howling scream of battle. From front doors, alleys, side streets, erupting from hiding places behind gates and hedges, an irregular army of running men. Old men, young men, bald men, men with sideburns, moustaches, men with teeth missing all banging on the side of the coaches, grappling with the phalanxes of police struggling to prevent them. As the convoy passed, the pushing became a scrum. The pickets began to chant,

'SCAB! SCAB! SCAB!' Rocks were thrown but the cordon held as the convoy screeched through the colliery gates.

Naz filmed the events from behind the police lines while Brian held a microphone boom aloft and struggled to get some usable sound. A number of other crews did the same. John watched the familiar sight and yawned. He wondered what the fuck he was going to say about the strike in today's news report. After five months, what was there to say that was different from yesterday?

An hour later, the street was calmer. The police and the pickets faced each other in an uneasy truce. Halfway up the street Naz and Brian were setting up their equipment, getting ready for John's piece. Standing with police and pickets in view behind him, John faced the camera. He was tall and slim with fair hair and restless deep brown eyes. On good days, he looked

43

handsome; today his face was blotchy and there were ugly bags under his eyes. He'd had a lot of bad days recently.

'All right?' John asked Naz. Looking through the viewfinder, Naz squared up the shot and muttered to himself.

'You still look like shit,' then louder to John, 'Perfect.' At twenty-eight, Naz was the baby of the team. A good-looking Ugandan Asian, he kept his nose clean and got on with the job.

John looked at Brian, 'OK, big man?' Brian in his headphones gave the thumbs up and nodded. Brian was forty-nine, a competent sound-recordist and an Olympic drinker. Married with four kids whom he rarely saw, he had a nose like a red avocado and a D-Day haircut. Violently short, brilliantined with a centre parting, his grey-flecked hair looked like the skins of two undernourished rats lying on his head.

John checked his reflection in a small window in a terraced house. He combed his hair and turned to the camera when the front door opened. A harassed, overfed woman in her thirties appeared. 'It's you! Off the tele!' she announced. With a comb still in his hand, John nodded a weary smile.

'If you wouldn't mind?' he said apologetically, nodding towards the camera.

The woman looked at him and sniffed. 'Eeh, you reek of drink!' she yelled. Brian sniggered asthmatically. Naz grinned. A child of around nine appeared in the doorway beside the woman.

'Who is it Mam? Is it the busys?' the child asked, holding onto her skirt. The woman ignored him and nodded towards the police at the bottom of the street. 'See them down there?' John looked as the woman continued, 'They're not from round here, you know. Bunch of thugs... no sodding numbers on their shoulders... Do what they like...'

'I know, I know. Now if you wouldn't mind, I'm trying to...'

'Why don't you show it on the news, then?' the woman interrupted. Without waiting for a reply, she yanked the child out of the house, slammed the front door and hurried away, dragging the boy by the hand. John looked at Naz with a shrug, then took his place for the camera. Brian gave a thumbs up as Naz did a 3,2,1 count-down. Taking a deep breath, John began his piece.

'Just after dawn, the small mining village of Willington found itself in the front line as...' he broke off, distracted by the sound of running footsteps. Naz signalled him to keep going. '...as police fought a running battle with pickets. The...'

He didn't get any further. He was interrupted by the nine-year-old from the house, 'It's your car isn't it, Mister?'

'Get out of the shot,' Naz shouted, but the boy took no notice.

'It's your car isn't it? The one with NTV on the side?'

Brian lifted his headphones. 'What about it?'

'It's fallen over,' the boy sniggered and ran off. John, Brian and Naz exchanged a puzzled glance as the comment sank in. Then John ran towards the end of the street. He turned the corner to see the NTV crew car being bounced by a group of pickets. Something about the action got to him. It felt like a personal insult.

'What the bloody hell d'you think you're doing?'

'Getting our own back!' replied a big, good-looking miner in his thirties. The other pickets left the crew car and milled round John, jostling him.

'What for?'

'Being stuck up the rozzers' backsides...'

'I'm a journalist, I'm not on anybody's side!'

'That's why you always film from behind their fuckin' lines.'

'That's why he's full of shit,' said the big man. Laughter erupted from the pickets.

'I'd like to interview you.' A few pickets sniggered. John tried again, 'Why not? Tell your side of the story.'

The big man grabbed him by the lapels and hissed gently into his face, 'You're a wanker but worse than that, you're their fucking wanker.'

'I'm not on anyone's side. I'm caught in the middle of this thing.'

The big miner chuckled and shook his head. 'There is no middle ground,' he said lightly, as if stating the obvious to the village idiot. At that moment, Naz and Brian appeared round the corner with twelve policemen in riot gear. Naz began filming the scene as the pickets backed away. The big miner looked at them, then back at John and grinned. 'See what I mean?' he said, joining the other pickets. On a count of three, they tipped the crew car onto its side with a roar of triumph. The big man turned and winked at John. John couldn't help liking him. His fearlessness and good-humoured energy were attractive, admirable even. John envied his certainty. Life was so much simpler if you knew which side of the barricades you were on.

Later, John remembered hearing a brief sound of drumming and a cry of alarm before two snatch-squads of shield carrying riot police charged in from both sides, trapping the miners. They scattered in all directions, but the ringleader tripped as he began to run. The police fell on him, swinging their truncheons at his head, brutally kicking at his body, shouting obscenities as they did so. In an instant, the good-looking miner's face was a bloody pulp and his body limp. John shouted in protest and tried to intervene only to be pushed back roughly by one of the officers. Finally, the miner was dragged away to a police Transit. John looked at Naz; he was still filming. Great.

FOUR

The NBC team drove back with the nearside bashed in. The doors on the nearside wouldn't open and the front wing was bent but the car still drove. Brian and Naz joked about the brutal beating but the memory stayed with John. Brian stopped outside a dowdy looking country pub next to a scrap yard. Without commenting, he got out and stared at the unprepossessing pub exterior.

'Does it do food?' Brian asked.

'Is it open?' Naz asked. 'It looks dead.'

'Only one way to find out,' Brian said ambling towards it. John looked at Naz and shrugged. They got out of the car and followed.

Outside, the pub was nondescript, quiet and unobtrusive. Inside, it was down at heel, with bald carpets and badly in need of redecoration. It was also noisy and full to bursting with the percussive sound of clinking glasses and men drinking and talking loudly. Brian examined the extensive bar menu. John and Naz looked round the large bar trying to work out what was going on. How come the bar was so full at eleven in the morning? Over the hubbub, a cockney voice shouted harshly, 'Who let the fucking paki in?'

The talking in the bar subsided and stopped. John, Naz and Brian were the only show in town. Brian looked up from the menu. Naz stood dead still, his face impassive. John produced his press card from his suit pocket and smiled.

'Press, Northern TV.'

'He's still a black bastard.' Someone laughed, then thought better of it.

Brian leant towards John and whispered, 'Coppers.' John

scanned the bar. The smirking, whispering faces staring back were in white shirtsleeves, black trousers and boots. At the back, he caught sight of tunics, helmets, truncheons and other gear. He remembered the picket's bludgeoned face again; his fury returned. Brian nudged him. 'Let's go. Come on,' he said firmly. The three journalists turned to find their way blocked by two burly figures.

'Not yet, Sooty,' one said. The two men sniggered unpleasantly. John wondered if there was going to be a fight, when the two men began making strange animal noises. Quietly at first, then growing in volume and intensity until they were howling and jumping up and down, teeth bared, their arms flailing in their simian dance. 'Ooh ooh ooh,' on and on accompanied by the rest of the pub. Then, as if by some prearranged signal, 'Ooh ooh ooh,' segued seamlessly into 'boo boody boo boody boo boody boo' as they began the Peter Sellers Song, 'Goodness Gracious Me'. The rest of the pub joined in. Just when it seemed a fight was inevitable, the two London coppers moved to one side, still singing, allowing John, Naz and Brian to exit the bar.

Outside, John was furious. 'For fuck's sake!' he said. 'If they aren't reined in, someone's going to get hurt.'

Naz shrugged. 'Forget it, happens all the time,' he said getting into the car. John looked at the pub impotently. Then he remembered the footage they'd shot of the beating. Just for once, the boys in blue were going to have their cage rattled.

FIVE

John walked through the newsroom and entered Clemmy's office without knocking. She was busy watching news footage on a video monitor and didn't look up straightaway.

Clemmy Harris was thirty-four, short with huge eyes, violent red hair and drop dead gorgeous. She smiled, pausing the tape when she saw John. Then something occurred to her. She stood up and closed the door of her glass-panelled office. John had had breakfast and was feeling better. Apart from anything else, he was off for the next forty-eight hours. He watched Clemmy as she walked back to her desk.

'Did you see the stuff we got this morning?' She smiled and nodded, but something about the gesture was half-hearted. 'Not bad.'

'Not bad. It was sensational! You are going to use it?'

Clemmy nodded. 'Yes, we're leading on the car.'

'What about the beating?' She grimaced slightly and shuffled some papers on her desk. He thought she was teasing him. 'You're not going to use it!?'

'We can't.'

'I don't believe it!' he shouted. 'It's an assault, on camera. A bloody beating!'

'Or a difficult arrest. The police claim he assaulted an officer with a brick. The injured officer is now in hospital.'

'That is total bollocks! The only one in hospital is that bloody picket. I saw it happen, Clemmy. I'm telling you, the police are out of control, we've got proof!'

In the open plan newsroom, the raised voice caused people to look up from their typewriters. Outside, the sky darkened and rain began to spatter the office windows.

'We could find him, the picket I mean, get his side of the story. Why not? They've got to you, haven't they?'

'Come on, John. Who pays our bloody wages? With TV franchises up for renewal soon, the company has to be careful. The government is very sensitive.'

'It's great stuff.'

'We've seen it all before.'

'Twelve riot police beating a miner senseless!' he said angrily. 'And it's not an isolated incident. They do what they bloody like! Me, Brian and Naz went in a bar, it was full of them drinking.' Clemmy cut him off.

'After five months, the audience is bored with the strike and frankly, so am I.'

'What do you suggest? More Bugs Bunny?' John retorted.

'We haven't had a decent murder in ages,' was Clemmy's response.

'I'll see what I can do!'

John marched out of her office. Clemmy watched him go and sighed. Outside, the rain hammered desperately on the office windows.

SIX

Silhouetted against the glowering cloud, the giant golf balls of Menwith Hill RAF base crouched like an alien colony; a place of secrets in a secret world. A thousand yards distant, lying hidden in a clump of wet fern and grass, Billy Hatton was another secret as he scanned the base through binoculars. The rain came on harder. He shifted his view from the base itself to a makeshift encampment outside the perimeter fence. Tents and crude shelters surrounded a fire. A few women were sitting chatting. He picked out a beautiful, soulful woman with black hair and held on her. She was laughing and talking with a vibrant, sensual energy. A blonde thirty-something woman smiled back at her. Spiky, angular, fidgeting restlessly, she appeared the opposite of her black-haired companion, but she too was a looker. Hatton wouldn't kick either of them out of bed.

Hatton put down his binoculars and consulted a photograph. He nodded to himself; it was her all right. The rain came on harder still. Perfect. Hidden in a clump of trees near the road, Hatton knew he was practically invisible and the rain would keep dog-walkers and casual visitors indoors. Looking round carefully, he drew a telescopic rifle sight from his pocket and lined the black-haired beauty up in the crosshairs. As he watched, he saw her touch the blonde woman gently on the knee in a furtive, tender gesture. A serious, troubled look appeared on the blonde woman's face and she took hold of the other woman's hand. Even through the telescopic sight, the meaning of this stolen exchange was inescapable. Despite being a professional, something about the moment touched Hatton, awakening a tenderness he'd almost forgotten. He felt the beginnings of an erection. *Down boy.*

Shoving the telescopic sight back in his pocket, he got to his feet in a single, agile movement. A hard man given to hard living, he'd screwed down his own emotions until he felt nothing. But like every other living human, he carried the vast, invisible secret of his own past buried inside him, the dark and difficult memories that came unbidden in his dreams and against which he weighed and tested every new experience. And just as buildings and matter dissolve, so feeling and memory fade leaving behind their own flinty deposit. Pain leaves an indelible mark.

Despite being a natural loner, he was expert at what he did, well trained and part of a team. He knew not to ask too many questions. He looked around then shook himself violently like a dog, expelling the excess water from his waterproof jacket and trousers. Satisfied there was no one about, he walked the short distance through the rain to the lay-by where he had left the van. The situation was perfect, do the job now, get away. In and out, no fuss.

He was opening the back door of his Escort van when the police panda car pulled up behind him. Hatton looked round to see the young constable getting out of the vehicle and swore softly to himself. *Shit. What the fuck does he want?*

As he did so, he stood up straight and smiled good-naturedly.

PC John Roberts was in a bad mood about being on the two to ten shift. He'd had a blazing row with his wife Linda over missing his son's first birthday party. Their shouting had made the boy cry before he left. It wasn't his fault. The station was short-handed because of the strike but the row stayed with him, playing on his mind. He couldn't say what had made him stop but something about the man and the vehicle bothered him and anyway, he felt like nicking someone. PC Roberts walked through the rain towards Hatton.

'Coming down in ropes, officer?' Hatton smiled. The young, rugby-playing constable towered over the weathered scouser.

'Would you mind telling me what you are doing out here, sir?' Roberts asked in his blunt Yorkshire way.

Hatton smiled, 'I was going to ask you the same thing. Shouldn't you be on the picket line earning overtime?'

PC Roberts didn't smile. 'If you wouldn't mind, sir?'

Hatton kept on smiling. 'Been for a walk...'

'In the rain?'

Hatton grinned, 'It's only just started like...' He kept smiling but he didn't like the way this was going. *Why the fuck don't you piss off? Get back in your fucking car and fuck right off.*

The policeman looked across at Menwith Hill base and then back at Hatton's binoculars hanging round his neck. Hatton caught the policeman's look and the unspoken question. Touching the binoculars, he grinned and volunteered, 'Bird watching... travel all over...'

Roberts looked at Hatton; he didn't look like a bird watcher. 'Looking for anything in particular?'

Hatton shrugged. He was out of his depth and he wanted to go. 'Thought I might see a kestrel but er the rain put the kybosh on that.. Look, I'd better be going... we're both getting soaked, eh?'

'Would you mind opening the back of your vehicle?'

Yes I fucking would, you thick cunt...' is what he thought. What he said was, 'Any other time, but I'm in a hurry, mate...'

'If you wouldn't mind, sir?'

Shaking his head, Hatton opened the back door of his van to reveal the holdall inside. *From here on in, it's shit all the fucking way.*

'What's in the bag?' asked PC Roberts. Hatton pulled the sides of the holdall apart and the policeman found himself looking at a rifle barrel and some cartridges. He'd been right to stop. The moment of exultation was followed immediately by fear. As the adrenaline pumped into his system, he looked up to see Hatton pointing a handgun at his midriff. Hatton was calm and his eyes were dead cold.

'I wouldn't do anything hasty if I were you...'

Billy Hatton shot him twice in the guts. A small, surprised cry erupted from PC Roberts' mouth as he slid down the back of the van and slumped to the floor. 'You aren't me,' Hatton said as he stepped over Roberts and closed the back door. Throwing the holdall into the passenger seat, Hatton got into the Escort and drove away.

Lying on the road in the lay-by, the policeman drifted into unconsciousness. The road around him turned crimson before the rain sluiced the blood away to mingle again with the damp, dark earth.

SEVEN

In bed, in a Leeds hotel room, John listened to the noise of the storm as he dozed, luxuriating in the sound and the soft, cool sheets. Ever since he was a kid, he'd loved the feeling of being safe while the storm raged around him. Clemmy, lying naked beside him, stretched.

'I should get dressed,' she said looking at her watch.

'Not yet, Clemmy.' He rolled over and kissed her. She responded before pushing him away and sliding out of bed. He watched her as she began to dress.

'D'you like meeting in hotel rooms, Clemmy?'

'What's wrong with the room? It cost enough.'

'We could be anywhere from here to Istanbul. It's so impersonal.'

'No ties, no problems. That's what we agreed, John.'

'It would be nice to meet somewhere less functional, that's all.'

She'd got hold of him after the argument. She was sorry about spiking the story; she wanted to make up. They'd been seeing each other for several months and when it came to sex, they seemed made for each other. She had a wonderful body and he loved her hunger but things had changed. Despite agreeing there would be no ties, John had fallen for her. She was married and, more dangerously, she was his boss but he couldn't help it. He hadn't told her he loved her. She'd run a mile so he affected a lazy indifference which he half-felt and half-meant. Clemmy was the contradiction, the chaotic chemistry he couldn't live without. He opened the minibar and took out a whisky miniature.

'Fancy a livener?' he asked opening the Scotch.

She shook her head. 'You should drink less.'

She was right and it annoyed him. 'Suit yourself.' He emptied the miniature from a height into his open mouth like a Greek fisherman drinking from a gourd. Irritated, she gathered her things and prepared to leave.

'Don't go yet,' John said.

'I have to get back.'

'They'll manage without you.'

'What do you want, John?'

'Apart from a great big joint? I'd like another job.'

'You should try doing the one you've got first. I can't keep making excuses for you.'

'What's the point of doing a good job when you spike the best stories?' Clemmy took a small mirror and reapplied the lipstick she'd lost. 'The Thatcher government is deploying all the forces of the state to smash the miners. Isn't that important?'

'She is the prime minister,' Clemmy replied.

'You're on her side? '

'I'm a woman! The miners may be the soul of the left but they're sexist and male-dominated and they're fighting for a world that's dying, thank God.'

'I don't believe this.'

'Would you work down a mine? Would you let your kids?'

'They might end up better people if they did.'

'Romantic rubbish,' Clemmy responded.

'The fact remains their way of life has been ambushed,' he said slowly, 'and bad things are being done in our name. We've got proof on film that you won't use. So much for the noble trade of journalism.'

'You don't care about the miners or journalism these days.'

'I'm too busy shagging you'.

'You're too busy getting drunk.'

For some reason, her barb stung. It had been a particularly shit day but he hadn't realised his disillusion was so obvious. A better journalist would have followed up the miner's beating and maybe linked it to the racism in the pub. He would have done once. He stared out of the window at the city, the lights winking on against the stormy sky. Journalism had started out as a crusade; his reporting was going to be a dynamic mixture of Hemingway's virility and James Cameron's discursive power. Now, he realised that he didn't write like his heroes and that he never would. It wasn't the stories he worked on or the deadlines he was given, he had a nose for a good story. It was just that at its best, his own prose style was staccato, sensational and tabloid. He wrote in headlines. It had never occurred to him that he might despise what he was good at even if it did make him ideal for television reporting. He'd lost his faith and he didn't know if he would ever get it back; that was the real problem between him and Clemmy. In another time and place, maybe, he would have made a commitment but right now, he couldn't tell her he loved her because he was so dissatisfied with himself. He was lost, empty, as if he was waiting for something to happen to give his life some meaning, but he wasn't sure what it was. He wasn't even sure if he really felt it.

Clemmy interrupted his thoughts. 'Sorry,' she said gently, 'I didn't mean to be so brutal.'

'It's not your fault, it's the strike.'

'It's a good story. Any other time, we would have used it,' she said, stroking his hair. She kissed his forehead gently.

'Leave him, Clemmy. Come and live with me.'

'Me, you and kids in the suburbs, John? I don't think so.'

'I think you'd suit kids.'

The idea of settling down wasn't unattractive but Clemmy wasn't ready. She'd worked too hard to get where she was, she didn't want to throw it away. John was a good reporter but he was a loose cannon; that's what she liked about him. Their relationship was driven by anger and sex. They met, made love, argued, made love again, went back to work and argued some more. She did like him though. Clemmy stroked his hair again. 'Sorry, I don't want to hurt you.'

'You didn't,' he lied and turned to kiss her again. She responded and they became aroused all over again. She loved having this power over him. And as they made love, she told him that she couldn't live without him. It was a lie but she was momentarily scared by the possibility that it might be true.

Across the road, sitting in a greasy spoon with a mug of cold tea and an unread evening paper, a secret watcher stared at the hotel through the rain, at the distant rooms with their lights on and imagined the drama within.

EIGHT

As the lovers climaxed again, the storm over the moors reached its zenith. The driving rain revived the fatally wounded constable. He was dying, he would never see his son again but he wasn't dead yet. With a tremendous effort, he roused himself and began to crawl back to his panda car. It was a painstaking, terrible journey. The rain eased abruptly. The car radio kept calling.

'Lima three zero nine, come in please? Come in, three zero nine. State your location.'

Blood oozing from the holes in his stomach, Roberts couldn't reach the handle to get inside the car. In agony and rapidly losing strength, he scrawled the registration number of Hatton's Escort in blood on the door of his vehicle. As his pulse faded, the rain streaked the bloody numbers down the side of the car. In one of those unknowable coincidences of the universe, at exactly the time that PC Roberts stopped breathing, the rain stopped too.

NINE

Hatton drove the Escort quickly but not too quickly. He went by back roads, slowing occasionally while he consulted the map on his knees. He knew the drill. Stay calm, return to the forest rendezvous point and wait. He didn't know how long it would be before the panda car would be discovered. Then he got stuck behind a combine harvester ambling along a single-track lane. It showed no sign of turning off. His hands began to sweat on the wheel. *For fuck's sake get off the bleeding road!* He wanted to honk the horn; he even considered shooting the driver but that wouldn't get the damn thing out of the way. Stay calm; that was easier said than done. Meeting that police twat at Menwith Hill was unbelievable bad luck.

Finally the combine turned off. Relieved, he accelerated away but he overcooked it and went into a skid on some slurry. He was heading sideways for a ditch full of water. *Christ all fucking mighty.* He struggled with the vehicle, turning the wheel back and forth desperately. At the last moment, the wheels gripped again. He took a deep breath, slowed down and drove carefully for another fifteen miles. Finally he was back in the road beside the forest. He forced himself to check that the coast was clear, then swung the van onto the private road and skidded down the muddy track between the trees.

Once in the glade, Hatton removed the holdall and tried to think what to do. He was struggling to stay in control of himself. He kept getting flashbacks of the shooting. He made himself stand still and breathe deeply. If he stayed in the glade undercover, Eric would come and find him eventually, help him go to ground. That's right.

As long as the little twat doesn't fucking bottle it.

60

He pushed the thought away and walked a short distance into the forest where he hunkered down to wait. He knew what to do: stay calm, play the grey man. It was a waiting technique they'd been taught – slowed down, like in a trance, your mind emptied – he could go for hours without moving. Ninety percent of his job was waiting.

After two hours, he had a pee and stretched his legs. He looked at the Escort van and remembered another line from his training. Escape vehicles should be destroyed, burnt out to reduce forensic evidence. Hatton paused, then took a jerry can of petrol from the back of the van, emptied it over the Escort and threw a match onto it. The vehicle ignited in a whoosh of purple flame. That was his second mistake.

PC Fred Scullion was going home when he saw the smoke. He and his four-year-old Alsatian dog, Sassie, had just done a full shift at a pit thirty miles to the south and they were tired. In his late forties, Fred Scullion didn't enjoy strike duty. His Dad had been a miner and two of his brothers still were. Using Sassie against pit lads felt wrong. When he saw the smoke rising out of the forest, he was inclined to let it go. The evening was damp and uninviting and the light was going, but this was their patch.

'What d'you reckon, Sass? Should we 'ave a look?' he said. 'Probably kids.' The dog panted cheerfully and seemed to agree with him. Afterwards, PC Scullion couldn't say why he'd turned into the forest. Maybe it was Hatton's tracks or some sixth sense or maybe it was just plain bad luck.

TEN

John stayed on in the hotel room after Clemmy left. He'd paid for the room, so he might as well enjoy it; not that he did particularly. He didn't even raid the minibar. Clemmy's barbs stayed with him, entwining themselves with images of the beaten picket and racist police. It was true, he liked a drink, but he hated the idea of being a drunk. He didn't know what he wanted but he knew he didn't want to end up like Brian, famous for his ability to down pints, and he had to admit that he was really stuck on Clemmy. He'd just had a shower when the phone rang, which was a surprise. As far as he knew, only Clemmy knew he was here.

'Clemmy?'

'No, John, it's me.' It was a bad line, and it took him a moment before he realised it was his big sister.

'Maria!? How did you know I was here?'

'I phoned the newsroom. Naz said you were in a city centre hotel. This is the fourth one I've tried.'

He knew that Naz disapproved of his relationship with Clemmy. Naz thought it would end in tears. John had worked hard to keep it a secret but now he felt embarrassed, like a naughty boy caught with his fingers in the jam. Not only had he been found out, he'd inadvertently given away Clemmy's name. His big sister always managed to make him feel guilty.

'What do you want, Maria? I thought you were busy saving mankind.'

'I'm scared.'

'Why? What's wrong?'

'There's been a murder near here, a policeman was shot...' she said only to be interrupted by the urgent bleeping of the pips.

'No, God, don't cut her off, please?' The line went dead. He swore at the room. 'Thanks, God, fucking thanks a bunch.' The phone rang again and he snatched it up. 'Maria?'

'I dropped my change on the floor.'

'Is the murder at the peace camp?'

'Just down the road. There's police everywhere and there's a lot of activity at the base.' She paused. 'Can I see you?'

'Come to the flat. No, second thoughts, I'll come to you.' She was cut off by the pips again and this time she had no more money.

'Shit,' she said into the phone but it wasn't heard by John or recorded by the banks of tape recorders in the blast-proof bunker under the base. As the line went dead, the servomotors driving the tape machines clicked off. The mainframe computer processed the information then sent a series of commands to the golf ball printer, which duly spewed out more print-out. Maria left the isolated phone box and walked back towards the camp.

Inside the base, the giant golf balls squatted ominously against the darkening sky. In the distance, the road was cordoned off; blue flashing lights formed a protective circle round the panda car. Within the circle, detectives and uniformed officers examined the body of the young constable and the number scrawled in blood on his vehicle. In the woods, rooks called their irritation at the disturbance below but no one heard them over the chatter of the emergency service radios.

Back at the hotel, John thought about his sister's call. It wasn't like her, wanting to see him, admitting she was scared. The one thing you could say about Maria was that she was fearless. She knew which side of the barricades she was on. He dismissed his doubts and phoned the newsroom to round up a crew but everyone was busy with the strike. The only person available was Naz.

'A policeman's been killed, near Menwith Hill.'

'Maria told me, but you're on leave and I'm about to go home.'

'We can't pass this up, Naz. The police are out of control, something like this was bound to happen sooner or later.'

'Like what?'

'The miners have been beaten, abused, vilified; one of them's snapped and decided to get their own back.'

'Do you know it was a miner?'

'No, but it's a reasonable hypothesis and it gives us an excuse to show the footage of the beating. Is there any info about it?'

'No. It struck me as odd. There's been nothing on the wire about it.'

'That means we'll be the first ones there! Come on, Naz, you've got to say yes. Think of the overtime.'

There was a pause at the other end but he heard Naz sigh, 'I'll pick you up John.'

ELEVEN

Billy Hatton had constructed a rough hiding place under a bush in a ditch. When heard the vehicle coming, he hoped it was Eric but he lay down in his hiding place. It was still early.

Fred Scullion parked his dog van near the burning wreck of Hatton's Escort van and got out to have a look. It was gloomy and very damp in the glade so difficult to see anything. He still thought it was kids but he let Sassie out anyway.

'Go on girl, have a shufti.'

Sassie barked and careered madly round the clearing, glad to be out of the van. When Hatton saw the dog, he swore to himself. *A fucking dog, Jesus.*

Hatton was good at fieldcraft, he'd come top of his class. He had an incredible ability to lie still in the most uncomfortable situations and knew instinctively where to hide. He sank back into the ditch, blanking out the discomfort as the cold water flooded into his boots and ran down his sleeves. The one thing he couldn't fool was a dog. He lay still, watching Sassie as she sniffed at the ground. Then she found his scent. She stood still and barked with her nose in the air until Fred Scullion noticed. Then she began to follow Hatton's broken trail across the glade. Hatton tried to send a thought message to the bloody thing. *Just fuck off. Go on, bugger off.*

It didn't do any good. The dog came over and began to bark furiously. Fred followed. 'Found something, lass?' he asked gently as Sassie sniffed at Hatton.

Hatton endured it for a minute but then he couldn't stand it any longer. He shouted, 'Piss off!' and stood up unexpectedly. Covered in mud and algae, he could have been the creature from the black lagoon apart from the gun in his hand.

'Bloody hell,' Fred Scullion began but he didn't get any further. Hatton fired two shots at him. One missed but the other caught him in the right shoulder, knocking him onto his back with a scream. Hatton prepared to shoot him again but the dog grabbed his gun hand.

'Fucking piss off, will you?' Hatton swore at the dog. He fired the gun, which made the dog let go but it wouldn't stop barking. The noise unsettled Hatton. Then his gun jammed. His wrist and hand were bleeding and for the first time that day, he panicked. He ran to the dog van, got in and tried to shut the door but the dog wouldn't let him. He started the engine and skidded away in the mud, the driver's door still open. The dog followed for a while, then thought better of it and returned to its master. Hatton slammed the door and drove away.

Back in the glade, Fred Scullion struggled to his feet as Sassie fussed round him. Losing blood and in a lot of pain, Fred didn't have much option. He'd have to walk to the main road and flag down a vehicle. He stood up, steadied himself and stuck a finger in the bullet hole to stop the bleeding. A doctor told him later, that doing that probably saved his life.

As Hatton thrashed the dog van onto the road, he thanked his stars it was almost dark. He had a few hours but things weren't good. He was in a stolen police vehicle, going away from his rendezvous point. He'd fucked it.

TWELVE

By the time the crew car arrived at Menwith Hill, it was dark and raining hard but the murder scene wasn't hard to find. Arc lamps flooded the area with an intrusive, violent illumination, which cast huge, ghostly shadows over the trees behind. The police kept the TV crew at arm's length and refused to name the officer. Despite repeated questioning, the only information John managed to extract was that there would be a press conference in Harrogate in the morning. He did a short piece to camera with the illuminated scene in shot behind. Naz had brought along a monosyllabic trainee to do sound but ended up doing most it himself. Tired and soaked through with little to show for the excursion, Naz was in a foul mood as he packed up the gear but John refused to be depressed.

'Cheer up. We were first here, it's our story.' Naz looked at him balefully, got into the car and drove away. John walked towards the peace camp.

A small fire spluttered and smoked under an old tarpaulin tied awkwardly between two saplings. A puddle of rain formed in the middle of the tarpaulin, which could only be emptied by flicking the middle up and outwards. A small collection of tents and benders, filthy with mud-spatters, surrounded the fire. Underfoot it was a quagmire. He caught sight of faces peering from tent openings and the occasional figure but couldn't tell if they were women. They didn't look human. When Maria embraced her brother, he hardly recognised her in her filthy waterproofs.

'Thanks for coming. Sorry about the mud.'

'The thing is, the flat's in a bit of a state.'

She smiled. 'Don't worry, we're not going back to your place.'

Alarmed, he asked, 'You have got transport?'

'Don't worry, men aren't allowed overnight in the camp.'

He looked round at the sodden camp. 'Good.'

'Come out of the rain and meet Jess.' They squelched through the mud to a large, brightly lit bender. Someone had rigged up a couple of hurricane lamps and it was possible to stand up.

'Hi, I'm Jess Maguire,' a husky, throaty voice said with a slight accent. He turned and saw a slim, blonde-haired woman with angular features wearing a diaphanous, multi-coloured smock of the sort he hated. She held out her hand and smiled. John shook it.

'Belfast?'

'Derry,' she smiled. She had bright blue eyes and a slightly awkward, restless energy. She kissed John on the cheek and gave him a 'come on' look with her eyes but there was something cool and detached about it. Then she stood back and looked at him in mock admiration. 'So this is John Bradley, the dashing reporter. Maria's told me all about you.'

'All lies.' He didn't take to her. She was another of those self-confident, hectoring women that the peace movement seemed to attract. He looked away and caught Maria watching him.

'What do you think of our camp?' Jess asked.

'Wet; wet and tiny.'

'Small but perfectly formed,' Jess replied laughing easily. Maria joined in.

'Shouldn't you be at Greenham Common? That's where the missiles are.'

'This is where the orders to fire come from,' Maria said and shivered. 'Come on. We're going to Jess's place for the night.' He frowned, confused.

Jess smiled, 'It's Maria's turn for a bath, and she wants to talk to you.'

Maria embraced her friend. 'Will you be all right?'

'Sure thing. Now go on. Nice meeting you, John,' she said with that look in her eye again. John smiled politely and looked away.

'Very nice,' he said as Maria steered him into the rain towards her battered Citroen 2CV.

'She's not available, John.' She started the engine and gave him one of her knowing, big sister looks. They drove along in silence for a while. The rain hammered on the canvas roof.

'Tell me about Jess.'

'She'd eat you for breakfast.'

'Who is she? What's she doing here?'

'She's rented the cottage to write a book about Tai Chi.'

'So what's she doing at the camp?'

'She believes in it.' He stared out into the wet darkness and wondered how much she'd left out.

The cottage was a converted barn on a lonely hill. As they parked and ran into the cottage, neither of them noticed the motorbike following them with its lights off. The motorcyclist was a big man in his forties with a full beard. He parked the bike behind a wall and climbed to the top of a small hill behind the cottage. With the rain cascading off his waterproofs, he watched as the lights came on in the cottage.

THIRTEEN

Hatton kept to the back roads but they were badly lit and poorly drained. The rain was still coming down heavily. He didn't see the flood until it was too late. As the van hit the water, it made bow wave like a lifeboat being launched. He had no option but to plough on, hoping the water wasn't too deep and praying the engine didn't die on him. When he reached the other side, he breathed a sigh of relief and gunned the engine. The little roads were too risky; he couldn't afford to get stranded. He had to put some distance between him and Yorkshire before daylight. He decided to take a chance and take the motorway south using the cloak of the dark and wet to mask his getaway.

His right hand had started bleeding again from the damn dog bite, when he saw the motorway sign and the lights of the slip road up ahead. *Thank Christ*. As he drove down the slip road, he was still trying to staunch the blood with a filthy handkerchief. He didn't notice the vehicles in front slowing until he looked up and had to do an emergency stop. He stared through the windscreen at the blue flashing lights up ahead. *Shit, it's a roadblock.*

Two patrol cars were parked across the three lanes. Another was sat on the hard shoulder, its engine running, facing oncoming traffic. The two lads checking the vehicles had drawn the short straws. It was late, they were wet, fed up and the people they were stopping were abusive and pissed off too.

As Hatton did his emergency stop at the bottom of the slip road, a Minivan carrying six burly miners pulled up at the roadblock. The driver wound down the window. 'We're visiting my mother.'

The policeman peered in at the miner and at the five large lads crammed in with him. 'Had six bastards, did she?' He was about to turn them back when a squeal of brakes and skidding tyres took his attention. He looked up to see Hatton's van reversing at high speed up the hard shoulder. It did a handbrake turn and disappeared back up the slip road causing other traffic to swerve onto the muddy verge. The police patrol car parked on the hard shoulder took after him, lights flashing, siren going.

FOURTEEN

Maria sat in a towelling robe drying her hair by the open fire while John made supper. After eating, they turned out the lights and relaxed in the flickering glow of the fire, which cast huge, weird shadows across the low beamed ceiling. He rolled a joint.

'You still doing that?'

'Are you?' he grinned, passing his big sister the joint.

They had the easy familiarity and rush to judgement of people who know each other well. For the first twenty-four hours, they got on like a house on fire. After that, they argued. It was a legacy of growing up. Two years older than him, Maria had everything first which had made him intensely combative. She was the idealist who didn't care about money; he was more practical. He preferred his ideals fur-lined and comfortable.

They were close because they had no one else. Their father had died unexpectedly at thirty-four from a heart attack, plunging their mother into darkness and the family into poverty. He was two and Maria four. Mum's family had emigrated. Dad was an only child; his parents were killed in the war so the three of them were alone. John shivered as he remembered the humiliation of growing up poor, brother and sister looking after each other while Mum went out to work. The bitterly cold house in winter, the humiliation of free school meals, free trousers and shoes. Perhaps because of this, they both did well at school and left home as soon as they could escape. Things were easier for their mother then but that's when she began to suffer with backache. Only when it was too late did they discover it was cancer. He remembered her pale and sweating with the pain but she never complained about the rotten hand life had dealt her. That had been twelve years ago.

The dope flooded into his limbs and he felt his body settle. He relaxed, self-doubt banished by a new optimism. His mood had gyrated wildly during the long and eventful day. Hardly surprising, but he despised the way trivial events had the power to remake his world. Not that the police murder was a trivial event but he sometimes worried that his characteristic nonchalance was a merely a cover for an inner darkness. Maybe he had inherited his mother's pessimism. Maybe he smoked too much dope. He pushed away his gloomy thoughts; he was cheerful because for once, he wasn't blind drunk and he had a good story. A cop murder was good at any time but during the strike, it spawned so many possibilities which he could put together. The rain hammered on the French windows. Maria shivered and pulled the towelling robe around her. John looked at her and remembered.

'So what are you scared of?' She looked up, wide-eyed and alarmed as if he'd glimpsed into her soul. 'You said it on the phone.'

'I've fallen in love.'

'Why should that make you scared?'

'I don't want to lose it,' she said staring into the fire.

'And?' She looked at him, uncomprehending. 'Big, small? Fat, thin? Bald, hairy?'

She giggled. 'Wonderful, fantastic.'

'I'm surprised you can find the time but if it makes you happy, that's great.'

Maria smiled. 'It's a bit one-sided at the minute.' She was about to say more but a loud bang somewhere in the house silenced her. Maria stared at John, wide-eyed. John put a finger to his lips, tiptoed out of the room, into the hall and switched on the light. It was empty. Another bang came from the kitchen. The back door was open and swinging back and forth in the storm. John looked out into the darkness but couldn't see anything. Up on the hill, the bearded watcher saw him though, silhouetted in the frame before the door was slammed shut again and bolted.

'Back door was open.'

Maria frowned, 'I'm sure I shut it.'

'It's shut now.

She looked at him fearfully. 'Give me a cuddle, will you?'

He went over to her and held her. In his arms, she was slight and vulnerable, and she was shaking. 'What's going on, Maria? It's not just love that's scaring you, is it?'

She looked at the darkness beyond the French windows. Lately, her nights were full of demons. She took a deep breath. 'The man who shot the policeman,' she paused, 'I think he was after Jess.'

'Why?' His face was etched with doubt. Maria could have hugged him. For once, her brother's worldly scepticism was reassuring. She wanted to tell John everything so he could demolish it. Fear made her cautious.

'Jess had to leave Ireland in a hurry. She got involved with some bad people.'

'Why would they want to kill her?'

Maria shook her head. 'It's dangerous. I can't tell you. It's something to do with the camp.'

'Menwith Hill??'

Maria leant forward and lowered her voice. 'It's a Trojan horse,' she said, a faraway look in her eyes.

'For Christ's sake, Maria! It's an American listening base, that's all.' Maria came back from her nightmare and looked at him.

'They record every phone call in this country.'

'Is that possible?'

'They know everything that goes on. Everything that's happened, that's going to happen. All the dark secrets.'

'That would be all the dark *male* secrets then?' She looked up at him, confused by his sarcasm. 'As opposed to the sisterhood?'

'If you could get inside, you could find out anything you wanted to know.'

'What's this got to do with Jess being on an Irish hit list?'

'I can't tell you any more.'

'Apart from some paranoid imaginings, you haven't told me anything.'

'Someone shot the policeman.'

John nodded. 'I think it was a miner, getting his own back. The police have been getting away with all sorts. Somebody finally snapped. There's a police press conference tomorrow, I'll keep you posted if you like?'

Maria smiled weakly, hoping he was right. He sat down and regarded his sister seriously. 'That camp isn't doing you any good.'

'If you feel powerless and scared, you have to try and take control.'

'A few women sitting in filthy tents isn't going to stop the missiles.'

'Women are making a difference, John. Thirty thousand joined hands at Greenham.' He shrugged, unimpressed, and demolished the closeness she'd felt. She looked at him with a sad, faraway expression that he would recall many times afterwards.

FIFTEEN

The rain stopped just before dawn. As Maria drove John over the moors to Harrogate, the sun warmed the saturated land. Mist rose into the vast sky. The sun still hadn't penetrated the sombre glade where Hatton had shot PC Fred Scullion, but the police had. Emergency vehicle radio chatter droned in the background as dog handler Scullion, his arm in a sling, pointed to the place where Hatton had shot him. Sassie barked enthusiastically and charged about while a police forensic team examined the burnt-out shell of Hatton's Escort. A DS reported to base that they'd found the vehicle they'd been looking for, the vehicle whose number John Roberts had written in his own blood.

A few miles to the south, Billy Hatton lay on a steep hillside, concealed in sodden undergrowth. He'd outrun his police pursuers the night before. The night and the storm had helped but the downside was he didn't know where he'd ended up. To conserve fuel, he parked in a field below the road and slept fitfully until first light.

Hatton surveyed the sleepy village nestling in the valley below. It looked quiet enough. A thin plume of smoke curled contentedly from one of the chimneys but the village was changing. Beyond allotments, new executive homes were being erected. No humble farm labourers' dwellings these but expensive commuter lodges for successful city folk. Dirty, hungry and wet, Hatton settled down to wait until the village came to life. That's when he heard whistling.

He peered back up the hill and saw a flock of sheep ambling into view followed by a sheepdog. A shepherd appeared, spied the van and walked over to examine it. Hatton wondered what to do. He didn't fancy staying put. His wrist was still bloody sore, he'd had enough of dogs for now. He checked his gun, grabbed his holdall and slithered down the steep bank towards the bridleway at the bottom. Once there, he shook the excess moisture from his clothes, wiped the mud from his trousers and set off towards the village.

Hatton walked past the church and on down the main street, stopping by the village shop. A Morris Thousand was parked outside. Hatton entered the shop. The shopkeeper was in his seventies, twisted and bent with arthritis, his knuckles fused into two bunches of bulbous, blotchy grapes. He wanted to chat; he didn't see many strangers.

'Not a bad sort of day?' Hatton managed a smile and caught sight of some car keys on the counter. The key fob was engraved with the word Morris. 'Better than all that rain we've had?' the shopkeeper continued. Hatton scanned the top shelf, saw the name Fray Bentos on a tin.

'Got any corned beef?'

The old man shook his head. 'Don't get much call for corned beef.'

Hatton pointed to the top shelf. 'What's that up there?'

The old man chuckled bronchitically as he set up some rickety steps. 'I know where it is all right, just don't get much call for it. It's all burgers these days,' he wheezed as he climbed up.

Hatton reached for the car keys as the old man reached a gnarled claw for the corned beef but at the last moment, the old man turned. Hatton snatched his hand away.

'Anything else while I'm up here?' the old man asked looking down at his customer. He told the police later, 'He was a dirty beggar, unshaven with a bloody wrist. Been in the wars, by the look of him.'

Hatton willed the old man to hurry. He didn't want to be in the shop a second longer than he had to. The old man tried again. 'Well?'

Hatton scanned the shelf. 'A tin of spam.' The old man turned back and reached for the spam. Hatton pocketed the car keys. 'Forget the spam,' he rasped, 'I'll just take the corned beef.'

'Hold your horses, they'll run away if you don't,' the old man laughed at his joke.

'Just give me the corned beef!' Hatton snapped, reaching over the counter and taking a loaf of bread and some cigarettes.

'Ayup? What's occurring?' the old man said, worried he was about to be robbed.

'I'm in a hurry!' Hatton replied, slamming a fiver down on the counter, grabbing the corned beef from the old man and hurrying from the shop. The old man stared at the shop door, a tin of spam in his wizened hand and a puzzled look on his face. He put the tin on the counter and examined the five-pound note, cautiously holding it up to the light. It looked fine. The rumble of heavy traffic outside made the shelves rattle and the doorbell tinkle.

Hatton hurried from the shop with the keys in his hand. A Morris Thousand wasn't the fastest get-away vehicle but it wouldn't stand out. With a bit of luck, the old fucker wouldn't realise for ages and he'd be clear away. Traffic noise caused him to look up, his face twisting in horror at what he saw. A convoy of four armoured police Transits full of police followed by a couple of police cars rumbled down the street. Hatton recovered himself and began to unlock the old man's car but one of the police cars screeched to a halt. The policemen inside, pointing and gesticulating, their heads twisting and turning like stick insects. He'd been recognised, they knew who he was. *They knew who he fucking was!*

The thought flashed like a beacon as he dashed up the street and turned up an alley followed by the younger of the two policemen. After a night without sleep or food, Hatton was knackered. He knew he couldn't outrun the fit young plod. He stopped, still facing up the alley, his holdall at his side with the gun in front of him. The pursuing policeman stopped running and walked towards him. Hatton turned shot him in the leg just as his partner appeared round the corner. The wounded policeman screamed and fell, clutching his leg while his partner backed away. Hatton aimed another round at the fallen officer's head and the gun jammed. Hatton's pulse went off the scale. A smile appeared on the able-bodied older policeman's face. He walked towards Hatton who backed away, swearing and pulling the trigger twice more as he did so. Both times the gun jammed again; the third time, it fired. The bullet ripped into the heart of the older officer, killing him instantly. He crumpled to the floor, watched by his horrified, wounded young partner. Hatton turned and fled up the alley, disappearing into the gardens at the back of the houses. A distant siren began to wail; others began a burgeoning descant.

SIXTEEN

The tape decks at Menwith Hill recorded non-stop as the wires hummed about Hatton. Chains of command consulted, secret decisions made, orders given. Police reinforcements were rushed to the village, thinning picket lines and emptying police stations. An hour after the second policeman was murdered the village was surrounded. Villagers were warned by loudhailer to stay inside and lock their doors and windows. Three hours after that, the army arrived and set up roadblocks. No one was allowed in or out. Armed police began searching the gardens and the allotments. They didn't hurry; they were careful, methodical as they moved across the ground in lines, prodding compost heaps, peering into water barrels and tool sheds. No one gave a second thought to the bit of old plastic sheeting by the bins, no one noticed the darting fish eye peering out of a tiny hole. Hatton lay still as a corpse, gun in hand and watched the police pass. This was what he'd signed up for, the buzz, the ultimate adrenaline rush.

John, Naz and Brian arrived at the village mid-afternoon and joined the media scrum encamped in front of an army roadblock. Camera crews competed for space to get a clean shot of the roadblock and the village beyond.

'For fuck's sake!' John swore to himself, pissed off at losing the head start he'd had the night before. He reversed the car up the road at high speed before skidding round violently.

'Easy, Tiger,' Naz said. Ignoring him, John continued back up the road and turned off down a muddy farm track.

'We'll be lucky to get back up here after all the rain,' Brian observed as they slithered down. John said nothing. He was on a mission. They stopped on a small ridge overlooking the village. From their vantage point, they could see army and police vehicles at the end of the main street.

The word had gone out at the press conference, everyone looking like shit, bored with the strike, wanting a piece of the action. William 'Billy' Hatton, 31, territorial SAS, ability to live off the land, armed and dangerous, killed two police officers, attempted to kill two more. It fucked John's miner theory but he still wouldn't have it. Something didn't add up. They'd been given two and two but Hatton made six. Normally John would have accepted the discrepancy but something about today, about this story was different.

There are moments when the tide turns and begins to flow in the opposite direction. Occasionally, we feel our destiny upon us. Occasionally, everything goes tits up.

No one else gave a flying fuck whether the story made sense or not. They had a rip-roaring, mad cop killer story to run with. Days of bloodlusting headlines, rage, cold-blooded murder, tearful widows, lucky escapes and a bad, mad dog to be hunted down. Roll up, roll up, all the fun of the fair.

'Right,' announced John, 'we'll set up here.'

As they unloaded the gear, an army helicopter buzzed overhead. Brian looked up. 'Christ, they're mob-handed.'

'Yeah, it's odd,' Naz responded. 'Nothing on the wire last night, yet this morning everyone knew about Hatton.'

'Come on, Naz, he's killed two coppers already, tried to kill two more,' Brian replied forcefully but Naz wasn't finished.

'How did they get his name, then?'

'From the number plate of the burnt-out van,' Brian muttered, headphones half-on, holding the boom mike aloft and fiddling with his sound levels.

'It wasn't his van,' Naz said. Brian and John stared at Naz, absorbing the import of what he had said.

'Are you saying it was stolen?'

'Why would he use his own vehicle?' Naz asked. 'Territorial SAS, killed two coppers, tried to kill two more. This is a bloke, who knows what he's doing. Why else is the army down there?'

'That sounds like one of my sister's paranoid fantasies.'

'All men are fascists according to the Greenham women,' Brian said in mock seriousness.

'Men make war, women make babies,' Naz responded.

'And if all the politicians in the world were women, there wouldn't be any wars.' John added. 'That's the theory, anyway.'

Brian removed his headphones, looked round furtively then said quietly, 'but every twenty-eight days, there'd be some really difficult negotiations.'

John and Naz looked at each other and then at Brian. Their faces held briefly, then collapsed. A moment later, they were hooting with laughter, faces contorted emitting shrieks and squeaks and in Brian's case, long wheezing coughing guffaws. It kept on going; a long, cathartic, hysterical outburst. Each time they stopped, one of them started again. It was funny because it was unexpected, because it was forbidden, because it vented the tension of the last few days. And their laughter was precious; a shared moment of affection and warmth born of shared hardships that they would remember long after.

After they'd calmed down, John began his piece to camera. 'In the small village behind me, a desperate police manhunt is searching for Billy Hatton...' he trailed off giggling helplessly, shouting through his laughter, 'For fuck's sake, Brian, stop it!' but that just made it worse. After a couple more goes, he succeeded.

He looked down at the village while Brian began packing up the gear. Hatton was down there and he had a feeling about this story. He didn't trust the police and yet, he didn't believe Maria. He wanted to prove to Clemmy that he could still hack it but it was more than that. He felt impelled in some way.

'Wait here, will you?' Naz looked up. 'I'm just going to stretch my legs.'

'Are you mad?' .

'I'm a reporter, it's my job,' John smiled, adding, 'don't worry, I'll be careful.' He began to walk away.

'If you're not back in half an hour, we're going back,' Brian shouted after him, 'or we'll miss the evening bulletin. I've got a darts match.'

He waved without looking back. Naz muttered, 'He'll probably get shot.'

'Lead fucking story if he does,' Brian grinned. Naz grinned too, then realising it could happen, hoisted the heavy camera back onto his shoulder and began filming John.

SEVENTEEN

As John walked into the village, Maria and Jess were unpacking shopping at Jess's cottage. After the recent heavy rain, the camp was waterlogged and they'd decided to have another night dry and warm.

'God, I'm glad to be back here again.'

'Don't beat yourself up over it,' Jess loaded the fridge. Maria stared at her and bit her lip. Jess caught the gesture and stopped what she was doing.

'Maria? What is it?'

Maria looked round guiltily as if to check they were alone. 'I told John.'

'For Christ's sake!' Jess threw the loaf she was holding across the kitchen. It knocked a cup onto the floor and shattered it.

'He's my brother.'

'He's a bloody journalist!' Jess said picking up the broken pieces. 'He was in the army in Northern Ireland.'

'That was years ago.'

'They'll use anything to stop us.'

'I'm sorry, Jess.' Jess ignored her and dropped the pieces of cup into a waste bin. 'I was scared.'

Jess looked at Maria and relented. She came over to Marie and put her arms round her.

'How did he take it?'

'He didn't believe a word of it.'

'Good.' Jess kissed Maria on the cheek and went back to loading the fridge.

EIGHTEEN

Hatton crouched in a deserted cottage, close to a back wall which gave a view of the road. He was hungry and exhausted but he wasn't beaten yet. He fished in his holdall and drew out a walkie-talkie. It was state of the art technology with an in-built scrambler. He switched it on, checked his watch and tuned into a frequency. A squeal of static sent his pulse racing before he turned down the volume.

'Demeter Control, this is Orion, come in please,' he said quietly and urgently. He was just about to try calling again when there was an answering pulse of static followed by a Belfast accent.

'You screwed up.' The voice was gentle, quiet and without emotion.

'There was nothing I could do, the policeman,' Hatton said, his voice rising despite himself. He took control of himself again. 'It was just bad luck.'

'It was your bad luck,' the Ulster voice replied calmly, as if stating the obvious. Hatton found himself sweating.

'I need out, can you set up a meet?'

'Don't worry, we'll be seeing you,' the voice replied again without emotion. Hatton grabbed the walkie-talkie excitedly.

'Where?' he asked desperately but his answer was a surge of static. He tried again. 'Demeter Control, this is Orion, come in please? Demeter Control, come in please,' but there was no reply.

He threw the walkie-talkie onto the floor and began to pace up and down the room. He was trapped. Obviously he could try and get away after nightfall but he was on his own. Unless he could find an edge, he was dead meat. He glanced out of the cottage window and checked the street. It looked like it was going to rain again. Good.

John walked into the village down an unfinished road, past half-built executive homes. A police car cruised in the distance. A dog barked half-heartedly, another joined in. No one stopped him, no one shouted. The place seemed deserted. It was weird and it wasn't very bright. His confidence deserted him. There were hundreds of armed police looking for a killer. What on earth did he think he was doing? The clouds were gathering – it was going to throw it down again. The first few drops made up his mind for him and he turned back. He turned back and began to retrace his steps. That was when he heard a noise coming from a cottage close to the new houses. Empty, it was being renovated. Old slates and building rubble littered the garden. Polythene sheeting covered the roof. The rain began to sluice down. He hurried up the path and tried the door. It was open. It was pissing down outside, so he went in. Billy Hatton shut the door behind him, smiled and pointed his automatic at John's head. *Shit.*

Hatton pushed the gun into John's mouth forcing him back into the cottage until his back hit a wall.

'Who the fuck are you?' Hatton rasped. 'Who're you with?' John tried to answer but Hatton pushed the gun into his open mouth until he could feel the barrel against the roof of his mouth. It was cold, unyielding, with a bitter taste that filled his mouth. He couldn't answer so he raised his eyebrows and made a noise which Hatton seemed not hear. Hatton was snorting like a wild beast. His hair was wild, his breath was rank and the veins in his neck throbbed and pulsed like a hydraulic pump.

John was more scared than he'd ever been. It was a surging, debilitating, enervating emotion, which swirled around his body, made him hyperventilate and stopped him thinking. His mouth dried up, his hands began to sweat and he badly needed the loo. Hatton withdrew the gun.

'I'm a journalist,' he said, reaching into his inside pocket. Hatton shoved the gun back into his mouth,

86

'Don't fuck with me.'

'I'm not. My press card's in my pocket.' Hatton ripped open the pocket, spilling the contents onto the floor. He picked up the press card and looked at it, then back at John. John shrugged. 'See?' he said. Hatton was unimpressed.

'Could be a cover. How come you're walking through the village on your bloody own?'

'I wanted to meet you.'

Hatton frowned, distracted, then looked at the press card again. 'Why?'

'I have a theory about you. You're connected to the strike, aren't you?'

Hatton regarded him thoughtfully. 'In what way?'

John was confused. He'd hit a nerve but it wasn't the one he'd intended. 'You're political. Killing the policeman was a political act, a protest.'

'Policemen,' Hatton said emphasising the 'men'. 'I've killed two.' Hatton shook his head, 'but I'm not political, I'm a soldier.'

John was an experienced interviewer; he was good at it. People were always suspicious at first. Often they needed to insult and humiliate the interviewer but if you let them take control, they usually wanted to tell their story. And once started, they wouldn't stop.

'Whose war are you fighting?' John asked.

'Mine.'

'Why?'

'I get off on it,' Hatton replied, his eyes somewhere else, 'the feeling when it's about to kick off. I can't get enough of it.'

'Why did you kill the policeman?'

Hatton returned from his preoccupation and looked at John anew. There was unpleasant look around his mouth and his eyes were cold. 'If it wasn't political?'

'Are you trying to interview me?'

'If you like?'

'I don't like.' Hatton hit him hard across the temple with the gun. He heard the blow as a sickening thud and he slumped to the floor. A throbbing, searing pain began to grow in his temple.

87

'I am a journalist.'

Hatton nodded calmly, then kicked John several times in his ribs causing him to moan. 'I know, seen you on the tele. You were a squaddie in the province.'

'How d'you know that?'

'I know lots of things.'

Hatton turned away distracted by a noise in the street. He crouched by the window and peered out. 'They're getting busy,' he said. John struggled back into a seated position, holding his arms round his midriff, trying to control the pain. Hatton turned back from the window. 'What did you say about me? That I was a vicious killer? A mad dog?'

'I said you'd murdered two policemen and attempted to murder two more and that you were trapped.'

'I've got a bargaining chip.' John frowned. 'I've got you,' Hatton said with a wink and began to tie him up.

NINETEEN

Clemmy phoned the police when Naz got back. She was angry with him for letting John go. She was worried sick about John but it was a great scoop for her and NTV. Their intrepid reporter had walked into the lion's den. Naz's film led their bulletins before cutting to John's last to camera piece about Hatton and the siege of the village. By the News at Ten, it led every bulletin. Fantastic stuff.

Eric Guttridge watched the news in the front room of his new bungalow, on an estate of new bungalows. He watched in the dark, with the curtains open, the ghostly blue light of the TV spilling into the darkness outside. Eric sweated as the photo of Billy Hatton was flashed up and his membership of the territorial SAS discussed. He sweated as the bulletin reported two murders and two attempted murders committed with the weapons Eric had transported. Hatton was surrounded but he had a hostage. If he was caught, what would he say, who would be implicated? Eric slurped lager from a can and pulled hungrily on a cigarette but his stomach remained knotted with fear. He'd left the curtains open so he could see anyone arriving but so intent was he on the TV that he missed the darting figure passing the window. The sound of a key in the front door made him start and stare wide-eyed, his heart racing.

A cheery voice called, 'Eric? It's me, Helen, are you in?'

He relaxed as a well-fed woman in her forties bustled into the room and put the light on. 'What are you doing sitting in the dark?' she asked, drawing the curtains. Eric got up and switched the TV off. Helen turned back to him, a look of concern on her face. 'Are you all right, love? You look pale.'

Eric nodded and went to get another can of lager. A reckoning was coming but not to Eric, not yet anyway. Army Land Rovers were moving through the darkness towards the surrounded village. Roadblocks opened to let them through, troops nudged each other and whispered about the cargo. Men in black, men of the shadows, unseen, covert, ordered by a nod and wink, nothing on paper, an arm's length deniable strategy. The villagers heard the traffic, checked the bolts on their doors and waited anxiously for the night to pass.

Jess and Maria knew nothing of the unfolding drama. After a bath and something to eat, they sat in front of the cottage hearth, watching the flickering mysteries of the fire. Maria luxuriated in the warmth and comfort. Jess was less comfortable. A decision had been taken which made her uneasy.

'God, a second night away from the camp. I can't believe it.'

'I'm not sure, Maria.'

'Someone has to do it and it can't be you.' Jess tried to smile but she could only manage a grimace. She felt unworthy; Maria was so damn decent.

Maria caught the sadness in Jess's face and came over to her. 'It's all right, Jess.'

Jess felt safe with Maria, happy even and yet, she felt like a shit. She was about to say something when she caught a look in Maria's eye. Maria moved close to kiss her but Jess pushed her away. Maria looked at her for a moment, then slid down to the floor. She leaned against Jess's legs, wrapping her arms around them, sighed and stared into the fire.

TWENTY

John's spirits declined with the fading daylight. As the hours slipped past, the pain in his temple eased slightly but the ache in his ribs throbbed hideously. Simultaneously drained and excited, he felt sick and shivery, a bitter taste of bile in his mouth, but it wasn't a cold he was suffering, it was fear. The comfort of religion might have helped but John had been an atheist since his teenage years and besides, he believed in the here and now. It was part of why he became a journalist; he wanted to think for himself instead of accepting orders without question. He tried to think clearly about Hatton and his situation but just when he thought he was in control of himself, his insides would lurch alarmingly again as another tidal surge of fear swept over him.

He discovered a kind of solace thinking about the people who cared for him. Despite the fact that he argued with her constantly, Maria was the only family he had and perhaps the only person who would always be there for him no matter what. Then there was Clemmy. He resolved that if he got the chance, he would tell her how he felt, that he wanted to make a go of it. If she said no, well so be it. That thought helped him to focus on survival.

The turning point came when Hatton gave him a drink of water. The water revived him and the gunman appeared more relaxed as he ate some corned beef. They sat on the floor, the room illuminated by the weak glow of a distant street lamp. Occasionally, Hatton would peer out of the window or disappear into the back room or upstairs to check outside. John watched him as he ate.

'It was an accident,' Hatton said abruptly, his mouth full of corned beef. John looked up without speaking. He didn't want to be hit again. 'The policeman,' Hatton explained, inviting a response.

'And the others?'

'They just happened.' A clatter outside brought him to his knees, gun in hand peering out of the window. After a moment, he relaxed. 'Fucking cat,' he grinned.

Seeing Hatton smiling, John risked another question. 'Territorial SAS?' he asked as neutrally as he could manage.

Hatton nodded. 'We were recruited. Lot of ex-cons, mad bastards, strange fuckers; had to sign an oath.'

'Queen and country?'

'Britain for the British, kick out the foreign scum,' Hatton said without emotion.

'The policeman wasn't foreign scum.'

Hatton sneered unpleasantly and John flinched as he anticipated another blow but this time, none came.

'I told you about him.' John's spirits started to rise as Hatton's fell. His hope of using John as a negotiating ploy veered from wild optimism to deep gloom. There wasn't any point in running, they knew who he was. They would save him because they looked after their own. On the other hand, they all knew the drill, he was expendable.

Despite the fear, John still wanted to know the truth. If he survived, it would be a hell of a story. If he didn't, well... 'You were after someone else weren't you?' Hatton reacted as if a pulse of electricity had gone through him. John tried again, 'A woman from the peace camp?'

'You're guessing.' Hatton threw the empty corned beef can into a corner.

'I'm right though aren't I?' Hatton didn't react. 'Maguire? Jess Maguire?'

Hatton stared at him trying to work out if he was guessing. *What the fuck does it matter now? You're fucking dead meat anyway.* He got to his feet in a single, cat-like movement and went to his holdall. He rummaged round, pulled out a battered photograph and showed it to John. 'Is that her?'

John shook his head slowly. 'No, no, it isn't,' he replied,

struggling to sound calm. Hatton sat down again, pleased at confounding his journalist hostage. John stared at the picture of his sister, her head ringed in red felt tip. She'd been right, her paranoid fantasies were fact except she'd got the wrong person. He had never for a moment considered the possibility that his sister might be Hatton's target. The idea reverberated round his head. A right-wing conspiracy, territorial SAS recruited from ex-cons, a plot to murder members of a peace camp.

'Why?'

Hatton shrugged. 'Fuck knows, I'm just a soldier like you were.'

'Who gave the order?'

Hatton shook his head. The cottage shook violently as a large helicopter flew low overhead. The deep, industrial, relentless clatter of the engine calmed and signalled its landing. Hatton hurried to the window and peered out. 'They're here,' he said excitedly.

A hundred metres distant, out of sight of the cottage, three men in black fatigues jumped down from the Sea King helicopter and ran towards a group of waiting soldiers. Specialist snipers with blackened faces crept and slithered into firing positions around the cottage. Behind them, a squad of armed police formed an impenetrable ring Two coffins were unloaded from one of the Land Rovers.

Inside the cottage, Hatton caught sight of shadows moving in the darkness. He grabbed his holdall and began checking his weapons. 'They know where we are.' He checked the back door was bolted and moved a table over to the window. The activity felt like a training exercise and reassured him. John watched his jailer.

'Who's they?'

'Get in the corner!' Hatton ordered. Sitting down, hands tied behind his back, John had difficulty moving. Hatton cut his bonds and hustled him into the corner. 'Do it!' he roared.

'You could give yourself up.' Hatton ignored him, intent on events outside. 'Why not? You're not going to shoot me, are you?'

'I might.'

'Tell me the story, Billy. Let me tell the world the truth.'

Hatton smirked, 'They won't let you.'

Outside, the sound of hurrying feet could be heard. A loudhailer called out of the darkness. 'Come out, Billy, with your hands up, or we'll have to come and get you,' an Ulster accent shouted.

'They know you.'

'They trained me.' Outside, running footsteps sounded all round them. Short bursts of running followed by silence. They were very close now. Hatton flattened himself against the wall and peered out

'Did they order you to kill Maria?' Hatton nodded and checked his weapons again.

'Who's they, Billy?'

'It's like that Eagles song, 'You can check out anytime you want but you can never fucking leave'.'

'Tell me, Billy. Who gave the order?'

'Gladio,' Hatton whispered.

'Gladio?' Hatton nodded as a stun grenade came through the window and rolled fizzing across the floor. It exploded, deafening him and filling the room with smoke. The smoke grabbed at his lungs, twisting them inside out.

Hatton cocked his weapons, opened the door and charged out shouting, 'Come on, you bastards!' but his voice was cut off by a long fusillade of shots. Two men in black fatigues, wearing gas masks, charged into the cottage and raked the room with fire. They grabbed John under each armpit and dragged him, still coughing, down the path out into the street, yelling at the tops of their voices, 'Move! Move! Move!' The explosion had deafened him and the sound was oddly muted. He seemed to see everything in a distracted slow-motion. Lights, men running, mouths opening and closing, smoke – a smell of excitement and death.

Afterwards, he remembered being dragged past Hatton's body. Under his armpit, he saw Hatton's corpse being dropped roughly into a coffin; his face and body covered in blood spatters. Then he was lifted up and thrown into the back of a Land Rover.

One of his rescuers shouted, 'Get him out of here!' and he was driven away at high speed, a young corporal holding onto him so he didn't fall out. Bumping up and down, he watched the village recede. As he left, the Sea King took off with a deafening roar, carrying the three men in black fatigues back into the black sky. It was over.

TWENTY-ONE

The next morning dawned as if nothing extraordinary had happened. A clear blue sky heralded a baking late-summer day but the zenith had been passed. The leaves were beginning to droop; there was a change in the air. The storms of autumn were coming.

When the phone rang, Jess and Maria were doing Tai Chi on the lawn in front of the cottage's French windows accompanied by the purifying strains of a Bach cello Sonata. Jess preferred the quicker yang short form of Tai Chi and performed the movements with a practised athletic confidence. Although not as accomplished, Maria covered her difficulty with a natural grace. She didn't know about John's ordeal because they'd taken the phone off the hook the night before; she wouldn't know until Naz phoned later that morning. The phone kept on ringing. Maria frowned,

'I thought it was off the hook?'

'Sorry, I put it back this morning,' Jess continued her movement. Maria shrugged and went to answer the phone. A few moments later, she came back, frowning.

'It's for you. Jack, in London?' Maria hadn't heard the name before. The ghost of a shadow crossed Jess's face. She stopped her Tai Chi and smiled uncertainly, wishing she'd left the bloody phone off the hook.

'You know him?'

Jess nodded, 'An old friend. Look, you carry on, I won't be long.' Maria watched Jess go, perplexed. She shrugged and continued her Tai Chi again.

By that time, the army and most of the police had pulled out of

96

the besieged village. Forensic teams and a few uniforms guarded the scene but little trace of the drama of the previous night remained. John had been driven to an army base and examined by an army doctor who diagnosed broken ribs and dressed his head wound. Then he was given a shower and something to eat followed by a few hours' sleep. He was walking wounded, numb, in shock, externally coherent but gibbering mentally, endlessly replaying the time with Hatton in his head.

He woke exhausted but daylight calmed him. After breakfast, he was taken to a Leeds police station where he sat in a baking, airless, overlit room and told his story to a bored detective sergeant. The DS explained that CID hated the strike. It starved them of manpower and funds and they were massively overworked; as if John cared. As far as the police were concerned, Hatton had killed, he had been killed; case closed. The rest was formality. Everyone had a huge caseload; no one gave a fuck.

After he had written out and signed his statement, he was taken to a room on the top floor. It was mid-afternoon and a hot day outside. Sunlight glinted off cars and buildings under a pale shimmering haze that hung over the city. There was a mirror in the room and he caught sight of himself. Unshaven, with a black eye starting over his left eyebrow, he looked terrible. He didn't care, he was preoccupied with Maria. He was scared for her, upset, worried but the main emotion was anger. He was angry with her for getting involved, because it concerned him and she hadn't told him, which made him feel foolish, which made him angry all over again. And the question that kept coming back round was, why? Why would they want to eliminate her? What did she know that was so dangerous? Maybe it was a mistake but Hatton had been real enough. The door opened and a tall, erect, well-dressed man entered carrying a file.

'Sorry to keep you waiting, John,' the man said in a neutral accent. In his thirties, he was well built, tanned and fit looking and wearing an expensive suit. He smiled politely, opened the file and began glancing through it. Somewhere outside, a siren began to wail. Another joined in, then a third. The man stood up and looked down at him. 'What are your plans now?'

'Haven't really got that far... er?'

'Sorry. Gimlet, Jeremy Gimlet.' The man held out his hand and John shook it. The handshake was firm and confident but Gimlet's eyes were far away, like a man weighing up possibilities. They came back to John. 'So, why did you do it? Why put yourself in harm's way unnecessarily?'

'I'm a journalist; I wanted a story. I've already told the police all this.' Gimlet nodded and went to the window with the air of a disapproving headmaster. John spoke to his back. 'Who are you then, Special Branch or something else?' Gimlet turned back and regarded him quizzically. 'Like I said, I'm a journalist. Hatton was a big story, still is.'

Gimlet looked out at the view. 'It's terribly fragile, all this,' he said indicating the view.

'Isn't that why we need a free press? Look, I know what I'm doing, I've reported from war zones before.'

'England isn't exactly a war zone, yet.'

'Depends on your point of view.'

'Mmm.' Gimlet examined the file, apparently bored.

John tried again. 'Why would a member of the territorial SAS kill a policeman during a national strike and then why, instead of being arrested, was he killed by the army?' Gimlet didn't reply. 'Aren't you interested or do you already know the answer?'

'Bad things are happening out there, John. Bad things, bad people.'

'Like Hatton? I mean what were his orders? Who controlled him?' Gimlet looked at John, his eyes black and narrow. 'I presume you know something?'

'Most of the detail is classified,' Gimlet replied, still examining the file.

'Who were the Ulstermen?' Gimlet's head looked up. 'They came in on the helicopter. Hatton said they'd come to kill him. He said they'd trained him, for his mission.'

'Why didn't you put any of this in your statement to the police?'

'They didn't ask, they just wanted to know what happened, the bare bones. They weren't that interested.'

98

'As I said, most of the detail is classified.' Gimlet closed the file and put it on the table.

'It'll come out at the inquest.' The ghost of a smile feathered Gimlet's lips.

'There will be an inquest?'

'Briefly, and for the most part in camera.'

'In camera, why?'

'National security.'

'Look, can't you at least give me a steer about Hatton? He killed two policemen. Isn't that important?'

'Of course.'

'And he may have been involved in a serious conspiracy. Surely that's worth following up?'

Gimlet shrugged. 'Insubordination is just a cheap thrill, John. You should know that.'

'I'm a good journalist. That's how I got to Hatton.'

'Lacks discipline. That's what it says in your file.'

John stared at Gimlet.

'You're talking about my time in the army?'

Gimlet smiled thinly. 'Not officer material.'

'I was twenty-one when I came out!' Gimlet looked out of the window again. 'So you're not interested in Hatton?'

'Lurid theories aren't my province.'

'What is, then?'

Gimlet turned back. 'Dealing drugs...'

John thought he'd misheard. 'Dealing drugs?'

'We found a quantity of cannabis resin in your clothes.'

'What?'

'It's a serious criminal offence.'

John frowned as he struggled to adjust. Gimlet took a step forward with cat-like grace and bent forward so that his mouth was close to John's ear. 'Forget Hatton, John. It'll end in tears if you don't.' Gimlet took a step back and stood up straight like an officer on parade. John looked at him puzzled.

'What now?'

'You're free to go.' Gimlet turned back to the window and looked out at the city.

John stood up and went to the door, where he stopped and turned back.

'In that case, there's only one thing left. Murder.'

Gimlet turned to look at him. 'Murder?'

'Yes. I'm going to murder a drink,' John winked and left the room. It was a cheap, saloon bar shot but it made him feel better as he shut the door and headed down the stairs. Behind him, Gimlet smiled to himself. The hot-headed young journalist had potential.

John emerged blinking from the police station. The city was in full evening mode, commuters hurrying home, revellers off for their first drink. On the corner the SWP collectors, T-shirts covered in 'Coal Not Dole' stickers, were still banging their plastic buckets and shouting their relentless mantra, 'Support the Miners, Support the Miners.' It was all instantly recognisable, just the same as yesterday and yet everything had changed. Twenty-four hours ago, John had been Hatton's hostage with a gun in his mouth. His world had shifted a gear; a critical mass reached. He wandered across the main road and into a pub.

TWENTY-TWO

An hour later, Clemmy embraced him enthusiastically. 'You're a bloody idiot, Bradley, but it's wonderful to see you.' She hugged him and smothered him with kisses. The sensation was comforting and he held onto her, enjoying her warmth and the softness of her body.

He'd phoned Clemmy to say he was OK. He knew they'd want to interview him before the other hacks found him but he hadn't expected her to drop everything and come straight over. It was after eight and the pub was starting to fill. He'd downed two quick pints and was a bit unsteady on his feet. He was overcome at seeing her and clung onto her.

'Gin and tonic?' he whispered.

She nodded, then passed a hand gently over his dressing and his still aching head. He winced and she frowned with concern.

'Are you all right?'

'Never better,' he smiled but feeling suddenly weak, he had to sit down onto a leather bench. He pulled her down next to him.

'I was scared I might not see you again, Clemmy.' She smiled. 'I love you, you know?' He had never said it before; not out loud, away from the pillow.

Clemmy smiled generously. 'I'm pleased to see you too.' She planted a kiss on his earlobe and left to get the drinks. She returned with a large G&T and another pint. He took a gulp and felt better. Clemmy raised her glass.

'You are clever. Here's to you.'

'How's that?'

'We've got a scoop! You're going to be in every news broadcast on the planet!' she exclaimed cheerfully. 'I thought we'd go for the human angle. How did it feel? Were you scared? That sort of thing.' John nodded unenthusiastically, struggling to suppress a growing unease. Clemmy caught the look in his eye and misunderstood. 'Sorry to talk shop, it's just that I'm so pleased to see you, I can't help myself. I promise not to mention it again.'

John sipped his pint. Somewhere in the bar, someone laughed raucously. 'What about Hatton? There's a story there and I've got it.'

'You're the celebrity. People want to know how you felt. Hatton is secondary.' John absorbed this without comment. Clemmy caught his coolness and squeezed his hand. 'I'm sorry. You're tired and battered, you need me to bathe your wounds.'

'That would be nice,' he murmured.

She sighed, concerned, then looked at her watch. 'I can't stay long. I'm on early tomorrow.' He shrugged, but she wasn't finished. 'Arthur's away, Friday till Tuesday, on a course.'

'I see.' The reality of their relationship was reasserting itself. He didn't want it to be like this. He wanted to be open, straightforward but above all, he wanted her to let him do his job, properly. She slipped her hand under the table and onto his crotch. Despite himself, he began to respond.

'Hatton is the key to something big, I can smell it,' he said trying not to react to her.

'I love it when you talk dirty.'

'They tried to warn me off.' She stopped playing and looked at him. 'Just now, in the police station.'

'Apart from the interviews, you're on holiday. Take a week, two if you need it.'

'You don't want to use it?' On impulse, she kissed him. He shook himself free. 'Well?'

She sighed.

'We've had a call. Tell your lad to go easy.'

'I've been warned off before.'

'This warning came from the board. Our board.'

'Ignore them for fuck's sake.'

'We're a television company up for franchise renewal; the government has us by the balls. Like this,' she demonstrated subtly under the table so that no one could see.

But someone did see; someone was watching intently.

John looked down at her hand, then at her. She was gorgeous. She saw his look. 'So how about Friday? Is it a date?' John nodded. He was tired. He sipped his beer. 'Same hotel, usual time?'

'I did some thinking when I was...' She smiled. 'Why don't you come to the flat, Clemmy? I want to talk to you.'

'Whichever?' she said evenly. Behind the din of the bar, a phone started ringing.

'Is there a Mrs Clements in the bar?' Clemmy snapped into professional mode and stood up.

'I've got to go. Get some sleep before Friday, will you? I want you to have lots of energy.' She took his head in her hands and kissed him hard, then pulled away.

'Look, better make it the hotel, easier to get to and from work. Save the flat till Saturday or Sunday when I've got more time.' And then she was gone. He watched her sashay away. He felt exhausted, tired and beaten. Life had hung him upside down and smacked him about. He downed his pint and left the bar. Hidden in the alcove, the big man with the beard watched him go.

TWENTY-THREE

He slept for over twelve hours. Walking to the bathroom, he was stiff and sore but after a shower and breakfast, he revived. He set about tidying the flat. It took time and he was methodical. He threw open all the windows, emptied the rubbish and washed his disgusting crockery. Then he washed the kitchen and bathroom floors and vacuumed everywhere else. He popped out to the shops and bought fresh flowers, which he distributed around. It was a long time since the place had looked this good. He enjoyed being there alone and sat looking out of the window, allowing his mind to wander.

The doorbell interrupted his reverie. It was Maria. He'd phoned her earlier and left a message but he hadn't expected to see her so soon. She looked great but was in a bad mood as she marched into the flat, but the flowers, the airiness and the state of the place took the wind out of her sails. John made some tea and they sat by the open window looking across the park. Like Clemmy, Maria looked at his dressing with a concerned frown.

'I'm fine, Sis.' Maria look unconvinced. 'All right, a bit shaken up but really, I feel pretty good considering.'

A serious look appeared on her face. 'Why did you do it, John?'

'You asked me to, remember?'

'I didn't ask you to nearly get yourself killed.'

'It wasn't just for you. It's my job too.'

'When are you going to stop behaving like a kid in an adventure story?'

'Now seems like a good time.'

'It isn't a game, John. At some point, you'll have to commit to something.'

'I'm committed to this story.' It was an old sore between them but it had become very important lately. 'What are you so angry about, Maria?'

She didn't reply. John's kidnap had ambushed her and taken her over. Anxiety had drained her and knocked her off course, when she couldn't afford to lose focus. 'I'm sorry, I've been worried about you.'

He relaxed. He could see the strain in her face. 'I'm sorry too. It must have been hard.'

For the first time since arriving, she smiled. Then she leant forward conspiratorially.

'Was I right? About him being after Jess?'

'No.' Relief flooded through her and she began to relax. 'He was after you.'

She shook her head but she could see he was certain. 'Are you sure?'

'He had your photograph. Why do they want to kill you?'

'I don't know;' but she did.

'Don't lie to me,' he said quietly. 'I had his gun in my mouth, the one he killed two policemen with and wounded two more. The gun he was going to kill you with.' She stared at him and shook her head.

'I can't tell you, John. It's for your own good.'

He wanted to tell her how he felt but the words wouldn't come. He and his sister were close but it was a silent intimacy. Somehow an unspoken agreement had been reached not to burden each other. Even now, he couldn't express his real feelings. Instead, he went back to the story.

'Tell me about Gladio.'

She shook her head.

'Well, let me tell you what I've managed to dig up.' He'd done some phoning around to old journalist mates on the anti-Nazi, anti-missile, CND peace camp fringe, called in a few favours and heard the latest conspiracy theory gossip. It'd taken an hour or so, but finally he had some background. 'It was a CIA initiative set up in Western Europe in the 50s and 60s. They wanted to create guerrilla units to fight on in the event of a communist takeover. The CIA ceased their involvement in 1969 but the Gladio network continued. The word is that an Italian Gladio unit was responsible for the Bologna Station bombing.'

Maria nodded, 'It was.'

'Are there Gladio units in Britain?'

'It's always been denied.'

John looked at his sister. Any other time, he wouldn't have believed her but Hatton had been real enough.

'But you know something else, Maria?' She nodded sadly. 'Tell me and we can work on it together. Gladio is a big, mainstream story, we could...' but she just tossed her head in dismissal. He tried again. 'All right, then, how did you hear about it?'

Despite her reticence, she seemed to feel the need to unburden herself. She looked round furtively and said quietly, 'I met someone at a European Feminist Conference.'

John laughed despite himself. 'Who?'

Maria smiled at the memory, 'A woman, an Italian.'

'What did she tell you?'

'I can't say, John.'

'For fuck's sake!' He tried again. 'There were a lot of women at this conference?' Maria nodded. 'So why pick you?'

'I had a drink or two and sounded off. I mean, the movement is my life, but well, it's like you said, we don't really change anything. I wanted to do something more strategic.'

'And on the back of that, this woman just came up to you and told you something so important that people now want you dead?'

Maria nodded. 'We slept together.'

'Right.' He paused. 'Even so, if it's such a big deal, why did she give it up in the first place, why tell?'

'She didn't want the secret to die with her,' Maria answered quietly. 'She disappeared a week after the conference.'

John shook his head. Any other time he would have dismissed the whole story as the paranoid ravings of the lunatic fringe, but Hatton had been real enough and so had the photograph with his sister's face ringed in red felt tip. He changed tack. 'Is Jess involved?' Maria nodded. 'Why? Was she at this conference?'

106

Maria shook her head. 'So what do they want? '

'I don't know.'

None of it made any sense. Maria looked fragile and vulnerable. He felt close to her and a million miles away.

'What do you know Maria? Why do they want to kill you?'

She wanted to tell him, to confess but more than that, she wanted him to be safe. 'John, promise me you won't get into any more trouble.'

'Are you going to promise the same thing?'

'All right,' she lied. 'There are other stories, go after them.' Before, he would have been angry and argued but now he felt differently and she had a point. Hatton was dead, Gimlet had warned him off and someone had warned off NTV. Maybe he should cut his losses.

'Promise me you'll leave it.' John nodded slowly. Then the phone rang. It was Naz.

'They want you to do an interview, well two, actually. One for us and one for Newsnight tonight.'

'I'm having a day off. Tell them I'm still recovering.'

'Tomorrow then?'

'All right. Is that all?'

'Are you OK?'

'Fine. A little tired perhaps but OK, you know?'

'How long are you off for?'

'Don't know. Clemmy said to take a week, two if I needed it. Look, I've got Maria here.' Maria waved her hands to say it was OK but John wanted to go.

'Hatton's funeral, it's on Friday.'

'That's quick.'

'In Belfast.'

'Belfast?'

'Hatton was born there, left when he was five.'

'Right.'

'One more thing,' Naz added, 'Brian said to tell you, there's easier ways to blag extra leave.'

'Tell him I love him too.' He put the phone down and smiled at Maria.

'Is there a problem?' John shook his head. 'And you meant it, you will keep your promise?'

John nodded again. 'If you promise to keep out of trouble?' Now it was her turn to smile and shrug.

Strictly speaking John's response was a lie but not a proper one. He'd keep his promise to Maria, after he'd been to Belfast. Naz's phone call had snapped him back into the world he knew. Hatton's Belfast funeral confirmed that the story had legs. Why else would he be warned off? Why threaten him?

On the six o'clock news, the strike had already replaced Hatton. The final events of his kidnapping kept replaying in his mind's eye, sometimes in muted black and white, sometimes in noisy technicolour. Whether out of emotional need, professional curiosity or both, he couldn't say. He kept hearing the helicopter, the sound of running feet, the fizz of the stun grenade; then the shooting, Hatton's lifeless body, the Ulster voice on the loudhailer. And now, he kept imagining a Belfast funeral.

As evening drew on, a wind got up, agitating the weeds in the small garden. He sat in the open window wondering what Gimlet did in his spare time, who he loved, what he cared for and why. Outside the flat, under cover of darkness, a convoy of armoured police Transits rumbled past on the main road while the gale lifted the litter into the air, rattling metal shutters. In the Radio Rentals shop, the late news played soundlessly on fifteen television sets. Standing in the shop doorway, a figure watched unseen.

TWENTY-FOUR

Late Thursday evening, John flew to Belfast in a twin-engine propeller aircraft that resembled a flying wardrobe. It rattled and shook alarmingly but it didn't bother him, he was in a good mood, pleased to be getting away, even if it was to Belfast.

Eighteen when he'd arrived and twenty-one when he'd left, he'd grown up in the city. At first, he'd enjoyed the excitement and the banter. The physical exercise was good for him; he was good at map-reading and telecoms and liked being part of a team; until the platoon was ambushed. One of the lads was killed by an explosion, another lost his legs and in the brief firefight that followed, everyone changed. John had been identified as officer potential but after that he began to query orders and make his own decisions. Too many things happened that shouldn't have. Sometimes they'd mount a roadblock in the middle of nowhere, only to discover later that a group of suspected terrorists had been slaughtered in a farmhouse nearby. He hadn't liked the feeling of being an accessory to something he hadn't agreed to. He wanted out, and while he waited, reading became his refuge. At first he read anything but then he gravitated towards the great novels. That's when the idea of becoming a journalist first occurred to him. He would cut through the lies and tell the truth.

The plane threatened to shake itself to pieces as it banked over the city before landing. Picked out by the evening sun, the cranes of the Harland and Wolff shipyard reached up like giant Meccano swans. An army helicopter buzzed north towards the darkening night like an angry wasp.

Ten pm. Belfast was a city under siege, a place of secrets, intrigues, treacheries and fear. Ordinary people lived here, ordinary people with shoes and coats and faces. Ordinary people who laughed, joked, walked the streets, rode in black cabs, marked out territories, sang songs, betrayed, murdered, mutilated and terrorised. In the dark hours of the night you might hear screams, the distant thump of a bomb, the occasional burst of gunfire but you never opened your door. You never took a cab to your door either, in case someone came back later and shot you. You never talked politics in public, except in low tones with people you knew and even then, you were careful. Belfast was the future; paranoia made manifest. The community were dancing in ruins, dodging bullets. Anybody with a shred of imagination drank. John joined them.

The bar was bedlam, the last stop before hell, an engine roar of agitated voices over the animated, energised, wild-eyed drinkers crowded aboard the oblivion express. Civilisation was on the operating table; the bloody veneer had been peeled back revealing the turmoil of twisted guts and gore beneath. Yorkshire and the miners' strike was the Battle of Britain, a Brylcreem confrontation where the combatants went home each night. Belfast was over the water. Belfast was occupied. There were checkpoints, curfews, no-go areas, troops, sabotage and reprisals. John liked it. For once, he felt at home, among like-minded souls who saw the same shadows. He drank heavily and slept little. Daylight brought a groggy hangover, the energy of the night crushed by inertia and reality.

The church was on top of a hill. Serried ranks of houses ran down three sides into Belfast like formations of troops drawn up for a battle. The fourth side held the graveyard and the church. A lone piper began a lament as the hearse stopped by the red, white and blue kerbstones outside the Protestant churchyard. Across the road, a Loyalist mural adorned the end wall of the terrace opposite – a day-glo King Billy with a clown's face sitting on a deformed horse, juxtaposed with a crudely drawn Armalite rife and the initials UVF. Beneath it, an army foot patrol lounged watchfully. A knot of people had gathered and stood back respectfully as the hearse was unloaded and carried by six large, black-clad shaven-headed men towards the church. A couple of older women walked past weeping, quietly followed by a small crowd. John brought up the rear.

At the exact moment that he entered the church, Clemmy paid off a cab and entered the revolving doors of the hotel in Leeds. She was excited, anticipating the afternoon. Slightly late, she hurried through the lobby and into the bar. Scanning the room for John and realising he wasn't there, she checked her watch, bought a drink and settled down to wait.

Forty minutes later, a cold wind blew as the coffin was lowered into the grave. Men in ski masks shouted in unison incoherently, their voices drowned by the army helicopter hovering overhead. They fired a salute with revolvers over the coffin and the coffin was lowered. Shivering, John was having doubts about the trip. The service and graveside oration had been a mixture of sectarian sentimentality, Loyalist propaganda and downright lies.

What the fuck am I doing back here? Getting a story? Fat chance. All I've got is a half-baked conspiracy theory. Not that fucking half-baked.

Leaving the churchyard with the other mourners, John's way was barred by a young, pink-faced man with fat cheeks and piggy eyes. He wasn't tall but he was wide. A black and orange shell suit one size too small stretched over his bulk and shone dully in the pale light. A black Ford Granada stood by the kerb, the rear door open.

'Get in the car.' The Belfast vowels elongated and twisted the word 'car' into a strange bird-like call.

John took out his press card. 'Northern TV, I'm a journalist.'

The man didn't even look at the card but indicated the car again. 'You'll be insulting Billy's memory if you don't.' Across the road, the army foot patrol had disappeared, as had the helicopter. John shrugged and did as he was told. The man got in beside John.

As they drove away, John asked, 'Where are we going?'

'Fucking King's Arms, for the fucking wake. Now shut the fuck up, will you? Tommy!' Tommy, the driver, looked about twelve. He nodded and inserted a tape into the tape deck. Van Morrison singing 'Carrickfergus' at a million decibels exploded into the vehicle rendering further conversation impossible.

By the time John got into the car, Clemmy had been sitting waiting for fifty minutes, her drink untouched. After checking her watch for the umpteenth time, she went to one of the hotel pay phones and called John's flat. When she got his answerphone, she slammed the receiver down, marched into reception and asked if there were any messages for her. When the receptionist said there weren't, Clemmy made her check again just to make sure. When it was clear that there weren't any, she turned away. She felt foolish, humiliated and very angry. With a great effort she pulled herself together, thanked the receptionist and walked out of the hotel, her face a rictus of fury.

The King's Arms was a new building just off the Crumlin Road, a one-storey concrete bunker with tiny windows and a flat bombproof roof out of the Ceaucescu crematorium school of architecture. Inside it was just as functional, the crowded island bar decked out in blue Glasgow Rangers' banners and Orange sashes. It was a hard-drinking, hard-man's bar. The only women were the barmaids, who served at high speed without ever making eye contact with anyone. Looking at the hard faces and dead, cold eyes, John was reminded of the coppers' bar in Yorkshire. The same brutality, the same hardness and suppression of feeling; the same unspoken fear. He'd come to the right place.

'Fuck me, lads, it's that reporter Billy held hostage.'

The shout jerked him from his musing. He looked up to see three grinning RUC officers, pints in hand leering at him. As he reached for his beer, a hush descended on the bar. The throng parted to make way for a heavy-set man in his forties. The big lad with the shell suit followed at a discreet distance. Two more heavies guarded the door. The big man came over to him.

He had a collapsed toad's face, the chin and forehead receding from his prominent battered nose. His protruding eyes were a startling blue colour. His head was shaved but his face and arms were recently tanned. He wore a number of sovereign rings on both hands.

'You were on Newsnight last night, so you were,' he said in a surprisingly high-pitched voice.

'Not for long.' The day before, he'd done forty minutes down the line to London and been told to expect twenty. In the event Newsnight broadcast just three minutes, the rest cut to make room for another initiative by Ian Macgregor in the Miners' Strike. Plus ça change. A barman hurried over and put a pint on the bar beside John and the big man. The man took it, gulped down a quarter and looked at John again.

'We're not pleased with you. That shite you put out.'

'What shite would that be?'

'Telly shite. Fenian propaganda, so it is.' He looked round the bar, then back at John. 'Why did you come to his funeral?'

'I got to know him a little. I was with him when he died.'

The man stared unpleasantly.

'Billy was a patriot.' He pronounced it 'Bully'.

'Is that why he was brought back here to be buried?'

The man sneered. 'Go back to your wanking pit.'

'But...'

'But, but, but...' the man interrupted, 'Too many questions.' He turned away.

'Billy took orders from Ulstermen. From Gladio.' The man stopped and turned back to face John. 'Billy told me.'

'Go back to the mainland. You're not welcome here.' He turned and walked away. John went to follow him, but found his way barred by the shiny shell suit.

'Leave it.'

John shrugged and returned to the bar, annoyed with himself. He was sipping his pint disconsolately when he felt a tug on his sleeve. He looked down to see a tiny, wizened, rat-faced man in an ancient crumpled suit.

'Can I stand next to you?' he whispered in a loud rasp.

'What?'

'Can I stand next to the man from Newsnight?'

John shrugged. 'Why?'

Rat-face's age could be anything between forty and sixty. He looked round the bar furtively, then pulled John down so he could whisper again. 'You'd want to stand next to you if you were the only Catholic in this Loyalist loony bin.'

John looked at the man, who grinned open-mouthed, revealing a dental catastrophe of blackened stumps and missing teeth. He caught the stench of his breath and recoiled involuntarily but the little man held onto him and pulled him back.

'Who are you?'

Rat-face shook his head impatiently. 'Your man who was just talking to you, Loyalist executioner, so he is. Big friend of the Shankill butchers.' He drew a grubby thumb across the sagging crop of his throat and down his midriff and made a gurgling noise to indicate being slit in pieces. 'Real piece of work.'

John nodded and downed his pint. 'Well, I must be going.' He turned to go but Rat-face tugged at his sleeve again. John pulled his arm away. 'I've got a plane to catch.'

'You want to know about Billy Hatton?' Rat-face hissed. John stopped and looked at the little man again. Rat-face winked, his face collapsing into a thousand creases as he smiled in triumph. 'I t'ought you did.'

'Well?' John asked impatiently. 'What about him?'

'Jack's bar on the Cliftonville Road. Ask for Kevin.'

John nodded. 'Right, thanks.' Then he remembered something. 'Cliftonville Road? Isn't that the er...?'

'Murder mile? Got it in one,' Rat-face grinned. 'Ask anyone where it is.' John sighed and made to leave but found his way barred again, this time by Rat-face's outstretched open palm. John looked down at it puzzled, then at Rat-face who smiled like a genie.

'What now?'

'You can spare the money for a pint, can't you? Intrepid reporter John Bradley, star of Newsnight?' the little man hissed cheerfully. John fished in his pocket, pulled out a note and gave it to Rat-face who clutched it gratefully. 'Jack's, eh?' He winked. John nodded and left.

TWENTY-FIVE

John decided against a taxi. Instead, he walked back into Belfast and then out along the Cliftonville Road. He was taking a risk but this was the last throw. He would go to Jack's bar and see what he could find out. If he drew a blank, so be it; he'd given it a go. The lovely evening was disfigured by an army foot patrol coming down the other side of the road. A soldier on point, rifle at the ready moved quickly to a new position where he crouched down scanning the street ahead. He was followed by another soldier with a radio, while behind him two RUC officers in flak jackets walked nonchalantly, chatting to each other, apparently unconcerned. Another soldier followed the policemen while a last soldier crouched, weapon at the ready, looking backwards and giving cover. Although John had on been on those patrols himself, he'd never got used to seeing troops on a British street.

Cheered by evening sunlight, he relaxed and looked for Jack's bar. He didn't see the man appear from the doorway behind him, or the second follower who crossed from the other side of the road to join the first. John stopped and scanned the street, searching for Jack's. He turned, saw the two men and decided to ask them where it was. As they came near, he caught a look in their eyes. Oh fuck! No! The foot patrol had disappeared and he heard the screech of wheels as the car appeared from a side street. Then he was bundled roughly into the car by the two men and it moved away at high speed while he struggled.

'Lie down, you Brit bastard,' one of them said, kicking him hard in the kidneys and shoving a hood over John's head. He did as he was told and the kicking stopped. They dragged him upright and after tying his hands behind his back, sat him between them on the back seat. 'That's better. May as well enjoy the fucking journey, eh?'

John did as he was told and tried to contain the terror surging through him. The hood was made of a heavy cotton fabric. It reeked of damp, body odour and decay. John wondered how many condemned men had worn it before him. A crash of sound exploded into the car as, for the second time that day, Van Morrison singing 'Carrickfergus' erupted from the sound system. The four lads in the car immediately joined in, singing lustily.

In an instrumental lull, he tried making contact. 'Which Loyalist bunch are you? Ulster Freedom Fighters?'

Someone giggled; another snorted a suppressed laugh.

He tried again.

'UVF then?' More sniggers. 'Red Hand Commando?' This time the car erupted into guffaws of laughter.

'I'm Sean and he's Seamus. They sound like 'hun' names to you?'

'But Carrickfergus is a Protestant anthem?'

'True, but your man is a great singer and you've been kidnapped by the Provos, so you have,' someone said with a chuckle, breaking off to join in with the final rousing chorus.

Two hours later, the kidnap car turned onto a muddy track and bumped along at high speed before pulling up. He was pushed out, still hooded, hands still tied behind his back, and propelled into a building, then down a corridor to a staircase at the back which he fell down, landing in a winded heap at the bottom. He heard a door being slammed and a bolt rammed home then he was alone again and quiet. His back ached and his temple was sore where he'd banged it again but he was alive, for the time being. He was scared but growing accustomed to the feeling. With Hatton, fear had been an enveloping presence which possessed and engulfed him; now it was small, nimble and came in short staccato bursts, violently tap-dancing through his innards.

Evening passed into darkness, darkness into night. In the guardhouse at Menwith Hill, a bored sentry yawned, leaned back in his chair and watched the news on a small black and white TV ignoring the security monitors. When the klaxon went off, he was laughing at the news footage of Ian MacGregor holding a plastic bag in front of his face. He shot upright, struggling to get his feet off the table and glanced at the security monitor. Three figures were clearly visible inside the perimeter. The guard pressed a switch, which turned on the security lights and let out the attack dogs. The klaxon continued to blare. The women stood, frozen, then turned back and ran towards the wire.

Other sirens began to wail inside the base. Vehicles accelerated round the perimeter road. Outside the fence, women from the peace camp began singing 'We Shall Overcome', banging dustbin lids, rattling the wire fencing and encouraging the returning intruders as they scrambled through the hole in the fence. With the dogs practically upon them, two succeeded but the third was caught and wrestled screaming to the floor.

At that moment, a lorry full of RAF police screeched to halt outside the perimeter fence. Guards jumped down and began pulling the protesting, screaming women back from the wire, preventing them from seeing the fate of the remaining intruder.

TWENTY-SIX

'A chair in here. Now!' The voice woke John from a fitful sleep. He'd heard the commotion upstairs, the door opening and the clattering down the wooden stairs but it had all been in his fitful dreaming. Despite the hood, he could tell a light had been switched on. Hands reached under his shoulder blades and lifted him up roughly. His hands were untied and he heard the voice again. 'Sit down, Mr Bradley.' A hand guided him to a chair and sat him down. 'That's it, there you go.' It was a gentle, southern Irish voice with a beguiling playful note. 'Now let's get that hood off you.'

The hood was removed and John blinked at his surroundings. He was in a cellar with a concrete floor. Two walls were covered in empty Dexion shelving. A bare bulb hung from the ceiling. A tall man with a large bulbous head, grey thinning hair and pin-bright blue eyes under old-fashioned, black-rimmed glasses tutted and undid the cap of a thermos flask.

'Fancy tying you up,' he said, pouring some hot liquid into the cap and offering it to John. 'You just can't get the staff anymore. Don't you find that?' John looked at the cup suspiciously. 'It's just tea. English breakfast tea actually but it's the best and as it's practically dawn, well why not. Go on, drink it.'

He took the cup and drank. It was hot, sweet and very welcome. The man grinned. 'That's the ticket. I'm Kevin, by the way.' Although tall, he didn't stand out; his face seemed to shut down when not in use and it was difficult to place him. He could have been a bank manager, a teacher, a professor, a farm worker but when he spoke, it was like switching on the power. His eyes filled with a restless, mischievous intelligence and his mouth smiled easily. He liked to talk but more than that, he liked to debate.

'What do you want, Kevin?'

'I'd say that was putting the cart before the horse. You're the one who's been asking about Billy Hatton.' Kevin walked round the room, then stopped and regarded him. 'What do you know about Gladio? You must know something; half of Belfast heard you mention them in the King's Arms.'

'Hatton said they trained him.'

Kevin nodded then began to pace back and forwards in front of John. 'It began as a guerrilla army set up in Europe after the war by the CIA in case of a communist takeover.'

'Yes, I know.'

'They selected people sympathetic to their cause, freemasons, ex-fascists, bankers and the like, trained them, set up secret arms dumps.'

'Then the Yanks pulled out but Gladio continued?'

'That's right. In Italy, France, Spain, Portugal, Germany.'

'And Britain?' Kevin regarded him thoughtfully.

'The British government has always denied their existence but here in the province, we have a healthy scepticism for British denials. They have been known to lie, you know, but then you'd know that from your time here.' He smiled. 'Yes, when you were part of the occupying forces.'

'So you think there is a British Gladio cell?' John prompted.

'Oh yes. They're around all right, linked to extreme nationalists.'

'Like you?'

Kevin ignored him. 'It's driven from high up, on the British mainland. They think democracy's a sham.' He paused. 'They may have a point.'

'What do they want?'

'The usual: power, racial purity; the strong lead, the weak follow. Your Maria must have really got up their noses.'

'What do you know about that?'

Kevin smiled. 'We hear things.'

'Who from?'

'Friends, and friends of friends,' He sat down on the chair. 'Are you a football fan, John?'

119

'Why the fuck does everyone want to talk to me about sport all of a sudden?'

'I'm a Liverpool fan myself, but that Mr Clough, now, he's a genius. He took Forest, a little club, and made them champions of Europe, not once but twice. Doesn't that inspire you?'

'In what way?'

'David and Goliath?'

'What does this have to do with my sister?'

'There were two other members of Hatton's Gladio unit, Tony Stubbs and Eric Guttridge. Maybe you should ask them?'

'Hatton was part-time SAS.'

Kevin shook his head and stood, serious again. 'Hatton was a crim, so he was; the part-time SAS crap is just cover for deniable freelance operations, like going after your Maria.'

'Do you know why they went after her?'

'Let's just say they have a very strict security policy.'

'What do you want? I presume you brought me here for a reason?'

Kevin smiled. 'Gladio runs guns to the Loyalists. My friends and I would like them to stop.'

'And?'

Kevin took off his glasses and began to clean them with a handkerchief. 'As a well-known journalist, you could help us,' Kevin said, inspecting the lenses. 'Gladio would shrivel under the glare of publicity.'

'You want me to help you?'

'We could help each other.'

'I can't work with terrorists.'

'Terrorists? Us?! We're the ones with the white hats, so we are.'

'You murder people in cold blood.'

'So you won't help us?'

John shook his head slowly, 'I can't.'

'That's a shame,' Kevin said sadly, then brightened. 'The name's Dillon by the way, Kevin Dillon. If you change your mind?' he winked. John didn't reply. Kevin stood for moment then roused himself. 'Sean, Jim! Get in here!'

The door opened and two guards clattered down the stairs, guns in hand, their faces hidden by ski masks. 'See to him.' Kevin hurried up the stairs, slamming the door behind him.

John's arms were pinioned and tied behind his back and he was hooded again before being frogmarched up the stairs and out to the car. Two hours later, he was pushed out of the car, which didn't stop but merely slowed down before screeching away. He rolled awkwardly across soft earth then struggled to stand, but fell again on the uneven ground. He knew it was light and there was traffic but that was all.

Rush-hour commuters crossing the Ormeau Bridge were surprised to see a hooded figure with its hands tied floundering on the grass in the park by the road.

TWENTY-SEVEN

Naz took two phone calls in the newsroom while John was in Clemmy's office. The first one he didn't say anything but listened intently and sighed as he put the receiver down. The second call was from Jess; she wanted to speak to John. Naz looked across at Clemmy's office and smiled. She was reading John the riot act. 'He's, erm, tied up right now,' Naz said quietly, hoping the shouting in the background didn't carry into the phone.

'It's about Maria. It's important.'

'Give me your number, I'll get him to...' Jess cut him off.

'Not over the phone. Tell him to come and see me today, at the cottage.'

'All right, I'll tell him.' Naz replaced the receiver. Behind the glass panel, Clemmy was in full cry.

After interrogation, debriefing and some tedious local TV interviews, John arrived back in Leeds exhausted. The news of his kidnap hadn't made it to the national news but that suited him. He'd survived without having another attack of the terrors. It was only when he was back in Leeds that he realised there was something there; something he could follow up. Arriving back, he didn't expect garlands of flowers or an orchestra at the airport or even a greeting card, but neither did he expect to be in a shouting match with Clemmy on his first day back at work. He tried to tell her what had happened but she wouldn't listen.

'What the hell did you think you were doing?'

'Going after a story!'

'You had no bloody right! We're short-handed because of the strike.'

'I was on leave, remember?'

'I told you to lay off that story.'

'I'm a reporter. It's my job.'

'I tell you what your job is.' He went over to her but she turned away.

'Gladio is dynamite, Clemmy, I can feel it.'

'That's all you do feel.'

'I'm getting close.'

'All you've got is a dead killer and the unsubstantiated allegations of an IRA terrorist.' She began making notes on a news bulletin script.

'Let me chase up Stubbs and Guttridge.' She frowned and went back to her script. 'Sometimes you have go into the shadows.'

'This isn't Guatemala, it's Yorkshire for Christ's sake! You can't go off on freelance fishing trips whenever you feel like it.'

'Why are you so angry?'

'You don't remember, do you?'

'Remember what?'

'Friday afternoon?'

'I was at the funeral.' Then he got it. 'Christ, the hotel! I'm sorry.'

'Why? I only waited an hour.'

'Let me make up for it, then?' He put his hands on her desk and leant towards her. 'How about a drink after work?' but the shutters were down.

'Can't tonight, I've got a meeting with the Controller.' Her eyes were bright and passionate, her cheeks flushed.

'I'm a good reporter.'

'Were, John. You've lost your objectivity.'

'Are you angry because the company was warned off or because I stood you up?' She ignored him. He tried again. 'Look, I'm sorry. I won't do anything else without telling you first.'

'I don't want to hear about Gladio again. From now on you do as I say or you're looking for another job.'

'So what now?'

'The miners' strike is at a critical stage.' He began to interrupt but she overrode him. 'The pit deputies' ballot is in two days. Take Brian and Naz and get the word on the pit village street.

Just a few vox pops. See if the pit lads think the deputies will side with them or not. Think you can do that without invoking a wild conspiracy theory?' She glared at him then went back to making notes on the script. He turned and left the office.

It was Naz's idea to call in at Jess's cottage on the way to the gig.

'Why couldn't she say over the phone?' John asked. 'Why couldn't Maria call me herself?'

'She sounded worried.'

John was pissed off. Pissed off at having to do pointless interviews, pissed off about Clemmy. Pissed off with himself for forgetting their date and pissed off with her for not listening to him. Maybe she was right, he was paranoid. Lately, he couldn't shake the feeling that he was being followed. He pulled the driver's mirror over to scan the rear-view.

'For Christ's sake,' Naz exclaimed, dragging the mirror back.

'Just checking we aren't being followed.' Naz slowed for the turning to the cottage.

'Don't be long, now,' Brian called as he got out. 'Try not to get yourself kidnapped this time.' John ignored the jibe and hurried up the path. Jess was back in her peace camp uniform, a loud, loose cotton dress and a hundred bangles on her wrist. She shushed him theatrically when he began to talk and led him out onto the lawn at the back of the cottage before she would speak. Her cloak and dagger paranoia irritated him.

'What's this about?'

Jess spoke quietly, 'Last Friday, three women breached the perimeter of Menwith Hill.'

'Broke in?'

She nodded, 'They were a diversion.'

'What for?'

'Forty minutes earlier, Maria entered the camp from a different location. Her aim was to break into the recording library.'

'She went alone?'

'It was her idea. She wanted to get proof about Gladio, some hard evidence that they exist.'

'For Christ's sake!' Jess didn't reply. 'And? Did she get out? Was she arrested? What?'

'I don't know.'

'What do you mean?'

'Menwith Hill and the authorities have acknowledged apprehending one of the three women who created the diversion, and issued arrest warrants for the other two.' She paused, then continued, 'but they have denied all knowledge of Maria.'

He stared at her. Jess looked tired. She hadn't slept since the night of the break-in and it showed. From out front Naz honked the car horn impatiently. Jess's fingers caressed his arm gently and she leaned in close. He looked down at her hand on his bare arm. Her touch was unexpected, diverting.

'That's why I rang you. I thought you might be able to help.' Naz honked his car again and the moment was broken.

TWENTY-EIGHT

Tony Stubbs arrived back from his run along the towpath, drenched in sweat. Despite the warm day, he wore tracksuit bottoms and a plastic bin liner over his vest to make him sweat even more. Added to this, he carried a fifteen-kilo rucksack on his back. Without breaking his stride, he jumped the eight feet down onto the deck of his houseboat and began doing high-speed press-ups, calling out the total in blocks of ten. Stubbs was thirty-five, thin and wiry with a lean, feral bone structure. If you passed him, you wouldn't give him a second glance, which was just the way he liked it. His press-up count had reached 223 when he heard a car pull up. A crowd of blue exhaust smoke appeared followed by Eric Guttridge on the towpath carrying two holdalls, who stood watching Stubbs uneasily.

'Two forty,' Stubbs gasped as Eric struggled down the ladder with his bags. 'Two fifty!' he announced triumphantly. He stopped the press-ups and jumped to his feet. Eric held up the holdalls without speaking. Stubbs nodded and led the way below into the boat.

The cabin was a hot, airless midden. Unwashed saucepans on a rusting camping stove, clothes scattered about, it was more workshop than living space. Stubbs cleared the top of the galley table with a forearm, cascading tools, crockery and papers onto the floor. Eric lifted the bags on to the table and stood back. Stubbs opened one and lifted out a heavy parcel of greased polythene. 'Any problems?' he asked, unwrapping a machine pistol and beginning to assemble it.

'It was hairy, roads are crawling with coppers.' Eric's eyes darted back and forth around the cramped quarters.

Stubbs snapped the gun together and checked the firing

mechanism with practised ease. 'You made it, Eric. It's my problem now.'

Eric nodded uneasily, hopping nervously from foot to foot. He was scared shitless. Hatton had been a catastrophe and he had expected to lie low for a while, at least until things had died down. Yet here he was, not two weeks since he delivered to Hatton, on another mission. It was madness. Stubbs glanced at him and frowned. 'What's eating you, Eric?'

'It's crazy. 'Kill another copper so soon after Billy's job? It'll never work.'

Stubbs examined the barrel of another smaller gun. 'It'll work long enough to affect the pit deputies' vote.' He opened the second holdall and removed a box of ammunition.

'Two hundred rounds of ammo, gas mask and two silencers, as you requested,' Eric volunteered. Stubbs unpacked a silencer and fitted it to the Uzi. Eric watched as he examined the equipment; Stubbs lacked the curiosity to worry about the possible consequences. When they were training, his nickname had been 'The Grinder' because he ground his teeth and displayed so little emotion. Eric, on the other hand, was cursed with a vivid imagination.

'What happens if it goes pear-shaped, Tony?'

'Same as Billy.'

Eric flinched, he didn't want to end up like Hatton.

'I want out.'

Stubbs stopped working with the weapons and looked at him. 'You knew what you were getting into when you signed up.' Eric had seen that look before, on Billy Hatton's face, and he was dead and cold.

'Yes, but we were training then. This is different.'

Stubbs finished checking the rest of the equipment. 'Are you going to give back that new bungalow of yours?' He replaced the stuff in the holdalls. 'Right, it's all here Eric. You can go.' Worried, scared, out of his depth, Eric stood there without moving. 'Piss off, then!'

Eric jumped back into life. 'Right. Er, good luck.' He turned and went back onto the deck. Stubbs appeared after him.

'And keep that gob of yours shut, if you don't want a visit some dark night.' Eric nodded and clambered awkwardly up the ladder onto the towpath. Stubbs watched him go, unsmiling.

TWENTY-NINE

Tensions were high in the pit village. A squad of mounted police in riot gear stood close to another mass of police with riot shields. An equally intimidating mass of pickets jeered from a safe distance. Everyone was on edge, preoccupied as if waiting for something to kick off. John was infected by the atmosphere too but he had other things on his mind. He was frantic about Maria. Where was she? What had happened to her? What on earth did she know that made her so dangerous? What the hell was going on? He'd phoned a couple of police contacts and drawn a blank but given the strike, that wasn't surprising. He needed to do something, anything other than hanging around on the picket line again.

John did three lacklustre vox pop interviews with the strikers but they were restless, unwilling to talk and his mind was elsewhere. The miners made a show of bravado; the deputies were on their side but it didn't matter which way they voted, the miners would never give up. In reality, however, the first fingers of doubt were starting to unsettle them. He gave up after the third miner gave the same response.

'Is that it?' Brian asked, pushing his headphones round his neck.

'Carry on if you think you can do any better,' John snapped and disappeared into a phone box. Brian caught Naz's eye. Naz shrugged and began to pack up the gear. Twenty-five minutes later, he was on his seventh call, talking animatedly into the receiver, burning up in the phone box. Gladio, Clemmy, the strike, Maria – he was running on empty again. Two mates from the nationals, another contact at Yorkshire Police HQ, a couple of answerphone messages, a duff number and an old flame at the

BBC in London; nobody knew anything. Abruptly, he slammed the phone down and left the box, swearing to himself. 'Got any change?'

Naz shook his head while Brian searched his pockets and produced one sixpence, two two pence pieces and a fiver.

'Is that all?'

'They'll be charging you rent if you spend any more time in there,' said Brian. 'Did you find anything out?'

He was about to reply when he saw something.

'Hello, what's he doing here?'

Brian and Naz looked over to where two senior policemen were talking animatedly to a tall man in a good suit.

'Get some footage, Naz.' Naz hoisted the camera and began shooting. Brian followed John's gaze.

'Who's the bloke in the suit?'

'We're about to find out. He's coming over,' Naz said as he continued filming. John detached himself and went to meet him. Gimlet smiled.

'You're a hard man to get through to, John.'

'Just doing my job.'

'I meant what I said.' John didn't speak. 'Oh and wipe that tape, please, or I'll have it seized.' Gimlet walked away. John went back to Naz and put his hand over the lens.

'Wipe it will you, Naz?' Naz and Brian frowned in unison. 'Just do it, please.'

'Who is that bloke?' Brian asked.

'Gimlet,' Naz answered.

'Who is he?' Brian repeated as Gimlet and the policemen disappeared behind the rows of police.

'Good question.'

'Any news about Maria?'

John shook his head. 'I'm going back to the flat.'

'Now? What about work?'

'Cover for me. If they ask, I'm sick. I'll be back tomorrow.' Bemused, Brian and Naz watched him go.

'Is it just me or is he losing his touch?' Brian asked quizzically.

'Both,' Naz replied. Brian looked at him puzzled.

THIRTY

When John arrived at the flat, he threw off his suit jacket and poured himself a large scotch. He drank it straight down, then began leafing impatiently through his filofax to see if he'd missed anyone out, but he knew he hadn't. He was frantic about Maria and upset about standing up Clemmy but Hatton was a big story and he wanted to follow it up before it went cold. He knew it was dangerous and that he was on thin ice but that's what gave the story legs. Done right, it was a passport to the big time. The memory of Maria's crumpled photograph ringed in red felt tip kept coming back. He needed to talk to Jess and find out what she knew. The doorbell rang.

John approached the front door cautiously. He wasn't expecting anybody and the figure blocking the light through the frosted glass wasn't small. 'Who is it?' he shouted cautiously, through the letterbox.

'Message from Mrs Clements, special delivery,' a voice replied in a deep baritone. He smiled to himself.

'Just a minute,' he said, unlocking the door. John just caught sight of a big man with a beard and a scowl before he was punched hard in the face. The blow cannoned him back down the small hall, knocking him onto his back. He tried to pull himself together as the bearded man approached him again. He picked John up and threw him into his small sitting room.

'What's this about?'

'As if you didn't know.' John managed to get off a punch before he was thrown against a wall and fell to the floor, winded. The man dragged him to his feet and this time John managed to punch him on the nose. It was a good shot and sent the big guy backwards but he came back and hit John again, hurling him across the room. He was a mess now. His lip was cut and his eye bleeding.

'What the fuck do you want?' He didn't have much left. Crumpled on his back, his right hand felt something hard and wet under the sofa – the neck of the whisky bottle. His hand closed round it and as the big man dragged him to his feet again, John hit him over the head as hard as he could with the bottle, which shattered in the process. The man crumpled to the floor. Still holding the neck of the bottle, John fell on top of him and held the jagged glass of the bottle against his throat.

'Who sent you? Gladio, eh? You another one?'

The big guy stared back, uncomprehending. Blood pumped rhythmically under the soft, pink flesh compressed by the broken bottle's razor edge. The man's eyes widened with fear.

'Special Branch, then? Tell me!' The man shook his head gently, trying to avoid the glass but John was out of control. He'd been pushed around too much. Now it was his turn. Spittle dribbled from his mouth onto the man's face. He tried again, 'The Provos?' The man shook his head again. 'Ulster Freedom Fighters then? Tell me! Who the fuck are you?!' John roared, his breath coming in snorts like an animal.

'Clemmy's husband.'

Time slowed. Air and passion were sucked from the room as if by a giant fan. John stared down at the big man in wide-eyed horror and shock. After a moment, he staggered to his feet. He looked at the jagged glass in his hand and shook his head. 'Jesus. What's happening to me?'

He let the bottle neck slip from his grasp onto the carpet. The man struggled to his feet and rubbed his head. The fight had lasted a minute, two at the most but the big man was bleeding from his scalp, John had a swollen lip, a blackening eye and the flat was a bombsite. John took a deep breath. 'Can we talk about this?'

Clemmy's husband stared at him then collapsed onto the sofa. He began to speak in a matter of fact monotone. 'She was a student when I met her. I was a big hard biker. She was impressed.' He paused and smiled at the memory, then shook himself and continued. 'Now she's a bigwig in TV and I'm just a telephone engineer. But I love her.' He stopped and sighed, looking directly at John for the first time. 'I miss her. Can you understand that?'

'Yes.'

'There've been others, but you're different. I think she's falling for you,' he trailed off. He shook his head slowly from side to side as if unable to accept this. Middle age was starting to fill and fatten his face.

'It's Arthur isn't it?' Arthur nodded sadly. 'Look, Arthur, I'm sorry. I knew she was married but until now, that was just theoretical but now I've met you, well, it's different...'

'You were just using her?'

John shook his head. 'No, I like Clemmy.' Arthur looked even angrier causing John to hurry on 'Actually, I love her.'

'I know,' Arthur said, his eyes narrowing with suspicion. 'I've been watching you, every time you met at the hotel.' He paused for a minute, his mind elsewhere. 'She'll leave me when she finds out I've done this.'

Arthur's air of beaten helplessness left John silent. Arthur hadn't killed anyone or plotted treason. His only crime was to be in love with someone who no longer loved him. John felt seedy and ashamed. Yes he was mired in conspiracy and deception but he wanted to step back out of the shadows and behave decently for once, but even that wasn't simple. John had fallen for Clemmy but she was married and now, standing with Arthur, that seemed important.

'She doesn't have to find out.' Arthur looked at him puzzled. 'Not if I don't see her anymore.'

'You work with her.'

'Outside work, like that.'

Arthur wasn't having it. 'You're lying.'

'No. No, I'm not.'

'Why would you give her up? She's lovely.'

'Yes, she is.' Arthur was scowling now and starting to rouse himself from the sofa. 'Look, Arthur, I've got problems of my own, believe me.' From the look on Arthur's face, it was obvious he didn't. 'I mean it, I won't see her again.'

133

Unconvinced, Arthur stared malevolently at him without speaking. 'It's been complicated for a while. We couldn't carry on as we were for much longer.'

Arthur struggled to his feet and stood silently, towering above him. Finally he nodded to himself. 'You'd better be telling the truth.'

John rubbed his eye and shrugged. 'Let's call it quits, shall we?'

Arthur lumbered slowly down the hall like a wounded animal. John followed. At the door, Arthur turned back, 'Cos if you're lying and you see her again, I'll kill you.' John nodded and shut the front door. Sighing, he sagged against the wall and slumped to the floor.

THIRTY-ONE

Tony Stubbs was flying, humming along to an old Stones track on the radio as he drove down the A1. He'd picked up his vehicle, stowed his equipment in the boot but kept the handgun in the door pocket, just in case. On the seat beside him was a pile of NUM strike leaflets. His brief was simple: do the job, scatter the leaflets about and get the hell out. It was crude but so were the press and the pit deputies were due to vote the next day. He'd found the target himself, an overweight country plod in his forties who because of the strike, worked alone answering every unimportant call in a radius of twenty miles. Every day he bought a bacon sandwich and a plastic cup of tea from Beryl's transport café, then parked up a small lane off the A1 to consume them. Perfect.

The vehicle was a bonus, a black BMW which went like shit off a shovel, and Stubbs enjoyed driving fast. He'd travelled forty miles south down the A1 at speed, enjoying the car, when he approached the small roundabout north of Doncaster. Traffic was light and he ignored the 'Reduce Speed Now' signs, breaking late, enjoying the BMW's superb ride and handling as he hit the roundabout. As he changed direction round it, he lost the back-end at sixty-five miles an hour. The car slewed violently to the left and went into a spin. He thought he'd had a blow out but he hadn't. After that, it didn't matter.

Stubbs might have remembered driving through a puddle in the scrapyard when he'd collected the BMW but he couldn't know about the mixture of oil and sand in the puddle which clogged the tread of his nearside rear tyre. Going down the A1 on a dry road, it didn't matter. It only mattered on the roundabout and only then because of coincidence. Subsidence had changed the camber but even that wasn't enough on its own. What brought all these disparate factors into a critical mass was the strike. Convoys of coal wagons had accelerated the damage to the road surface. It would have been fine if it hadn't been for the nearside rear tyre catching on a small patch of oil, allowing the back end to be driven outwards by centripetal force.

The driver of the Ford Transit remembered seeing Stubbs' head twisting back and forth as he wrestled with the spinning BMW but it was too late. The back end of the car caught the Transit a glancing blow and flipped into a roll. It rolled twice, hit a traffic sign a glancing blow, wrenching off the front passenger door, then flew off the road and down into a small gully, where it landed on its roof and rolled over twice more, before coming to rest in a clump of young trees recently planted by the council. The engine whined hysterically then stuttered to a halt. Wisps of smoke curled lazily up from the wrecked vehicle. The propaganda leaflets were strewn across the bank, marking the car's slide into the gully. A strong breeze picked up some of the leaflets blowing them this way and that, like outsize confetti in a comic opera. In the driver's seat, Tony Stubbs sat upside down, still in his seat belt, his lifeless hands grasping the wheel, his neck broken.

As the emergency chatter about Stubbs' accident reached its zenith, John climbed into the back of an ageing cab and directed the driver towards Otley and Menwith Hill. The driver, a rock and roll casualty with a destroyed complexion, didn't want to go. His Hillman Avenger was a maroon rust bucket and he was worried about being stopped. Apart from that, his face had a black eye, a split lip, a bad graze on his temple and other cuts and bruises. He was only persuaded when John counted out thirty-five quid in fivers into his hand for the round trip.

John had cleaned himself up as best he could but he'd needed to get out of the flat. He couldn't just sit there, he had to do something to try and get his life back under control. Besides, he'd had a phone call from Naz.

'There's news, about Maria. She's in the top-security wing at Hull Jail.'

'Why the news blackout?'

'She's being held under the Prevention of Terrorism Act.'

'What?! Why?'

'Don't know. It's just come down the wire.'

'All right.' John added as an afterthought, 'thanks,' but Naz had already hung up.

In the cab, John's self-absorption discouraged idle conversation. There was something about John that unnerved the driver.

When John walked into the little village of Bridgford to look for Hatton, it wasn't just Brian and Naz that he'd left behind. He'd crossed from the safe, known world into a parallel universe of paranoia, lies and death. Sitting astride Arthur with the bottle to his throat, he'd glimpsed how far he'd travelled. He could have killed Arthur, murdered Clemmy's husband. What was it Gimlet had said? In war, it's kill or be killed. He understood that theoretically everyone is capable of murder but what he'd experienced was real, visceral. It made him feel closer to Hatton. He shivered at the thought.

Was going after the Gladio story worth all this? But what choice did he have? Gladio existed. They had tasked Hatton to kill Maria. They probably ran guns to the Loyalists. There was a story and besides, Arthur would have happened anyway. He was from the 'old world' of affairs and drinking binges, but that was small comfort.

Telling the driver to wait, John strode towards the women's muddy encampment at Menwith Hill. The cab driver didn't like the place. The giant domes and the wire gave him the creeps but it was the military police patrol vehicle inside the wire which made up his mind. He'd been paid. Fuck it. Reversing at high speed, he skidded the Avenger round and drove off at high speed, belching smoke.

John shouted after the disappearing car but his intemperate language attracted the disapproving glances of the women in the camp. In his battered state, he had the familiar look of a violent ex-husband or boyfriend. Some made as if to challenge him, but there was a resolve in his face, a determination, which made them stop and let him past. He entered Jess's bender. She was in the middle of a discussion with two women but they stopped talking as soon as he appeared. He stood there, awkward and unyielding. He wanted answers. His enquiries had come to a dead end but she knew more than she was telling. She always had. Jess smiled apologetically to the women, 'Excuse me.' The women stared coldly, unhappy at the interruption. 'It's John, Maria's brother.' At this, their faces softened a little but their caution remained. He didn't give a fuck. Jess escorted him from the bender.

'You shouldn't just barge in like that, John.' She saw his face close up for the first time. 'Christ, what happened to you?'

John ignored her. 'She's in the top-security wing in Hull jail.'

'What!?'

'Being held her under the Prevention of Terrorism Act!' If Jess was surprised, she didn't show it.

'How did you find out?'

'I'll tell you when you tell me what the fuck is going on!' The knot of peace camp women watching from a distance became agitated. One of them called to Jess, asking if she was OK. Jess nodded, then glared at John.

'Why did Maria break in, what was she after?'

'I can't tell you, John.'

'Who the fuck are you, Jess? What are you doing here?'

She smiled. 'I'm on your side, John, really.'

'Why Maria? Why not somebody else?'

Jess shook her head sadly, 'Maria made me promise.'

'Fuck off!' He threw his head back and waved his arms about angrily. This time the women came over. A short dumpy woman with a shaved head spoke up.

'You have to leave now.' John stared at the group of dirty, hostile women in their muddy boots and outdoor clothes. They began to escort him away from the camp towards the road, pushing and shoving him as they went. He pushed them back.

'All right, I'm fucking going aren't I!'

Jess pushed to the front. 'It's for your own good, John.'

138

'Can you give me a lift to Otley?'

Jess threw him some keys. 'Take Maria's car, I don't need it.' She turned and walked back into the camp. He got into his sister's 'Deux Chevaux' and drove away, the knot of dirty women blurring long before the malevolent, sightless white domes.

THIRTY-TWO

Back at the flat, he tidied up and sat down by the window. In the untended garden, a late-flowering clematis was just coming into bloom amid the crowding nettles and uncut grass, a splash of beauty among the weeds. He got out a writing pad and began to make a list, trying to make sense of what he knew. The evening sun angled into the room, illuminating the names: Maria, Hatton, Gladio, Jess, Menwith Hill, Gimlet, Kevin Dillon – nothing jumped out at him. Things were moving, however, the tectonic plates holding his world together were shifting again. Plans were being hatched; conspiracies set in motion. Already it was too late.

For the second time that day, he was surprised by the doorbell. Frowning, he threw the pad down and walked to the front door. He couldn't see who was outside and he couldn't be bothered to ask. He opened the door to find Clemmy standing there, looking gorgeous. She was wearing another figure hugging, low-cut summer dress with a fitted linen waistcoat and cream high heels. Surprised, he didn't say anything as she marched past him into the flat. He followed her into the living room. She threw her arms round him and kissed him passionately. He responded briefly, then unhooked her arms and stood back. Clemmy began to walk round the flat, examining it.

'It's nice,' she said, turning to him with a smile. It disappeared as she saw his face for the first time. Her brow creased with concern and she came over to him. 'What happened to you?' she asked, touching his wounds gently with her manicured fingers. He let her, then pulled away.

'I walked into a door.' She surveyed the room, which still bore obvious signs of the struggle and shook her head sadly. 'It looks worse than it is.'

'What's going on, John?'

'I thought I was in your bad books.'

'I was upset, I don't like being stood up.'

'I'm sorry about that, really I am.' She kissed him gently and he felt himself responding. With an effort, he pulled away. 'We can't go on like this, Clemmy.'

She nodded. 'I agree.'

'No ties; that's what we said.'

'I've been thinking about things, John. When you were being held hostage and I thought I might not see you again; I got scared. I don't want to feel like that again. Then when we met in the pub the other night, well, I knew.'

'What about Arthur?'

'It's over; has been for a while.'

'I see.'

'Don't you understand what I'm saying, John. No more furtive meetings in hotel rooms. I'd like to try and make a go of it with you.'

'You're married to Arthur, Clemmy.'

She stroked his forehead. 'Sit down. Let me have a look at those cuts.'

John did as he was told. She went into the kitchen and reappeared with a cloth and a bowl of warm water and bathed his cuts. He enjoyed being fussed over. The sensation of her breasts pressing against him as she reached across him was delicious.

'Oh by the way, there's been something on the wire about someone you were interested in. Tony Stubbs.'

'What about him?'

'Car crash on the A1.'

'Anything else?'

'No.' She dabbed his lip, saw him looking at her and kissed him gently. He responded again. He knew it was wrong but he couldn't help himself. The kissing became passionate, then frenzied, and then they were attacking each other, pulling their clothes off in a frenzy. The alarm klaxon blared away in his head. He knew all the reasons he shouldn't be doing it but that's what made it so delicious. As they tumbled about the room, he began

141

to get flashbacks of the fight with Arthur. His erection faltered and disappeared. He rolled over and stopped. Thinking he was play-acting, she grabbed at him, wanting him to continue. Her face fell with disappointment when he didn't.

'Sorry. Don't seem to have it in me today.'

She looked at him, puzzled, then smiled sympathetically. 'It's all right, it'll come back. I'll help it.'

He shook his head. He'd promised her husband, and it felt important to keep his word. He stood up and began to dress, pulling on a pair of jeans. He took a deep breath and said quietly, 'I'd like you to go now.'

She was used to being in charge and getting her own way. 'John, didn't you hear what I said?' He nodded. 'I'll leave Arthur, come and live with you. Whatever you want.' It was all he'd wanted to hear but it was too late. He'd made a promise. "You said you loved me.'

'I did.'

'What's changed, then?'

'It's over, Clemmy.'

'I love you,' she began. Stony-faced, he said nothing. 'Don't you love me, John?'

'It's not enough.'

'Why not?'

He said nothing. Out in the open, his words sounded brutal and cold, like a dead thing. She felt foolish, then began to gather her clothes. He tried to help but she pushed him away roughly. He stood silent while she dressed quickly, hating his pity.

'What's happening to you, John? You're no fun anymore.'

'I think it's the decent thing to do.'

'Pity you can't do your job decently.' She picked up her shoes and waistcoat and marched to the front door.

'I'm sorry, Clemmy.'

'Don't patronise me, you bastard!' Then she was gone, slamming the door behind her. John winced, shook his head and kicked the wall. He was tempted to run after her and bring her back but he didn't.

He walked back to the room, poured himself a drink and put on a Jackson Browne LP. He thought about Tony Stubbs; another lead gone. Maybe she was right, it was a wild goose chase. Sometime later, he fell asleep on the sofa. The LP finished but the needle slipped and caught on the end of the record like a pencil being sharpened in hell.

Forty miles away, under cover of darkness, Stubbs' BMW was being loaded onto an unmarked recovery vehicle and towed away. The watching traffic police breathed a sigh of relief – at least there wouldn't be another tailback come the morning rush hour.

Police and ambulance crews had established that Stubbs was beyond help. The discovery of his handgun, which fell out when the driver's door was opened, changed everything. When the car boot was prized open and the contents of his equipment bag were revealed, an army special unit was on its way. They'd been summoned when the car number plate had flashed down the wires. After that, the police interviewed witnesses and watched the traffic jam get worse. At six o'clock, during rush hour, the tailback was seven miles. The Army Special Unit had top-level clearance. They didn't hurry; they just went about their job carefully. They didn't speak except to give orders and they ignored the police. The police weren't bothered. Lots of strange things happened during the strike. They'd learnt to take the overtime and not be too curious.

THIRTY-THREE

John came awake with a start, woken by the phone ringing. It was dark and he was disorientated. His head was sore and the base of his spine snagged with pain as he moved. He groaned and looked at the clock: it was four am. Who the hell was calling him at this time? The ringing was hideously loud in the dark. The silence returned and enveloped him when he picked up the receiver.

'Is that you, John?' The accent was unmistakable.

'Who is this?'

'An admirer of Brian Clough, I've got a story for you.' Christ, the last thing he needed was to be phoned up by the Provos when God knows who might be listening.

'I told you before, I'm not interested.'

'You'll be interested in this one, it's about Hull jail.'

His grip on the phone tightened. 'What about it?'

'Some of my lads are in there. They reckon there's a rabbit off.'

'What kind of rabbit?'

'If I were you, I'd get a crew down there, tout de suite, so I would.'

'What do you mean?

'The word is it's a set-up. It's been organised from outside, aye.'

'What the fuck are you on about?'

'There's a riot going on in there. The whole place has gone up; the top-security wing is cut off.' There was a click as the line went dead. He stared at the receiver impotently and put it back. After a moment, he dialled directory enquiries.

From the outside, Hull Jail was an imposing redbrick fortress that reassured the passing public. Inside, it was a crumbling,

144

insanitary mess dominated by the smell of stale sweat, sewage, old cooking and fear. A secret hell for the mad, the sad and the dangerous confined within. And lodged within each prisoner, the secret, tragic history of their own undoing. In the small hours of that late August morning, Hull Jail was a scene from Dante's inferno. Prisoners in C wing ripped out basins and piled up mattresses and furniture into a makeshift barricade but it was the noise that caught the attention. Echoing round the landings were the terrifying, unearthly, primal screams of caged beasts, driven by rage and frustration. Animated bodies were running and crawling over each other like excited primates. They'd got onto the nonces' landing, where the rapists and sex offenders and anyone else on Rule 43 were kept segregated. Cells were ripped open and terrified prisoners were dragged out, to be beaten and mutilated in the name of primeval justice, but not all. Dennis Murray had raped and murdered seven women before he was caught. A part time metallurgy lecturer with few friends, his victims had lived and worked in the Hull and North Humberside area. Murray's chosen hunting ground had been the leafier suburbs frequented by the well-spoken, educated women he preyed upon. He loved humiliating them.

A posse of three tattooed skinheads invaded Murray's cell. He crouched, gibbering in terror in the corner, holding onto the bunk bed but they ripped his hand away and dragged him screaming onto the landing. One of them kicked him and told him to shut the fuck up. Despite his fear, Murray sensed that something was afoot. Instead of being tortured like the other nonces, he was led down some steps through a series of doors. On the way, they passed two IRA prisoners screaming at a couple of screws watching from behind a locked grille, pleading with them to come in and sort things out. Normally the screws didn't mess with the IRA but Murray remembered that this time, they laughed and taunted the terrorists – they were going to get their fucking heads kicked in.

Two more screws watched on security cameras from a reinforced safe room. A phone rang in the room. One of the screws, a fat, middle-aged man called Trevor, picked up the phone and said without taking his eyes off the security cameras, 'HMP Hull.'

'John Bradley, NTV. Could you confirm that there is a disturbance in the prison?'

Trevor considered briefly, watching the nightmare unfolding in black and white on the TV monitors. He grimaced and said, 'Piss off.' As he put the phone down, he nodded to a fellow officer, who pulled the switch which cut the power to the prison and plunged it in to darkness.

Alone in an unlit cell, Maria manoeuvred a mattress against the door in an attempt to shut out the noise of the nightmare outside. The prison reminded her of the hospital her mother had attended in her last illness. It had the same smell, the same endless waiting. Her mother's cancer had been diagnosed late; it was inoperable but she'd undergone a course of radiotherapy. Neither Maria nor her mother ever said so but both sensed it was pointless. It was a ritual, an acclimatisation for the inevitable climax. And so it proved. Two weeks after the last appointment, her mother collapsed. Two days after that, she was dead.

Watching her mother fade away reinforced Maria's determination to make a difference. That's what had led her here, to this antechamber of hell.

A voice outside called her name softly. It was a gentle, friendly northern voice not unlike her brother's. Maria went to the door,

'Hello?' she said hopefully. 'Who is it?'

'Dennis. Put your ear to the door, I want to tell you something.' Maria did as he asked and Murray began whispering to her, explaining in graphic detail what he was going to do to her. Maria screamed and retreated from the door but Murray didn't stop. Maria stared at the door hypnotised, waiting for it to open while the whispering continued, a terrible compelling rhythm which she was unable to resist.

Next morning John, Naz and Brian set up for a piece to camera at the foot of the highest, most imposing wall of HMP Hull. The main problem was John's face. He looked like a bloody gargoyle and had had to apply a lot of makeup to hide his bruises but even then, he couldn't hide everything. They got round the problem by avoiding close-ups and filming more of imposing prison walls.

When the prison cut him off, John knew he had a story. He phoned the night desk of the Hull local paper and gave them the story, then did the same to a couple of nationals and the BBC. For once, he didn't want a scoop; he was concerned about Maria but the best thing for her was to get the story out there. At six-thirty, he hustled Naz and Brian into missing the morning briefing and driving to Hull. At eight am, the prison service issued a statement confirming the riot and screws going off duty gave them some more gossip. The riot squad had arrived at dawn to take back the prison. The word was they'd gone in hard, focusing on a core group of IRA ringleaders who would be tried later and made an example of. For prisoners like Murray, now safely back in his cell, this was a puzzle because the IRA had tried to stop the riot.

Brian waited for a police siren to pass, then gave the thumbs-up. Naz nodded, and John began.

'Eleven am outside an apparently tranquil Hull jail. But behind these walls, there's a massive clean-up going on after last night's riot. For three hours, prison staff lost control of the top-security wing, which houses some of Britain's most dangerous prisoners, many of them IRA bombers. Damage is estimated at over two million pounds.' He made the figure up but it was an educated guess based on other riots. 'It's expected that a large number of inmates will face charges. John Bradley NTV News, Hull Jail,' he finished with a flourish. He stood still while Naz stopped filming then looked up. 'All right?' John asked. Brian gave a muted thumbs-up and took off his headphones, then nodded glumly and began packing up the gear. 'Christ, will you two cheer up? It's a legit story.'

'The news editor decides who covers what, not you,' Brian said coolly. John scowled at him and gestured at the walls.

'Maria's in there!' Naz nodded.

'We've only your word for that,' Brian observed.

'They haven't bloody denied it. And there was a riot in there, we do know that.'

'All right John, but do us a favour will you?' Brian asked, 'try getting your arse to the eight am briefing like everyone else.'

THIRTY-FOUR

Naz and Brian dropped John off at the flat. He phoned Clemmy at work to apologise for the jail story but she wasn't there so he left a contrite message. If she phoned back so be it, but if she didn't, he'd keep his head down for a couple of days. Notionally, he was still on leave. As it was, John's piece made the lunchtime bulletin, the six o'clock and the News at Ten. That made him feel better and he hoped it would put him in a better position with Clemmy. She might be hurting but she was a pro when it came to her job.

Eric Guttridge, at home in his bungalow, crept silently from room to room. At first the news of Stubbs' accident had filled him with relief because he wouldn't have to do any more dangerous drops. A moment's reflection redoubled his paranoia. He'd outlived his usefulness and he knew from experience that his masters didn't like loose ends. Eric wiped his sweating palms on his shirt and tried to think. Mornings and evenings, the cul-de-sac was busy with people coming and going but during the day, the place was dead. Nothing moved and the silence in the empty bungalow seemed to bear down on him but he didn't put the radio or TV on. Every delivery van or approaching car made him start but he wanted to hear it, to hear them coming.

Three days later John was back outside HMP Hull but this time he was going inside. He had a visitor's warrant. The publicity created by the riot had forced the authorities' hand and they'd owned up to Maria's presence. After queuing for half an hour, being subjected to a detailed search and leaving his watch, money and keys in a box at reception, John was finally shown into a small, windowless room by a warder. In the middle of the room, which stank of cabbage and stale sweat, a small plastic table was screwed to the floor. Two plastic chairs were arranged on either side of the table. Everything: walls, floor, table and chairs appeared to be the same shade of mottled blue. The warder stood in the corner like a club doorman. Another door opposite opened and Maria entered or rather shuffled in. She seemed smaller, less substantial, as if she'd shrunk somehow. She was deathly pale and lines of fear were etched round her mouth and eyes. On seeing John, her face lit up and she hurried towards him.

'No touching,' the warder barked. John flashed a look at the screw but Maria accepted it and sat down. John sat opposite. He wanted to touch her and reached out his hand before remembering and pulling it back. 'Are you OK?'

'I am now,' she smiled, but the terror of her night twitched and flickered behind the smile. As she took in his black eye and bruised lip, her face fell. 'What happened to you, John?'

'I'm fine, really. What about you? The riot?' She didn't answer. Her eyes glazed over and she shuddered involuntarily as she remembered. 'I've got you a lawyer, a good one. You'll be out of here in next to no time, three days at the most.'

Maria smiled weakly, unable to conceal her apprehension.

'I hope so.'

'They can't keep you after the hearing,' adding for the screw's benefit, 'you're a peace-campaigner, not a bomber.'

Her face became serious again. 'Have you seen Jess?'

'A few days ago.'

'How was she?'

'Fine. I told her you were in here.'

'I'd like her to be at the hearing.'

'I'll sort it.' That's when he got it. 'Is Jess your new...?' he trailed off as Maria nodded and smiled. He was surprised but said nothing.

Maria put her hand towards his, her finger just touching the end of his. 'It's over, John. I don't want to fight them anymore, I want my life back.'

'When you get out of here, we're going to spend some time together. We'll go away somewhere.' Maria smiled.

'You'll be out of here in forty-eight hours.'

'I mean it, John. I want us to have our lives back.'

He looked at his sister and the screw standing in the corner and sighed. 'All right.'

'Time's up,' the warder barked. Maria flinched at his voice and got to her feet unsteadily. She kissed two fingers and planted them on the back of John's hand and whispered, 'Goodbye John.' She hovered, not wanting him to leave. The warder touched John's arm, steering him towards the door.

'We'll have a real celebration, day after tomorrow.' Then the door closed and she was gone.

On the way home, John weighed everything up. Maria was right; Gladio was too big, too powerful. She wanted her life back and he should try doing the same with his. Maybe he could work things out with Clemmy. After all, if she didn't love Arthur anymore, perhaps they could find a way forward together. For a start, he could try doing his job properly and drink less.

THIRTY-FIVE

Next morning, John hurried through Leeds early morning rush hour. Shaved, showered, rested, he was wearing a clean shirt, new tie and his best dark suit. He felt good for a change, alert and energetic. It was amazing what a difference not drinking made; well, not drinking, not smoking dope and going to bed early. He made a mental note to do it more often. The morning sun shone with a cool Nordic intensity, heralding another warm day. A church clock began to strike eight, causing John to swear and quicken his step. Having made the effort, he didn't want to ruin everything by arriving late.

By the time he arrived at the NTV building, he was jogging. He loped up the steps towards reception but as he pulled on the door, someone tugged at his sleeve. He turned to see a furtive, ill-dressed little man with a bad five o'clock shadow.

'John Bradley?' he said in a Geordie accent. 'I've seen you on the tele.'

John didn't break stride. 'I'm late for a meeting,' but the little man pulled him back.

'It's about your sister, Maria.' John stopped and looked at the hobgoblin.

'What about her?'

'I know about her and Billy Hatton.'

'Who are you?'

The little man looked round furtively and muttered, 'Guttridge, Eric Guttridge.' Eric was sweating and nervous. Unable to sleep, he'd left the bungalow at four and been waiting outside the NTV building since just after five.

'Guttridge and Stubbs?'

Eric nodded uneasily, 'I got something to show you.'

John swore to himself. He'd promised Maria that he'd leave it alone. He'd promised himself that he'd do his job; he'd promised Clemmy. On the other hand, he'd promised Maria that she'd be out of Hull in forty-eight hours and, despite the Herculean labours of his solicitor, she was still banged up with no date set for the hearing. Fuck. Fuck. Fuck.

On the fourth floor in the newsroom, the morning conference was about to start. Naz glanced out of the window and caught sight of John on the pavement below. Clemmy hurried in from her office, businesslike and efficient. She tapped a cup on the table and said, 'Can we get started, please?' The hubbub of morning gossip died. Brian cleared his throat. Clemmy looked at him. 'Er, John's not here,' he said. Clemmy looked at her watch and grimaced slightly. From the window, Naz watched John and Guttridge walk away. Clemmy clocked the activity.

'Naz?' she asked.

Naz looked up. 'I don't think he's coming.'

'Then we'll start without him. The pit deputies' vote, who's covering that?'

Naz frowned slightly at Brian but Brian didn't care. They'd been given a bollocking for doing the Hull Jail story without clearance; he was getting sick of being tarred with John's brush.

Following Eric's directions, John drove the 2CV north out of Leeds and then west towards the hills. As he drove, Eric explained about Tony Stubbs' mission and the accident that fucked it. John was incredulous and sceptical. Would Gladio really employ a sad loser like Guttridge?

'I need evidence.'

Eric nodded. 'That's where we're going, to get some.' He directed John to the forest glade where he'd met Hatton. Despite the day being warm and muggy, it was dark and gloomy. No birds sang there. Eric got out of the car and looked round nervously.

'What is this place?'

Eric began to clear away some debris from a tree stump. 'Arms dump. There's lots of them, hidden away in forests like this.' He finished clearing the debris and felt around in the undergrowth for something. Then he pulled and a small rectangular metal hatch levered up. Eric reached in and pulled out two bundles wrapped in heavily greased polythene. John watched fascinated as Eric unwrapped one of the bundles and revealed a black, new, metal and plastic machine pistol. 'All top quality stuff.'

John inspected it. 'You supplied Billy Hatton from here?'

'And Stubbs. I was the armourer. They were both mechanics.'

'Mechanics?'

Eric looked round furtively. 'Killers.' John handed the weapon back. Eric began to wrap it up again.

'How did you meet?'

Eric grinned. 'We knocked over a couple of supermarkets when we were in the TA. That's when we were recruited.'

'Into Gladio?'

Eric shook his head. 'No, it was the SAS that came first.' John looked askance at the unimpressive little man in front of him. He didn't look like SAS material. Eric caught the look on his face. 'We thought it was a bit iffy but the money was better and we were in a scrape after the robbery. They offered to wipe the slate clean.'

'And that's when Gladio recruited you?'

Eric nodded. 'They sent us to Ireland.' A pulse of fear contorted his face.

'Are you a fascist?'

Eric shook his head vehemently. 'I'm not political. I did it for the money.'

'Who else was recruited?'

'Don't know. You're put into three man teams, a need-to-know basis. You don't know anyone else.' Despite trying to stay focused, John felt himself growing excited.

'And you were trained in Northern Ireland?' Eric flinched, then nodded.

'Billy and Stubbs were really into it.'

'But you weren't?'

Eric shook his head. 'They gave us local targets to fucking practise on.'

'And you're prepared to say all this on camera?'

Eric nodded, hopping nervously from foot to foot, glancing furtively at the enfolding gloom of the forest. 'I don't want to end up like Billy and Stubbsy. If I'm on TV telling my story, they're going to think twice about...' he trailed off .

John put his notebook back in his pocket. 'Stay here.' Eric nodded agreement. He was used to taking orders and he felt better for unburdening himself. John climbed into the 2CV and drove away. Eric sat down and began to roll a cigarette. Above, a crow called a warning. Others answered. Eric shivered involuntarily. He didn't like the place.

It took John ages to find a bloody phone box. He had to drive about ten miles. He managed to get through to the newsroom and speak to Brian but when he explained the story, Brian didn't want to know. It was Naz who swung it. By chance, he and Brian were on standby in case anything broke at short notice. Nothing had and they were sitting about, following up traffic accidents in case they needed a filler.

John waited for them in the lane by the plantation and signalled the NTV car to follow him down the forest track. Ninety minutes after leaving Eric, the two cars arrived in the glade. Brian opened the tailgate and began unloading the equipment. 'We're supposed to be in Leeds.'

'Come on, Brian, we weren't exactly busy,' Naz replied. Brian wasn't comforted.

'Clemmy'll hit the roof when she's hears it's Gladio again,' he said, hoisting up the camera.

'She'll have to listen now,' John insisted. 'This is the arms dump that supplied Billy Hatton and Tony Stubbs. You know about Hatton? Stubbs was part of the same Gladio cell. He was killed in a car crash on his way to another mission.' Naz remembered something.

'Stubbs? A1 near Doncaster?' he frowned. 'I heard something about that.'

'Like what?'

'A traffic cop I play darts with. Guns found in the boot. It was hushed up. Army job.'

'See, Brian!'

Brian turned on Naz. 'Since when did you start playing fucking darts?'

'For Christ's sake!' John shouted. 'Let's get on with it.'

'We need something to film,' Naz said changing the subject.

'Over here,' John instructed, aware that he hadn't seen Eric. He called his name but there was no answer from the surrounding forest. He called again, louder but the only effect was to drive the crows squawking from their roosts.

Brian shook his head and looked skywards in disbelief. 'Here we go again.'

'It doesn't matter. The proof is the arms dump.' He levered the heavy hatch open with a gasp. 'In there, a secret cache, filled with automatic weapons, ammunition.'

Brian knelt down and felt around with his hands. After a moment, he looked up and shook his head, scowling. John pushed him aside and felt inside the hole. It was empty. He looked desperately at his two colleagues.

'It was here!'

'It's not there now,' Brian said roughly. He picked up the camera and walked back to the crew car.

'It was here and so was Eric!' John shouted after him.

Brian shut the tailgate and walked round to the driver's door. 'I'm going back to the office.'

John didn't reply. Naz looked at John sadly and patted him gently on the shoulder. 'You can't win them all, John.' John nodded dumbly and watched the crew car drive away.

John didn't report Eric's disappearance. He didn't trust the police and he didn't want to endanger Maria any more. He wondered what had happened to Eric. If he'd got cold feet, there was a chance John could get him to talk when he found him again but he couldn't shake the feeling that his best chance had gone. Without Guttridge, John had no proof of anything. Maria was right, he was beaten and like her, he wanted his life back.

THIRTY-SIX

He slept badly but was revived next morning by the news that Maria's hearing had been set for the next day. He phoned Jess three times and got no answer. It was evening when he finally got through. The late sun filled her cottage with a wistful light. As she picked up the phone, the tape decks at Menwith Hill had already clicked into gear and started recording.

'I'm glad you rang.'

'I saw Maria.' John said.

'How is she?' Jess said.

'You'd know if you'd been to visit her.'

'I had to go away.'

'The hearing; it's in York, tomorrow. Maria would like you to be there,' John added.

'Can you give me a lift? You've still got her car.' She asked.

'I'll pick you up at nine.'

'Why don't you come to the cottage and eat tonight? I'll cook.'

'I'm not very good company at the moment.'

'Come, anyway. I want to hear about Maria.'

John sighed, what the hell. 'All right.' The tape decks in Menwith Hill clicked off.

John spent the next day being a reporter again. A striking miner had gone back to work for two days then come out on strike again, only to be shunned by his former colleagues. He did a couple of pieces about the human cost of the strike, now beginning its sixth month, but the dispute was entering one of its periodic lulls. Pickets still screamed as the police convoys drove through their lines but it felt like the miners were going through the motions. A dull resignation seemed to infect the

157

strikers; a realisation that there would be no quick victory, just a long hard slog. The doubt and uncertainty resonated with John like a hangover, as he drove to Jess's.

It was a sultry evening. Dark clouds prowled the horizon like dreadnoughts accompanied by the occasional grumble of thunder. They ate pasta and salad outside. A Bach cello concerto played quietly in the cottage, mingling with the sounds of evening.

'That was good,' said John.

Jess smiled. She was wearing an ugly, loud, yellow and green dress and a lot of multi-coloured bangles on her right wrist. Her hair, which she ran her hands through habitually as she talked, was a mess. Then again, he wasn't exactly Robert Redford himself.

'No need to sound so surprised,' she said.

He pushed his plate away and offered her more wine. She declined but he poured himself another glass. He'd drunk most of the bottle of red he'd brought and opened a second. He was drinking to forget. Jess leaned forward.

'How is she?'

'Scared. Why haven't you been to see her?'

'I had to go away. I've been in London for a few days. I just got back.'

'She told me about you and her.'

Jess frowned. 'What? She has a crush on me, that's all.'

'Oh, I thought,' he struggled, embarrassed.

Jess giggled. 'Sometimes you are so fucking provincial, John.'

He found himself grinning back at her. Jess poured herself some more wine and changed the subject. 'You heard about the riot?'

'It was a set-up. Did you know that all the rioters are in court at the same time? York tomorrow?' John responded.

She looked genuinely surprised. 'You're sure?'

John nodded but didn't explain how he knew. Naz had told him as they were standing on the picket line. 'Any other time, it would be a really big story on its own but with the strike...' he tailed off and drank some more wine.

158

'You still haven't told me how Maria is,' Jess said.

'She wants her life back. She's had enough.'

'She'll feel differently when she gets out.'

'What gives you the right to sit in judgement?' he slurred.

Jess nodded, 'We have to stand together and fight.'

'Easy for you to say. Haven't noticed you putting yourself in harm's way.'

'You don't know what I do.'

'True.' He sneered.

'If we stand together...'

'Spare me the Socialist Workers lecture. People have a habit of getting hurt.'

'What happened to the intrepid reporter? The seeker after truth?'

'I want my life back too.'

'Fucking journalists,' she snapped.

John ignored her. He was tired of fighting and losing, tired of the paranoia. He stood up and swayed unsteadily then staggered, his hands fumbling through his pockets looking for his keys. She followed him.

'What are you doing?' Jess asked.

'Going home.'

'Don't go. I was out of order.' He shrugged drunkenly. 'Look, we're both wound up.'

'In a few weeks, this will just be a fading memory.'

'You shouldn't drive. Stay here. We're both going to York tomorrow. Why go home only to come back again?' He considered this. She took hold of his arm and led him back into the living room. 'Sit down while I make up the couch.'

He considered briefly, then collapsed into a chair and reached for his wine glass again. It was dark when he woke and he was disorientated. There was an insistent, offbeat banging which had woken him. His head throbbed and his mouth felt dry and furry. He got up and padded into the kitchen. The back door had blown open again and was swaying back and forth in the wind just like it had the night he stayed there with Maria. John stood in the doorway, enjoying the cold air on his flesh. He shut and bolted the door, turned and found himself confronted by Jess, wearing a skimpy vest. 'Going for a walk, John?'

'I heard the door banging.'

She laughed lightly. In the half-light, half-darkness, she looked ethereal. Despite the gloom, the outline of her figure was sharp and willowy and there was something else: chemistry. He tried to think. He was drunk, tired. He took a deep breath and tried to collect himself.

'Best go back to bed?'

'Probably.'

She didn't move. He went to walk past her but her hand brushed the back of his lightly, deliberately. She grabbed his hand and pulled him towards her and kissed him, exploring his mouth with her tongue. For a moment he didn't respond, then they were all over each other. After a moment, he got hold of himself and pulled away.

'This isn't the time,' he said quietly.

'You're right,' she smiled.

Next morning, he woke to find himself alone, unsure whether he'd dreamt the events of the night before. After all, he had been very drunk. Something snagged on his toe. He reached down, pulled out Jess's crumpled vest and sighed to himself. *'Christ'*. He tried to rationalise what had happened but the truth was, he felt numb inside. Hatton, Maria, finishing with Clemmy had all had an impact but sleeping with his sister's lover was pretty low. He pulled on his trousers and stood up with a groan. His head pounded. He really had been out of his skull. Best see how he felt when he was well again.

As he was shaving, a convoy of prison vans left Hull Jail. In the largest convoy of prisoners in peacetime history, twenty vans were required to convey the IRA hardliners and other malefactors who had wreaked havoc in the jail. As the only woman, Maria had a prison van all to herself. A posse of outriders, police cars and heavily armed guards escorted the convoy across east Yorkshire towards York.

John and Jess breakfasted in silence, their night-time intimacy making them strangers. When they spoke it was with studied politeness but there was no avoiding the nuances. In the car, John helped Jess with her seat belt and as he plugged in the clip, their faces were momentarily close. There was a moment, then it was gone.

'We'd better be going,' John muttered.

Jess nodded and he started the engine.

'About last night,' he began. She shook her head.

'Things happen in war. We went to bed together. No big deal.'

'Actually, I was talking about the argument.'

'I was out of order.'

'You were right about not giving up, carrying on.'

'You were certain I was wrong last night.'

'I've changed my mind and I feel better for it.'

'What about Maria?'

He shrugged. 'She'll feel differently when she's out.'

'Actually, I meant are we going to tell her, about last night?'

John sighed. 'I'd rather not. Why does everything have to be so complicated?' They didn't speak again and drove in silence.

Two hours later, they were waiting outside York Magistrate's Court for Maria to arrive. The first of the prison vans appeared followed by another and another.

'Christ, what is this, a prison van convention?' he chuckled. She smiled back. At that precise moment, their faces half-turned to each other, one of the prison vans rose fifteen to twenty feet into the air in a surreal ballet. A tongue of orange flame licked up its side and as it fell back, they felt the shock wave and heard the explosion. Streams of red-hot debris flew past like a firework display. Other fragments rained down on them like super-heated chaff. Although deafened, John was aware of the insistent noise of alarms and sirens overlaid with the sound of people screaming. Jess stared at the burning van with a sickened look on her face but it was John who cried out. Then he was running towards the burning van. A policeman tried to bar his path but John somehow shoved him aside.

'Get out the fucking way!'

Jess watched, ashen, unable to move as John ploughed on towards the back of the still-burning van. The back door was hanging off revealing Maria slumped on the deformed metal floor. John grabbed Maria and carried her to the roadside. She looked serene as if she had just fallen asleep but her head lolled like a rag doll and he knew that she was dead. John rocked gently back and forth holding her in his arms. People gathered round him to help but he wouldn't let them. His face was grimy, stained with blood and tears and he held Maria, repeating quietly to himself over and over,

'No, no, no, no.'

THIRTY-SEVEN

After the explosion, John's mind seemed to fragment as if it were processing a number of different realities simultaneously. Despite being some distance away, the blast had deafened him and he saw everything in a muted slow motion. He watched the crowd of excited onlookers closing in, shouting and calling, spreading their contagious hysteria. And despite their training, the ambulance men were in shock too, shouting to each other as they formed a cordon round John and Maria. John watched as they gathered Maria from his embrace and began a futile attempt at resuscitation. And as he watched the scene changed and he was back in Bridgford, surrounded by blackened-faced armed men, running and shouting watching another body. While he grappled with these competing images, another part of his mind was in denial, desperately trying to hold onto the world as it had been. As the doors to the ambulance were closed and the vehicle roared away, lights flashing, siren blaring, the crowd began to disperse until he was sitting on the kerb behind the police cordon, alone again.

He was interviewed briefly by the police and answered their questions without prevarication but he was distant. Not surprising given the circumstances, the officers told each other, he was in shock. They were right, up to a point. But there was something else that troubled him, an idea that wouldn't go away.

Three hours after the explosion, he found himself alone and, bizarrely, at a loose end. Jess had left before him and after his brief initial interview, the police gave him a lift back to Leeds. Walking through Chapeltown market on a busy weekday morning, everything looked normal so he went to work. Then it got a bit strange.

163

As he entered the office, he was aware of every head turning towards him as if in some bizarre formation dance exercise. A silence fell over the office. Naz came straight up to him and said, 'Hey man, shit. I'm really sorry, you know,' and squeezed his arm. Brian followed but unable to meet his gaze, he stared fixedly at John's knees and mumbled something similar before hurrying away. Even Clemmy managed a sympathetic hello adding he didn't have to be in work; the first direct words she'd spoken to him since their split. But despite their support, there was another, familiar look in his colleagues' eyes that John couldn't place for a while. It was predatory; they were sizing him up. He was the story, the sad bastard disfigured by tragedy, whose life would be forever marked by this before and after. He was today's fresh meat and they all wanted a piece of him. He'd been there often enough himself but seeing them hanging back at a safe distance like vultures waiting for the carcass to expire, he was overwhelmed by a wave of nausea and rushed from the office. He clattered down the stairs and out into the street where he vomited heavily into the gutter. He rang Jess but there was no answer.

The day after the explosion, two things happened to wake him from his torpor. First, he had to make a formal identification of Maria's body. He'd tried Jess's phone several times and left messages but there was no answer. He hadn't slept and he arrived early, impatient to get it over with. Beneath the streets of Leeds, in a windowless basement which smelt of disinfectant and cleaning fluid, an absurdly young PC showed him into a small bare room. Maria's body reposed under a sheet on what looked like a wooden kitchen table. John was surprised; he'd expected a metal gurney and a hi-tech forensic environment. He found himself wondering if there was a shortage of gurneys in Leeds. The police surgeon was a big, red-faced man who had trouble breathing. With a theatrical flourish, he pulled back the sheet to reveal Maria lying still and beautiful beneath, as if she'd just dropped off to sleep. The surgeon seemed to read his mind.

'It's not uncommon,' he wheezed. 'Bomb victims often look normal.' But it wasn't the normality that winded John; it was the

164

fact that she looked so happy and serene in death. The surgeon stiffened and drew himself erect in an attempt at formality. 'Is this your sister?'

'Yes, that's Maria.' The surgeon moved to cover her but John held up his hand, bent down and kissed her on the cheek. Big mistake. Before that moment, he'd half-hoped she might be a shooting star somewhere up in the heavens but feeling her flesh, cold and hard like lard, there was no equivocation. He shuddered involuntarily and took a step backwards which allowed the surgeon to replace the cover. He began to wheeze some words of sympathy but John was already gone, his step quickened by a new resolve.

The young PC walked John back up the stairs. 'They'll release the body in a day or two.'

'What about the inquest?' John asked.

'Don't need it for that, they know what happened.' Leaning in close, the PC whispered confidentially 'It was a mistake, it wasn't her they were after...' He was about to continue but the look of cold fury in John's eye stopped him dead in his tracks.

John hurried away, up the stairs and out through the frosted doors onto the busy street. The police investigating knew what had happened. Maria hadn't been the target. A Loyalist splinter group had been after big name IRA prisoners for a 'spectacular'. The press and TV were already hinting at the same conclusion. Inhuman monsters kill woman protestor by accident. It was fine as an idea except for one thing. It was wrong. A Loyalist splinter group might have been involved but they weren't aiming for the IRA. Right from the prison riot and maybe before that, the event had been planned so that it would look like a mistake. But it hadn't been a mistake. They'd sent Hatton to kill Maria and when he failed, they tried again until they succeeded. John had wanted his life back but that would never happen now; he had crossed over. He was a journalist with a big story but the rules had changed and so had he. John didn't understand what Maria had done to make her death so necessary but he intended to find out.

165

THIRTY-EIGHT

Next morning, John packed a bag, walked to the railway station and bought a ticket to Liverpool with cash. At Manchester, he waited till the train was pulling out and jumped off, checked that he wasn't being followed and then caught another train to Carlisle and a bus to Stranraer. Once there, he checked the ferry timetable then waited until the last possible moment before buying his ticket and sprinting onto the ferry. No one followed him but just in case, he found a gents loo and changed from urban city clothes into dirty jeans, an anorak and a brightly coloured bobble hat which he pulled down low over his face. The crossing was choppy and he felt queasy in the airless metal box as the ship lurched back and forth.

On leaving the ferry at Larne, he caught a bus to Belfast. The rolling countryside was populated with prosperous farms and pretty villages. It could have been anywhere in the UK except for the painted kerbstones, a tribal pursuit for a country in strife. In some places they were painted red, white and blue while in others, they were orange, green and white. The colours mirrored the flags, which flew everywhere. The Union Jack for the Loyalists; the butcher's apron as the republicans called it. They flew the Irish tricolour over their territory. It could have been anywhere in the UK except for the fact there was a civil war going on.

And although the mainland liked to pretend that the conflict in Ulster wasn't happening, it was already too late. The war had spread from the province to the mainland, to the coalfields where the battle lines were drawn and redrawn each day, where everything was filmed, recorded, watched, monitored, examined, reported, filed, cross-referenced, discussed; where even the watchers and recorders were watched and recorded. There were frontline troops to prosecute the war, support staff, volunteers, strategists and tacticians. And then there were the dark elements: spies, double-agents, saboteurs, assassins and the shadowy people who ran them. The province looked green and prosperous like so much of the UK. It was late summer; the harvest was being gathered.

In Belfast, John waited for another bus to Downpatrick, Newcastle and the hills beyond. Someone had spray-painted 'Bobby Sands is a skinny bastard' across the bus station wall, the insult celebrating the hunger striker's sacrifice. Nena was singing '99 Red Balloons' over a tinny loudspeaker. The record must have been stuck because she kept on singing as the bus pulled out. Two hours later, he got off close to the Silent Valley reservoir and as evening came on, walked three miles uphill. The walk was hard but in the evening light, the countryside was stunning. Looking back, the land fell away in a sweep of verdant, undulating turf ending in the distant darkening blue of the Irish Sea. Populated with small trees, the lush green grass looked like a vast bowling green, which a perverse giant had thrown over the hills. On the walk he passed a farmer driving a tractor towards the main road. He didn't see anyone else. He was exhausted, running on empty, driven by adrenaline and rage. He'd hardly slept or eaten but he was fine apart from the flashbacks.

The silent valley reservoir is a lonely place at the best of times. Flanked on three sides by steep, bare hills, even on a sunny day, it has a haunting, mournful beauty so redolent of Ireland. The car park was empty and uninviting, the white blockhouse of the public toilets shuttered and padlocked for the night. A few gulls skimmed across the blackening water of the lake, calling sadly. The temperature began to plummet and John wished he had another layer of clothes.

That morning, he'd received a letter from his bank; company envelope, London postmark and inside, a leaflet about interest rates. Nothing unusual about it except for the small square of paper which fell out. On it, handwritten in compact, neat

167

capital letters, was a note, which told him to be in the car park of the Silent Valley reservoir in County Down at dusk as soon as possible. Next to it was a tiny red tree-shaped motif – the emblem of Nottingham Forest Football Club. He'd stared at the small square of paper for some time then burnt it carefully in an ashtray. But standing there in the cold Ulster dusk, he had doubts. There was no way of knowing if the note came from Kevin Dillon. If it was a trap, well, so be it.

It was dark when he heard the car. It screeched into the car park and stopped, engine still running. John stood cautiously in the shadows waiting for what he wasn't sure. An irritated voice called from the car in a strong Belfast accent,

'Are you gettin' in the fuckin' car or what?' John hurried over to the rear door where rough hands grabbed him and threw him to the floor as the car accelerated away. 'Stop fuckin' struggling till I put the fuckin' hood on you, you Brit bastard.'

A hood was placed over John's head and he was allowed to sit up.

'Is that really necessary?'

'Oh I'd say it was very necessary, so I would.'

'Kevin?'

'I told you we'd be seein' each other, now didn't I?'

'I can't see a fuckin' thing.'

The lads in the car chuckled.

'A sense of humour in adversity, one of the few things about the Brits we admire, hey lads?' Despite the levity, there was an undeniable tension in the car that discouraged idle chatter.

John smelt the sea before he heard it. As he got out of the car, the fresh salt tang gusted into his face. The hood was removed and in the light of a full moon, he saw that they were standing on a rocky promontory above a tiny cove, battered by the swell. The direction of the wind suggested they were on the west coast somewhere.

'Come on, we haven't got much time,' Kevin whispered, propelling him away from the sea towards a large house screened by some low trees. The other lads stayed with the car.

'Where are we?'

'One of those places they send priests who've got themselves into bother.'

'In the south?'

'Aye, we're in the Republic.'

They arrived at a huge oak front door. Kevin pulled on a thick rope. A bell sounded in the distance. After a few moments, the door was opened slightly and an elderly, bearded face peered out.

'Father Uccello?' The door opened wide and Kevin led John through an oak-panelled hall and into a small, empty chapel. The place was decorated to the eyeballs. Statues and figurines lined the walls; a carved screen in front of the altar; intricate stained glass windows; walls and ceiling covered with frescoes and mournful paintings of the Saints in their passion.

'What's this go to do with Maria?' John was irritated by the lack of explanation. Kevin stopped by a carved wooden confessional. He opened the door, indicating the seat inside. John looked at him frowning. 'I'm not a Catholic.'

Kevin pushed him down onto the chair.

'Listen and learn. You've got half an hour.'

The inside of the confessional smelt of incense, lavender and body odour. The walls were decorated with a filigree of dark, carved wood. John was about to stand again when he became aware of a presence the other side of the grill.

'Uccello?'

'Yeah, that's me. Call me Pete.' The voice was a shock: southern English, working-class accent, almost cockney.

'You're English?'

'Bedford. My folks settled there after the war. Dad made ice cream. Wish I had now.'

'Did you know my sister, Maria?'

'No, never met her.'

'Do you know why she was killed?'

'I might.'

'What does that mean?'

'It means I might. Oh sod this.' John heard the confessional door opening. He jumped up, opened his door and collided with a short, overweight, sallow skinned man in a dark suit and grey silk shirt. He had receding, jet-black hair and the eyes behind his wire-rimmed glasses were intense, nervously darting back and forth like a wild animal's. John barred his way.

'Can we try again? My sister was killed two days ago, I'm a bit on edge.' Uccello hovered uncertainly, breathing heavily. 'You know something?' Uccello nodded and they returned to their confessionals.

'I didn't know Maria but I probably know someone who did. Annie.'

'Maria said she met an Italian girl at a European symposium on peace and socialism.'

'That'll be her. Antonella was her novice name. We worked together for a while.'

'Annie was a nun?'

'Until she lost her faith.' Uccello paused and took a deep breath. 'I was an accountant before I joined the church, good one too. Anyway, it turned out to be useful. Too bloody useful.'

'Why?'

'I was clever, a quick learner. I kept my nose clean and my head out of politics. I was unconnected. I got promoted, became a Vatican consigliere, accountant to the Pope. I looked after investments. Annie was my assistant.'

'What kind of investments?'

'The Vatican's a very private place. A lot of secrets.'

'Like what?'

'What do you think? Money.' Uccello paused then went on. 'I loved the church, the ceremony, the mystique. But I was clever, and I knew something didn't add up. I told Annie and we followed the audit trail back. We discovered a lot of accounts and documents. We were meticulous. I thought it was a mistake.'

'How much money are we talking about?'

'Lots.'

'What happened?'

'I thought I could use the information to my advantage, make myself indispensable.'

'What did Annie think?'

'She was an idealist. She believed every wrong can be righted.' Uccello paused, 'We argued. She tried to tell people but no one listened. She kept trying; I kept trying to stop her. I was threatened, blackmailed. She was recalled to her order.'

'What did they blackmail you with?'

'We worked late a lot. We became close.'

'That's it?'

'Not all.'

'And that's when she lost her faith?'

'She lost her faith in the church when she found out about the money and in me when I didn't do anything about it.'

'But she left the church and tried to tell people anyway?'

'Yeah.'

'She told Maria she didn't think she would live long.'

'She disappeared.'

John paused for a moment. 'And the money?'

'Looted during the war. Converted into various currencies and put in safe hands.'

'You mean the Vatican?'

'It's not there now if that's what you're thinking.'

'Where is it?'

'My Ma always wanted me to join the church. She used to go on and on about the war and the importance of having a big organisation on your side in case things went wrong. That's why she wanted me to be a priest. She thought no harm could come to me then.' He chuckled mirthlessly to himself.

'Uccello?'

'It's not my real name. Just while I'm here.'

'You're in hiding?'

Uccello snorted. 'You found me.'

'So where is the money?' But Pete Uccello was now gone. John pushed open the confessional and Kevin Dillon stood there.

'Time to go.' John was hurried from the darkened chapel back out into the night. 'Was I right? Did the sodomite tell you something about your Maria?' Biblical, harsh, the word caught John off guard.

'Sodomite? I thought he was caught having sex with a novice nun.'

Kevin grinned. 'Among others. Did he tell you something?'

'Yes, but I needed more time. Why did I have to stop then?'

'He's taken a vow, he only converses with the living for half an hour a week. Apart from his devotions, you're it for this week. You should consider yourself honoured, so you should.'

As they reached the car, Kevin turned to him and asked, 'So how about a quid pro quo?' In Kevin's soft accent, the Latin phrase could have been the refrain for a song. 'We've helped you, are you going to help us?'

'What did you have in mind?' John replied.

Kevin smiled grimly. 'Gladio is a vampire. Shine a light on it and it shrivels.'

'Sounds like the IRA.'

Kevin stared as if considering something. 'How would you feel about helping to end the conflict in the Province?'

'Is that what you want?' John replied.

'Some of us do.'

'Go ahead and end it then.'

'It's not that simple. There are factions,' Kevin commented.

'Who want to keep it going?'

Kevin nodded. 'If we helped to expose a far-right conspiracy at the heart of the British political system, well that would be evidence of our good faith, wouldn't you say?'

'How would we do it? All we've got is the word of a disgraced, frightened priest, an IRA terrorist and a paranoid journalist. We'd need proof.'

'You could dig around for some.'

'The story would be spiked.'

'Depends who you tell it to.' Kevin produced a photograph taken with a telephoto lens in a tree-lined street showing two men arguing in suits. One grey-haired and dignified, the other younger and more familiar.

'Gimlet,' John breathed.

'Aye, but it's the old man he's with that's important. Jan Swemmer.'

'Who's he?'

'A Dutch banker. Worked for the Nazis during the war.'

'What does he do now?'

'He's Gladio's banker.'

'Says who?'

'Pete Uccello for one.'

'Where was this taken?'

'Liege, Belgium.'

'What are they arguing about?'

'Money would be my guess.'

'It's all circumstantial evidence. We need something else.'

Kevin opened the car door for John. 'Well don't take too long.'

John had a thought. 'Has Uccello met Gimlet?'

Kevin shook his head. 'No, Swemmer. He took confession with your man.'

John felt the weight of events on him and swayed against the car. Kevin took John's arm. 'Easy there, we can't have you flaking out before you've done anything, now can we?' but his voice was gentle. As they sat in the car, Kevin said one more thing. 'I'm sorry about your sister, John. I know what it's like to lose someone close.' John nodded but felt his eyes well with tears so he sniffed heavily.

The drive back was the reverse of the journey there. John was hooded but instead of dropping him off at the reservoir, they disgorged him on the outskirts of Downpatrick. Before he got out of the car, he thanked Kevin for taking him there. Kevin regarded John, for once his face serious and troubled.

'You'd better be watching your back, then. Keep an eye on Kathleen.'

'Kathleen?' John was puzzled.

'She calls herself Jess now.' There was more to discover but Kevin leaned across him and opened the car door. John stayed where he was.

'Jess, what about her?'

'Exactly. Now get out of the fuckin' vehicle before we get a ticket.'

'What if I need to contact you again?' John asked as he got out but his question went unanswered as the car slewed away. As he walked towards the lights of Downpatrick, it began to rain. Somewhere above, a helicopter buzzed unseen across the black sky. Uccello had answered some questions but he'd raised so many more. John felt envious of Kevin and his boys, they knew what their destiny was and why.

THIRTY-NINE

John caught the first bus back to Belfast. In the bus station, Nena was still singing '99 Red Balloons'. He tried phoning Jess but all he got was the answerphone. He wanted to talk to her. At least now he had something to trade. He left the phone box and walked over to get the bus to Larne. That's when he was arrested.

He didn't see them coming. He was humming along with Nena and thinking that that damn song would be in his head for days now. Then he was aware of someone close by and heard a voice, speaking in a strong Belfast accent.

'John Bradley?' He nodded. Six burly men clad in flak jackets grabbed him and handcuffed him, then frogmarched him to a waiting armoured Land Rover and threw him in. As the vehicle sped away, John struggled to get up only to be kicked in the ribs. He relaxed a little when he saw the RUC badges on their tunics.

He spent the next seven hours in a cell. Finally, at about midnight, they dragged him to an interview room. A large man in a leather jacket came in, accompanied by a fat woman in her late thirties who chewed gum with the distracted intensity of a football manager. She had bright tiny green eyes, which stared at him unpleasantly. She didn't speak.

'I'm a British citizen. I want to see my solicitor.' At this, the woman giggled which made him angry. 'What the fuck is this? What's going on?'

'This,' said leather jacket, emphasising the word, 'is Castlereagh Police Station and we're the fucking Special Branch, so we are.'

Hearing the name of Castlereagh sent a pulse of fear through him but also a frisson of excitement. Guttridge was right, there was a connection with Gladio. 'What are your names? Who am I being interviewed by?' Still chewing, the woman giggled again. The man leaned closer and lit a cigarette. John could see blackheads on his nose and a myriad of tiny broken veins in his cheeks.

'We have a saying in the province, Special Branch, carte blanche.' He blew smoke into John's face.

'Why have I been arrested? I haven't done anything.'

'Conspiracy.'

'What conspiracy?'

'What were you doing in Downpatrick?'

'I'm on holiday.'

'Don't give us that bollocks,' the woman shouted abruptly in a working-class Welsh accent. It was the first thing she'd said and the accent took John by surprise. Despite himself, he couldn't help grinning; Ulster the place for surprising accents. She didn't see the funny side. 'It isn't funny. You've been talking to the fucking Provos.'

'Stranraer, Belfast, Downpatrick and then a little sightseeing at the reservoir?' the man continued menacingly. They seemed to know a hell of a lot; so much for John's cloak and dagger bollocks. 'Where did you go after that?'

'Two days ago in York, my sister was murdered.'

'Yeah, we heard,' the woman replied unconcerned, still chewing.

'I needed to get away for a while.'

'Where did you go after your walk to the reservoir?'

'You were with the fucking Provos, weren't you?' the woman yelled. The man gave the woman a hard stare. She stopped chewing and fell silent.

'We know where you were.' John stared at them both but said nothing. The man stood up and walked round John. 'Consorting with terrorists is a serious business. Look where it got your sister.'

'What's that supposed to mean? Did you kill her?'

'We're the good guys, we don't do things like that.'

'You get Loyalist death squads to do it for you.'

The man spoke again. 'You've been warned. Keep your nose out of what doesn't concern you.' They went to leave the room but the woman stopped at the door.

'Be a shame to miss your sister's funeral,' she giggled and left.

John was kept alone in a windowless cell with a single light bulb for four days. If they were trying to scare him, they succeeded. The two Special Branch goons knew a lot about what had happened but they didn't seem to know about Uccello. Maria had been murdered because of what she knew; now he was being threatened and softened up but he wasn't sure why.

After four nights, they opened the cell without warning and pushed him outside. It was first light. He walked out of the gates and down deserted streets back into the city centre. In the grey dawn John could just make out the security paraphernalia of pylons, aerials, microwave dishes and armoured lookouts on the mountain behind the city. A bright unblinking searchlight shone into the sky. Above the empty city, it looked like the gatehouse to Mordor.

He arrived at the deserted bus station and waited, shivering, for the first bus to Larne. For once, even Nena was silent. He stayed awake as the bus bounced along the small roads and caught the first ferry to Stranraer. As soon as he landed, he phoned Naz who sounded relieved to hear him but wondered where he'd been. John cut him off.

'Maria's funeral, Naz? When is it?'

'Four o'clock.' Naz sounded surprised.

'What day?'

'Today. This afternoon.' Naz sounded even more surprised and was about to ask something else but John put the phone down.

FORTY

John just made it. Unkempt, wild looking, his clothes a mess, he appeared at the back as the ceremony was about to begin. The sisterhood from the peace camp had organised everything. The funeral service was in a modern crematorium chapel near Otley – all concrete, pine and stained glass. The ceremony was a celebration of Maria's life and her outgoing spirit, a happy-clappy mix of poems, upbeat songs, feminist anthems and tearful eulogies. The peace campers were angry and upset but they had accepted the official explanation that Maria had died by accident. John knew that she'd been murdered, that she'd been onto something and that stopped him engaging with the ceremony.

After the cremation, Maria's ashes were taken, to be scattered at Menwith Hill. Her death seemed to emphasise the mortality of the peace camp itself. The day before, the government had moved against the Greenham Common women – a high-court judge had ordered their eviction. Fearing they would be next, the Menwith Hill women wanted to recommit to the struggle, which led to a row over who should carry the urn. The women felt it should be one of them but John told them either he carried the urn to Menwith Hill or no one did. The women scowled and muttered darkly but they couldn't deny his right.

It was a breezy day. High above the radar domes and aerials, fluffy clouds scudded west driven by a strong breeze. Clasping the urn, John waited as more poems were read out. Jess had reappeared. Clad simply in a long black silk dress she looked gaunt and haunted but there was something terribly attractive about her vulnerability. Forcing himself to look away, he waited patiently for the signal to upend the urn. When he did

178

so, nothing happened and he wondered if he'd forgotten to unscrew the top but he hadn't. The ashes seemed unwilling to leave their plastic container but maybe they were just waiting for the right moment. A strong gust and they fell out in a great lump of grit, most of it landing on the earth in an untidy mound. John watched briefly then threw the urn towards the fence. As he walked away, he found Jess in step next to him.

'Can you give me a lift?' John asked.

'Where to?' Jess replied.

'The cottage. We need to talk.' On the way back they hardly spoke at all. In the hallway, they looked at each other, examining each other's eyes. She kissed him but he didn't respond.

'Where were you, Jess? I couldn't find you after the explosion.'

'I was upset. I wanted to be on my own,' she replied.

'Here, at the cottage?' She nodded. 'Why didn't you answer the phone?'

She shook her head helplessly. 'After what had happened between us, I don't know, I felt... bad.' She paused. 'I tried ringing you yesterday and the day before.'

John considered this. 'I went away.'

'Where?'

'Why?'

Jess stroked John's arm gently. He pulled it away. 'Don't tell me if you don't want to.'

She looked vulnerable but Kevin's last question stayed with him. 'You know, don't you? You know why Maria was killed?' She shook her head. 'What are you doing at Menwith Hill, Jess?'

'I'm a peace activist. We all are.'

'How about Kathleen? Is she one?' he asked.

'Fuck off, John.'

'That's your name, isn't it?' he persisted.

After a moment or two she softened. 'I was christened Kathleen. Jessica is my middle name, after my English grandmother.'

'Catholic?'

'Atheist,' she paused, 'but I was brought up Catholic, in a small village, near the border.'

'Is your family still there?' John asked.

Jess frowned. 'My Dad was killed in a bomb blast. My Mum moved away with my little brother.'

'But not you?'

'I hated the sectarian stuff. I escaped to Sussex University and read English.'

'I've been in Northern Ireland, Jess. I know why they killed Maria.'

'I see,' Jess said quietly.

'And I know that you know why she went into the camp.' Jess looked away. 'What I don't know is why Maria went instead of you.'

'Who did you talk to?' she asked.

'Possible allies. How come the IRA know you, Jess?'

'Everyone knows everyone over there. My Dad was killed by them.'

'Did you know Maria was going to be killed?'

'No.' She shook her head.

'Then why won't you tell me?'

'Because it's dangerous and,' she paused, 'I like you.'

'I'll tell you if you tell me.' She smiled without answering. He didn't probe any further. He turned and left, then drove back to his flat.

John knew why they'd killed Maria, so why had Special Branch arrested him only to let him go? Did they know something or were they just following instructions? – Gimlet's presumably, but why? And then there was Jess, who was starting to take up a lot of his idle thoughts. On the other hand, he had just cremated his sister and his emotions were so upside down that he doubted whether anything he felt was reliable.

At the flat, there were a couple of messages on the answerphone – one from Clemmy asking him to ring when he had a moment and one from the police informing him that the inquest into Maria's death was in two days' time. It was just a formality and would be immediately adjourned until further inquiries were completed. When would that be? John wondered. *Sometime fucking never.*

FORTY-ONE

John slept for a long time then spent the next day at home doing his job. He worked the phone, chasing down leads connected with Gladio. For the first time in a while, he had an objective and it drove him on. He started with Eric Guttridge, following up leads about his TA recruitment, trying to trace other members of his regiment, details of his training. John found a couple of part-time squaddies who remembered Eric and backed up his claim that his territorial SAS regiment had been composed of an unusually large number of ex-cons. Nobody was willing to talk on the record but he got enough confirmation to satisfy him that if the story were exposed, it would take a lot of explaining. It was late when the phone rang. It was Clemmy asking him to come into work; she needed to talk to him. Her voice was clipped, loaded somehow but she gave nothing away.

Back at the office next day, the familiar atmosphere of the newsroom felt surreal. The other hacks went about their work. They didn't stare at John but then Maria's death wasn't headline news anymore and neither was he. Clemmy was in a meeting so he continued checking leads when he became aware of Naz standing by him, looking concerned.

'I thought you were on leave,' Naz's face crinkled with concern.

'I've been called in.'

Brian appeared behind Naz, an idiotic grin on his face. 'Had a good time?' he asked with a knowing leer. John looked up puzzled. Naz leant in and explained quietly.

'Clemmy's been away for the last three days.' John looked at him uncomprehending. 'There was a rumour you were together.'

'My sister was murdered last week!' The silly grin vanished from Brian's countenance. Foolish and uncomfortable, he backed away awkwardly. Naz looked at John.

'So how goes it? Are you sure you're ready for this?' John nodded but it was clear Naz wasn't convinced. 'Come on, John, it's me you're talking to.'

John sighed and nodded. 'I have a rocky moment every now and then but I'm coping.' It wasn't a lie but it wasn't the truth. He was a bit off his head but he wasn't floating weightless anymore; he had a purpose but he wasn't about to tell Naz that. Their conversation was interrupted by the morning briefing, which was taken by Clemmy. She was cool and businesslike, wearing a loose summer dress of a kind he hadn't seen her in before. It looked great on her; in fact she looked great, better than he remembered, there was a bloom in her cheeks and she radiated energy and competence. After the briefing, he caught her eye and she motioned towards her office.

'Shut the door, please.' He did as he was told and turned to face her.

'Is this important?'

'It won't take long.' She spoke in a clipped voice. He assumed she was still angry with him. Well, he couldn't blame her if she was.

'Look, sorry I didn't return your call. I've been away...' he trailed off. Something about her gaze intimidated him.

'That's understandable, given the circumstances. I'm sorry about Maria.'

'Thanks.'

'Actually, this isn't about work.'

'What is it about then?'

'I'm pregnant.' She looked at him, her eyes full and accusing. The words resonated round his brain. He shook his head to try and gain control of himself. She misunderstood John's gesture. 'Yes, it's yours; I'm certain of that.'

Of a million possibilities, he hadn't considered this. He knew he should feel something but he just felt empty as if he had been hollowed out.

'I thought you should know.'

He struggled to respond in a way that approximated to some notion of being civilised. 'What are you going to do?'

'You mean am I going to keep it?'

He shook his head. 'No, I, er, just wondered, I don't know, how you felt about it?'

'How do you feel about it?' she blazed. 'I've decided on a termination.'

'An abortion?'

'Got a better idea?'

He shook his head lamely yet even then, he sensed that it couldn't be that simple. 'No, er, well it's your erm, decision.' His response sounded brutally incomplete. 'If there's anything I can do, er... any help you want...' he trailed off.

'I've made my decision. It wouldn't be fair on Arthur.'

John felt numb. She regarded him for a beat, then shaking her head, she walked behind her desk, sat down and began looking through a script.

'Why tell me then? If you've made up your mind?'

'You have a right to know.' She softened again but a screech of brakes in the street outside snapped her back to reality. 'I'm not giving up my career; I've worked too hard for it and if I do have a family, I want the father to be there for the child.' She went back to her script. John looked at her then turned and walked out of the office.

FORTY-TWO

In the NTV crew car, Brian was cheerfully foul-mouthed as he drove at speed; Naz quiet, checking the map and making the occasional sharp response. It was like old times except for Brian's relentless sniping especially when John refused to disclose what Clemmy had said; old times except they'd moved on.

They were covering the strike again. After a brief lull at the end of August, hostilities were being rejoined. The last week of September, the nights were drawing in; there was a chill of winter in the air. The warmth had left the picket lines too. The occasional banter which had existed between miners and police had been replaced by cold-eyed determination and hate. The country grew nervous as peace talks between miners and the Coal Board collapsed again. The Archbishop of Canterbury and the Bishop of Durham inveighed against the hardline government tactics. They pleaded for dialogue, consensus, the importance of community, but it was far too late for any of that. Gangs of hooded vigilantes lay in wait for scabs and meted out brutal justice. The NCB withdrew the strikers' free coal; the government pursued the NUM though the courts to freeze their assets and stop the strike pay. For those left, it was No Surrender, 'No Pasaran', a fight to the death with a cold and bitter winter in prospect.

Police and strikers alike hated the press who now resorted to underhand tactics to get their stories. The miners were convinced the press were on the government's side. Fearful of being caught on camera beating up a striker, the police had turned against them too. Getting quotes was like pulling teeth.

John struggled to get material but he kept getting flashbacks of Clemmy telling him she was pregnant, Jess lying naked, Maria lying dead. Naz cut him some slack but Brian gave him a hard time. In one interview, John kept fluffing the same cue and later, he forgot to ask a question. Brian was straight on his case. On the way back, they passed close to a new housing development in a village on the edge of Leeds. He remembered something and asked if they could make a quick detour.

'It's where Eric Guttridge lives. He disappeared the day we went to look at the arms dump. His wife reported him missing.'

'For fuck's sake!' Brian exploded. John looked at Naz, who looked away.

'It won't take long. I just need to talk to her for five minutes, ten at the most.' Brian grimaced but John appealed to Naz. 'Five fucking minutes? That's not too much to ask, is it?' Brian swore under his breath but Naz sighed and nodded acceptance.

They parked in the quiet cul-de-sac populated with new bungalows. He checked the address and walked up to one of them and rang the bell. It had started raining heavily. John tried to shelter by standing close to the door and he nearly fell in when it was opened. Florid-faced, wearing rubber gloves and a holding a duster, Helen Guttridge stared out apprehensively.

'Mrs Guttridge?'

'Have you found him?' she asked breathlessly, her eyes brightening. Her face fell when he shook his head but she allowed him onto the mat inside the front door.

'I'm afraid not. I was wondering if I could talk to you for a few minutes?'

'I've already told the police everything and those other men. Are you the police?'

'No, I'm a journalist.' He showed her his press card. Helen Guttridge took a sharp intake of breath and began to close the door.

'I can't talk to you.'

'I saw Eric, just before he disappeared. I'd just like a few minutes of your time.'

'Those men said I shouldn't talk to anyone,' she said fearfully. 'From Eric's unit. He was in the TA, you know.' He nodded but stayed silent. She wanted to talk; it was just a question of getting

185

her started. She considered briefly then opened the door wider to allow him inside. He stepped into the tiny hall. It reeked of air freshener but it couldn't dispel the despair which inhabited the place.

'What else did the men say?'

'That he was in trouble and publicity would just make things worse.' She paused as she remembered, 'I mean, it was only the TA and he enjoyed it so much at the beginning. He was so happy when he bought the car and then when we bought the bungalow. I thought I'd died and gone to heaven.'

'Did they say what kind of trouble?' She shook her head.

'I had trouble understanding their accent, it was very thick.'

'Were they Irish? From the North?'

She nodded and then looked him in the eye. 'He's not coming back, is he?' The duster hand dropped to her side.

'I don't know.' She came closer.

'He's never been gone this long without getting in touch.'

There was an impatient honk on the horn which broke the moment and annoyed John. He gave her one of his business cards. 'If you want to talk again, ring that number, any time.' She nodded, still distracted. She was right, Eric wouldn't be coming back. He'd merged with his background, retreated into deep cover. The insects and microscopic creatures that processed him were alchemists transforming the base metal of his body back to the stardust from which everything comes.

As he hurried back to the car, John was still weighing things up. The men from the TA who came to talk to her had had Ulster accents. It wasn't enough on its own but it was another piece of the jigsaw. As he got in, Brian said, 'About bloody time,' and drove off at high speed. Afterwards, they stopped at a bar on the edge of Leeds. It was a watering hole for assorted hacks covering the strike. The air was thick with smoke and chatter as usual but the mood was subdued. Everyone knew they were in for a long haul. Brian took the order but when John asked for an orange juice, Brian turned on him.

'Fucking thin yoghurt, what's the matter with you?'

'Nothing, Brian, I just don't fancy a drink today.'

'Fuck me.' Brian stalked away.

'Who's rattled his cage?'

'He doesn't want to lose his overtime,' Naz said quietly. 'We got a bollocking over the last wild goose chase.'

'What wild goose chase?'

'Eric Guttridge and the non-existent arms dump in the woods?'

'I didn't know,' John replied.

'You can't just go off freelancing when you feel like it, no matter what the story is.'

'Even if it's about who killed Maria?'

'Especially if it's about that.' Naz leaned closer to John and whispered, 'Leave it alone John, I don't want to lose a friend.'

Brian returned with the drinks and passed John's fruit juice to him with ostentatious, exaggerated delicacy. John tried to defuse the situation.

'I'm sorry about the detour, Brian.'

'Next time, do it in your own fucking time.'

'Give me a break, will you?'

'Our brief is covering the strike. When we've done it, our job's over.'

'Since when did we stick to the bloody brief? I know you don't want to lose your precious fucking overtime but Guttridge happens to be a bloody story. You remember what that is, Brian? It's called journalism. It's supposed to be what we fucking do!'

Brian pushed his chair back and stood up.

'You used to have a laugh. Now you're just a sad fucker.'

'Where are you off to?' Naz called after him. 'It's bucketing down out there.'

'I've left my fags in the car.' Brian stomped outside. John glanced at Naz for support but he just gave a non-committal shrug, which further annoyed him.

'Come off that fucking fence, Naz. Brian's been needling me for days. Well? Hasn't he?'

'The difference between journalism and a personal crusade is objectivity,' Naz commented.

'Meaning I've lost mine?' Naz was about to reply when a low

bass rumble followed by a dull, growing roar took over. The room seemed to lift and shake and the front windows blew in. At the same time, the front door flew open and a blast of hot air ripped into the bar space, knocking over tables and chairs, picking up crockery and cutlery. As people started screaming, a full pint flew past John's face. John and Naz were seated at the rear of the bar in a corner behind a pillar. As the table settled between them, they looked at each other for a split second, then they were running towards the door, treading on people and glass. The crew car was parked round the corner in a narrow alley with high brick walls. The alley contained the worst of the blast. That was the reason for the relatively minor damage to the pub. The downside was that the narrow alley walls had focused and intensified the explosion. The car was a blackened, smoking hulk, a deep fissure ran down the middle like a bizarre centre parting. There was a bubbling crater where the engine had been. Parts of the vehicle fizzed and guttered as the rain fell relentlessly. Brian was half-in, half-out of the shattered vehicle. His legs were sticking out of the car at a crazy angle as if the explosion had happened as he'd leaned in. Naz and John reached him at the same time but it was apparent Brian was beyond help. John pulled at him maniacally, saying over and over,

'The bastards! The fucking bastards!'

Naz pulled John away.

'Leave it!'

John slumped back against the alley wall. 'He's got three fucking kids. They were after me.'

'They were after all of us.' John pushed Naz aside and tried to walk away but Naz grabbed him and turned him back.

'You knew the kind of risks you were taking. That's what made it such a good story.'

'What made it a good story is that it's fucking true,' John retorted.

'It's a fucking corker now!' Naz raged pointing at Brian.

'You want them to get away with killing Brian? Don't you care?!' John asked.

'Of course I care! He was my friend, our friend.'

188

'When you've got a story, you've got to go after it, that's the job.'

'Some things are more important than the job,' Naz spat.

'Like what?' John blazed.

'Don't you fucking lecture me. Amin kicked my family out of Uganda and thousands like us. He murdered countless others and nobody in the West gave a flying fuck. Sometimes you have to walk away.' He glared at John angrily, then threw him against the wall and turned and walked towards the main road. As the rain hammered down, the sound of approaching sirens grew louder.

FORTY-THREE

After yet another police interview, John drove over the moors in the deepening twilight to Jess's cottage on the off chance that she'd be there. It was the only place to go. Unlike everyone else, she at least believed him about Gladio even if there were too many questions.

As John drove, images of Brian and Naz kept popping into his mind unbidden. He remembered the three of them laughing hysterically outside Bridgford as he tried to do a piece to camera. When he'd walked down the hill to find Hatton, he hadn't just walked away from them, he'd walked away from everything that had gone before. He was part of a war, a vicious, secret war. It was kill or be killed. The world had moved on and there was no going back.

The rain had stopped, giving way to a cool, damp evening. Grey mist formed in the cold pockets and hollows, ghostly possibilities loitering on the edges of perception. The gathering gloom echoed John's mood. As he got out of the car at her cottage, a flock of lapwings took off in the next field calling sadly.

Jess opened the door, saw his face. 'What's wrong?'

'They killed Brian.' He pushed her back into the cottage. 'They fucking killed Brian!' He stared at her, eyes blazing.

'I'm really sorry.'

He took hold of Jess. 'Tell me the truth!'

Her face contorted in pain. 'You're hurting me.'

'Why did Maria break into the camp?' Jess shook her head. 'They killed her and they've killed Brian. Why?' Jess grimaced in pain and John let go of her arms. She rubbed them and shook her head. 'I don't know.'

'All right, then. Why did Maria break into the camp? Why not you?'

She turned away and looked out of the window. 'My Mum lives in a Belfast tower block and drinks. My kid brother has mental health issues and sleeps rough.'

'What's that got to do with it?' John asked.

'The IRA executed my father. He wasn't blown up. They cut out his tongue and shot him in the back of the head. My Mum never got over it. She and my brother were hounded out of the village.'

'Why?'

'They said he was an informer.'

'Was he?'

'No. He was a gentle man who wouldn't hurt a fly. That's when I was recruited.'

'Recruited?'

'I wanted revenge.'

'You work for the British, MI5?' John asked, incredulous.

'Something like that.'

'Christ.'

'I'm freelance now.'

'Sounds pretty full-on to me.'

'Look, I had a relationship with them when I was younger. It stopped when I went to university.'

'But it started up again?'

'When I joined the peace camp, they got in touch.'

'To infiltrate the women?'

Jess shook her head. 'They knew Maria was onto something.'

'Gladio?'

'They ordered me to let the break-in go ahead.'

'All right, but why arrest Maria under the Prevention of Terrorism Act if they know the truth? Why put her through that?'

'Gladio is a state within a state. They wanted to find out where it led, how far, how high.' Jess explained.

'You used her.'

'She knew what she was getting into.'

'She didn't know you were a spy under orders to seduce her.'

'Actually, she tried to seduce me.'

'She's dead and you're alive. Did they order you to seduce me too?'

'I hate terrorism, the IRA, Loyalist death squads, Gladio, all of them.'

'What about Gimlet? Is he part of this?'

Her eyes opened wide and she caught her breath but then she was talking. 'Major Jeremy Gimlet. Coldstream Guards seconded to secret duties.'

'Whose side is he on?' She shrugged.

'Is he part of Gladio?'

'Maybe.' She began to say something but he interrupted her.

'Why kill Brian? I mean, if they'd wanted to kill me, they could have done it anytime when I was in Northern Ireland. Why wait?'

'Perhaps you were lucky?'

'I wouldn't like to be unlucky.'

Jess sighed and ran a hand through her hair. 'You look done in. Sit down and I'll cook some food.' John stared at her without answering. 'At least let me get you a drink?' He nodded and watched as she poured whisky into a glass, her hand shaking. It was still shaking as she gave him the drink which he downed in one go. He held out the empty glass for a refill.

'Something happened in Ulster, didn't it?' She asked.

'You still haven't told me why Maria broke into the camp.' Jess smiled but said nothing.

'Well?' He persisted.

'You first.'

He told her about Kevin Dillon's note and the trip to Ulster, about his arrest by Special Branch. Finally he told her about Uccello. When he'd finished she put her hand on his.

'Is that everything, then.'

'Not quite. What did Maria break into the camp for?'

'Proof of Gladio's existence. Once a month, someone phones instructions to the Swiss bank holding the Gladio accounts. We were after the phone records.'

'But how did you know which ones to get?' John asked.

'We'd bribed a security guard. Not a Yank, one of the RAF

guys. We needed proof that Gladio was using Nazi money. It was one way of getting it.'

John examined her beautiful face, lines of pain arcing down from the corners of her eyes and mouth.

'You think the person who makes the phone calls is Gimlet?' John asked. She nodded. 'Pity it was all for nothing,' he said

'Actually, it wasn't. Maria didn't fail.'

'She was caught, she didn't get the tapes.'

'Someone else did.'

'But I thought the other women provided a diversion for Maria?'

She nodded. 'Maria's covert entry was another diversion. She knew how good the security was, she had to be sure.'

'Then who did get the tapes?' John asked.

'The RAF sergeant stole them during the commotion.'

'You could have stopped her?'

'It was her idea and a good plan. It worked.' Jess paused, 'We thought they would hold her for a while then let her go.'

'Why?' Jess looked at him. 'Why did the sergeant do it? I mean, I know why Maria would but why did he risk everything?'

'He needed money.' She saw the doubtful look on John's face and added, 'He has a gambling problem. He'd hit a losing streak.'

'How much?'

'Ten thousand.'

'Paid for by your employers?' She nodded.

'Then you've got the evidence on Gimlet and Gladio?' Jess nodded slowly and John felt a weight lifting from his shoulders. 'Then we've won. We've got the bastards, haven't we?'

'The tapes have to be decoded.'

'Your people can do that, can't they?' John asked.

'If they want to.'

'Why wouldn't they want to?'

'There are ramifications. Embarrassing allies, exposing powerful people isn't good politics,' she said slowly.

'They can't just ignore it.'

'They'll use the information privately, behind closed doors, to cajole and secure agreements.' And there it was. Finally he knew everything and it was a dead end, literally. Maria, Brian, Hatton and Guttridge dead, lives ruined, families torn apart, and for nothing.

FORTY-FOUR

John found a seat at the back of the fifteenth century C of E country church, away from family and colleagues. The reassuring atmosphere enfolded him. The certainty of the ancient oak ceiling and grey stone pillars appealed but he didn't belong. He had moved over to the dark side, the place of fear, paranoia and sudden death. That's why he sat at the back gazing at the stained glass windows, fiddling with the hymn book.

Clemmy arrived looking severe in black accompanied by Arthur, stuffed awkwardly into a dark suit in the manner of a big man unused to such apparel. Clemmy graced John with the coolest of glacial nods. He wondered if she'd had her termination. The thought of it came to him unbidden in his idle moments but there wasn't anything he could do about it, not after Brian. Nevertheless, it troubled him. When Clemmy wasn't looking, Arthur acknowledged him too, a look half friendly and half menacing. Naz nodded but sat near the front, as did most of his erstwhile colleagues, who exhibited a collective animus towards John. A rumour had gone round that he was jinxed, that there was bad blood between Brian and John and John was somehow implicated in Brian's death. John didn't mind, his time at NTV was drawing to a close. When the church was full, a less comforting melody signalled the arrival of the family and the coffin.

John had met Brian's wife once. She was only just five feet tall. Standing beside Brian, she'd looked like a perfectly formed, round-faced doll next to a giant. At work, people had sometimes speculated about their coupling but they'd produced three kids. Seeing the family group shuffling along behind the coffin, heads bowed, lost and sobbing, he felt himself overwhelmed too.

After the funeral, John walked through the village. He stopped at a public phone box by the village green and dialled a Belfast number. A clipped accented voice answered and John spoke briefly into the phone then ended the call. He sat on a bench by a duck pond, lit a cigarette and waited. It was a breezy late autumn day and the wind ruffled the feathers of the few bedraggled ducks circling aimlessly on the water. Leaves were lifted up and twirled in impromptu reels by the frequent cold gusts. Sensible people stayed indoors but John didn't feel sensible. Fifteen minutes later, the phone rang again. John listened for a minute or so before replacing the receiver without speaking. Then he walked away.

FORTY-FIVE

The police questioned John at length about Brian, normal CID plods this time but the result was the same. Tired, hard-faced men who'd seen too much pain to be anything other than cynical, they asked questions like automatons scarcely listening to his answers. They had a theory, which joined all the dots into a picture that made sense. An oxygen bottle used for welding had been left in the alley outside a garage and it had exploded. Conclusion: it was an accident. They didn't want to hear anything contradictory because that meant more work. Besides, after the Orgreave footage of mounted police charging miners like some banana republic crushing an uprising, they didn't like the press. John couldn't tell them anything anyway. He had his suspicions but as far as the police were concerned, Maria's killing had unhinged him so he saw conspiracies everywhere.

John told Jess he had found someone in Edinburgh who had information about Eric Guttridge. He asked her to go with him but when she tried to find out more about his new source, he was monosyllabic, saying only that it was important. Since their drunken intimacy before Maria's death, he had kept his distance from Jess and she from him. The trouble was, she was the only one who understood.

They left early but it was raining hard and the journey north in the 2CV was slow and uncomfortable. The tiny engine chugged along as they were overtaken by a procession of juggernauts hurling tidal waves of spray over the vehicle. Uneasy, Jess wanted to turn back but John was on a mission. Besides, the rain was good cover.

Just south of the Scottish border, John stopped at a country pub.

'Lunch,' he announced.

'This isn't a good idea, John.'

'Suit yourself, Jess, I'm hungry.' He got out and walked into the bar. After a moment Jess followed. The place was empty apart from a heavy-set, florid faced man behind the bar John gave Jess a sandwich and went to the gents, a corrugated lean-to at the rear. The barman disappeared too.

In the cool of the gents, the rain pounding on the metal roof, John smiled at the barman.

'Been a while, Matt.'

'What do you want, John?'

'Advice.'

Matt Hardwick had been John's corporal when the platoon was ambushed. Bluff, fearless and unimaginative, he nevertheless had smoothed John's passage out of the army. He had a reason. John had saved his life. When the first bomb was detonated, Matt had gone forward but John had rugby tackled him just before the second blast. The bloke next to John had been blown to pieces. Like John, Matt knew that shadowy forces allowed Loyalist nutters access to weapons to butcher and maim suspected terrorists. Like John, it was the ordinary squaddies Matt felt sorry for, the cannon fodder who ended up with no legs and half a life. He'd bought himself out of the army just after John and settled at the pub near Otterburn Camp. John told Matt what he proposed to do.

'What do you think? Will it work?'

'It might.'

'But?'

'Win or lose, you'll be a target, John. Those bastards have long memories.'

'But it's worth a go?'

'Make sure you have an escape kit,' Matt advised.

'Like what?'

'Passport, money, a weapon.'

'Anything else?' John asked.

'Don't come here again.'

Jess appeared. 'John? What the hell are you doing out here?'

'I thought I dropped something but it's fine.' Matt looked at her, then returned to the bar.

'John?'

'It's OK, Jess. Come on.' He hustled her out of the bar.

'What the hell is going on?'

'It's OK, honest.' They got into the car and drove away. Jess was angry but there was nothing she could do.

As they nosed through the afternoon Edinburgh traffic, the rain eased. They parked and caught a bus heading towards South Queensferry, before alighting at some shops near a park surrounded by serried ranks of neat, interwar grey stone bungalows. The atmosphere was severe and clannish, a northern gulag for a dreary respectability. People scurried past in the rain without looking. After scanning the street, John set off on foot towards the park with her in pursuit.

'Where the hell are we going?' she asked. It was still raining but he turned into the park and began to march across the expanse of sodden pasture. She swore fiercely and went after him.

They emerged on the other side of the park into a quiet street of well-kept, identical bungalows each adorned by an ugly, frog-like wooden dormer window. Lace covered every window. Nothing moved in the street, not a curtain or a car or a sign of life. John turned to Jess, the cold, determined look back on his face. 'This is it.'

'What? Who're we going to see?'

'Kevin Dillon.'

She gasped and stopped. 'I'm not dealing with him.' John showed no emotion. 'Why didn't you tell me?' she demanded, running after him.

'You wouldn't have come, would you?' Furious, she ran in front of him and barred his way.

'They're terrorists. I work for the British.'

'I think they want to take a risk.'

'If you're wrong, they'll kill us both.' Jess informed John.

199

'If I'm right, they won't.' He turned and walked into the drive of the bungalow next door. He marched up the gravel path to the front door.

He was about to ring the bell when she grabbed his arm. 'I already told you, my people won't release the tapes.'

John rang the bell and said, 'Maybe we can force their hand.'

The neat front garden had a handkerchief lawn surrounded by a well-stocked border, a magnolia, roses and a quince. A short, fat, balding red-faced man of about forty in a badly fitting suit opened the front door. He caught sight of Jess. 'Who's she?'

'She's with me.'

The balding man shook his head and began to shut the door 'No one said anything about a woman.'

John shoved his foot in the door. 'She's part of the deal.'

The balding man shook his head. Jess got annoyed. 'That's fine by me, I don't want to come in, anyway.'

John grabbed her arm and yanked her back. 'For fuck's sake, hear us out. What have you got to lose?' The balding man looked back into the house. John heard a muffled voice then the door was opened. Dragging Jess behind him, John entered the bungalow and went into the back room. The little man motioned to them to sit down. John released Jess who rubbed her arm angrily.

'Would you like something to drink? Tea or coffee?'

'Where's Kevin?'

'I'm Stephen, Kevin's interlocutor.' The last word sounded ridiculous in the skirl of his accent.

'I arranged to meet Kevin,' John insisted.

'Alone so you did. Not with your floozy.'

Jess took control. 'Come on John. This isn't working!' John followed her as she marched towards the doorway only to find it blocked by a large, shaven-headed man in a tracksuit. In his hand hanging down discreetly by his side, was a gun.

'I am authorised to speak for Kevin,' Stephen added behind them. 'Now why don't you sit down and tell us what's on your mind?' John looked at Jess who ignored him. He shrugged and they did as they were told. Stephen smiled and nodded to John. 'What did you have in mind?'

John took a deep breath, 'A press conference where we tell everything we know about Gladio, Billy Hatton and my sister, backed up by what I've uncovered about Eric Guttridge and the Territorial SAS regiment he'd belonged to.'

Stephen pursed his lips. 'Where does Kevin fit into this scenario?'

'He can talk about the guns being run to Loyalist death squads and their use by the British state for covert, arm's length assassination in Ulster.'

'Doesn't sound like much to me,' Stephen said dubiously. 'It's all circumstantial.'

'There is more,' John added.

'What would that be then?'

'Kevin will release photographs of a senior member of the British Security Services consorting with Gladio's banker.'

'What about her?'

Jess grimaced but John ignored her. 'She provides the piece de resistance, the source of Gladio's money. The names and numbers of the Swiss bank accounts where it's stored.'

'You'll have proof of that?'

'No, but if the information's accurate, it will be up to them to disprove it.' John watched Stephen for his response. 'Well?'

Stephen moved his head from side to side as if exercising a crick in his neck. 'Are we talking television here?'

'TV, radio, press, the works.'

'And where would this circus take place?'

'Dublin. Somewhere not part of the UK.'

Stephen shook his head slowly. 'I don't think so.'

'Why not? I can organise the press; they'll have to take notice.'

'Kevin is allergic to television.'

'Once a killer,' Jess laughed aggressively.

A banging in the hall followed by raised voices made them start apprehensively as the door burst open. 'True, but that's not the reason,' Kevin Dillon said as he entered the room. He was wearing a good suit and tie and his bluff face revealed nothing. He looked at Stephen and said, 'Get us some tea will you?' Stephen left the room, closing the door behind him. Kevin offered his hand to Jess. She ignored him and he withdrew it. 'Kathleen? You've grown up. Suits you.'

'What's the reason you won't be interviewed?' John asked.

Kevin passed a hand over his head. 'Vanity. I couldn't be seen on TV in my old glasses and bald as coot. What would that do to my image?' He looked troubled but then he grinned and his face came alive, his eyes dancing behind his glasses. A chuckle came from somewhere at the back of his throat. 'It's a grand plan.'

John felt the excitement growing in him. 'You'll do it?'

Kevin was serious again. 'On one condition.' John looked at him. 'Tell me about her.'

'No, John,' Jess ordered.

'She's freelance.'

'A mercenary?'

'An activist!' Jess spluttered.

'Who works for the British?'

Jess shook her head but John nodded. 'Yes.'

'For God's sake!'

'For the good guys against Gladio,' John added.

'Thin on the ground, good guys,' Kevin said quietly. 'So, Kathleen, how long have you been working for them I wonder?'

'Since you murdered my father.'

Kevin looked away for a moment. 'A lot of bad things have happened,' he paused then added, 'on both sides.'

'I told you this was pointless!' Jess hissed.

John tried again. 'You and some like-minded people want to end the armed struggle. So does Jess and others like her. Exposing Gladio would be a big first step.'

'The British love to fight so they do, but it's true, some would like an end to hostilities.'

'So?' John pressed. 'Are we on?'

'I will if she will,' Kevin said quietly.

'Come on, Jess'

'How do we know we can trust you?' Jess asked.

'That goes for both of us,' Kevin replied. 'Look, I'm sorry about your father...'

'Fuck off!'

'If we can expose Gladio and stop some of the killing, that's got to be worth trying, hasn't it?'

Jess sighed. 'Have we got enough to expose Gladio?'

Kevin spoke quietly. 'When Peter Uccello tells what he knows about the Nazi gold and the Vatican, that should make headlines in every country in the world.'

Jess was still boiling but John's plan had merit. 'All right.'

'We've got a deal?' Kevin asked. Jess nodded.

'How can you be sure Uccello will talk?' John asked.

Kevin stood up and stared at the garden. 'The Inquisition used to offer heretics the choice of recanting and being hanged or being burnt at the stake,' he said evenly as he turned to face them. 'I've offered him something similar: told him to confess but if he doesn't I'll reveal everything about him. He's a pragmatist.'

'Then we've done it,' John said, struggling to conceal the elation he felt. Piecemeal, the information they'd amassed didn't seem like much. They were so used to hiding what they knew, discussing it in hushed, fearful whispers that putting it all together in preparation for telling it to the world was simultaneously unnerving and stimulating. John realised that the story stood up and the more he thought about it, the more excited he grew about the prospects. After all the defeats they'd suffered, they might actually land a glove on Gladio.

If the plan came off, he would have avenged Maria and Brian as well as being proved right. It would also cement his career. No more flogging round country lanes at the crack of dawn competing for quotes with every other hack. Then again, if it didn't work...

They toasted success with a cup of tea, arranging to meet in Dublin the following week. The green light would be a press release early on October 11th followed by the press conference sometime in the afternoon at a yet to be decided Dublin hotel. Only the date was fixed. Every other arrangement would be left until the last possible moment to limit the possibility of any leakage.

'Any last questions?' Kevin asked as he led them to the front door.

'One. Why meet here? Why not in Glasgow?'

'Catholics are very loyal but terrible gob-shites. This is a Protestant area. Your Protestant is nosier than a cat but they keep themselves to themselves and they do look after their property.' Kevin smiled. 'I like a well-kept garden, makes everything seem right with the world.'

Jess and John stayed in a hotel in the centre of Edinburgh but their mood was sombre. Over dinner, they talked little apart from a spat while they were waiting for the main course.

'You had no right, John.'

'What right did Maria have, or Brian?'

'That's not the same.'

'No. They're dead.'

Jess didn't reply and they ate mostly in silence. Later in the twin room, they lay silently, alienated from each other and themselves.

FORTY-SIX

Back at work John was a pariah, acknowledged but largely ignored. He didn't care; he was moving on. He went to see his GP, talked about his sister's murder followed quickly by the tragic death of a close colleague. He was stressed out, kept having odd thoughts (which wasn't far from the truth). The GP listened sympathetically and promptly signed him off on a fortnight's sick leave and prescribed a course of Valium. Partly for cover, he collected his prescription then considered throwing it away. In the event, he kept it, 'just in case'. In case of what, he wasn't exactly sure.

On the 9th October, he told friends he was going on holiday and flew to Paris. There he bought a ticket and flew to Dublin. Jess made her own way to Dublin and once there, they met at the rear of a noisy bar overlooking the Liffey. Both were smartly dressed. She was wearing a dark business suit with fashionably large shoulder pads. He giggled; it made her look like someone out of Dallas. She retorted that he looked like a country bank manager in his suit and tie. Over a Guinness and a Martini, John talked through the final timetable.

Uccello would arrive in Dublin on the evening of the 10th October and stay at a Catholic seminary on the outskirts of the city. Kevin Dillon would travel down from the North in the early hours of the 11th. They would all meet at the Hilton at nine a.m. After a brief check of the agenda, John would send out the press release. They would all wait in the hotel for the press conference later.

With two days to kill, they booked into a penthouse at the Hilton and went to bed. Whether out of relief or exhaustion, they made love with a desperate energy, eating each other up.

At first, their abandon was exhilarating, but it didn't last. The world had shrunk to a universe of two.

In a lull between food and sex, Jess told him about growing up in Ireland and some tales of university adventures but, whether out of habit or some prescient caution about the future, she omitted several details. Perhaps it was because she was in love with him. She was into him and it was intoxicating. In their idle moments, they talked about places they'd like to go when it was all over, the kind of countryside, the weather. They didn't own up to it but both of them were thinking about a possible life beyond.

Late on the evening of the 10th, there was a phone call. Jess answered and said, 'Fine,' and put the receiver down. 'Uccello's arrived.'

John nodded and stared at the Dublin night skyline. The last act had started. One more night, twelve more hours, and they would be getting their own back.

FORTY-SEVEN

Kevin Dillon left Belfast in the late afternoon and drove to a small farm near the border where he waited. Shortly after midnight, he climbed into a Ford Sierra with his two 'bodyguards', Sean and Seamus. They drove south, crossing the border on a tiny road that wasn't patrolled. Ten miles into the republic they were flagged down by a roadblock; an armoured vehicle blocked the lane. A figure with a lantern waved it slowly back and forth. A sign announced a police checkpoint and asked drivers to slow down. Inside Kevin's car, they couldn't see who it was but it was obviously Garda or troops of some kind.

'What the fuck's this?' Sean said, slowing.

'Sink the boot, get the fuck outa here, Sean,' Seamus said quickly. Kevin calmed things down.

'Easy lads. Let's just have a look, shall we?'

'I've got a real bad feeling about this, Kevin,' Seamus repeated. 'Let's just get the hell out while we can,' but by then it was too late. Another vehicle appeared from a field and barred the road behind them.

'Have you all got your passports?' Kevin asked lightly.

'Fucking passports,' Seamus muttered as the car slowed towards the figure. 'Should have brought a fucking weapon or two with us.'

'But aren't we legit so we are?' Kevin said lightly. 'On our way to a stock market in Galway with me wearing my new glasses. Why would we be carrying guns if we were doing that?' The figure holding the lantern waved them to a stop at the side of the road. Sean wound down the driver's window.

'What the fuck's all this then?'

'Would you mind stepping out of the vehicle, sir?' He was

dressed in dark fatigues and it was difficult to make out any insignia. He spoke in a contorted southern Irish accent.

Kevin leant over from the passenger side. 'Is there a problem here? We're on our way to the horse auction in Galway. We're late as it is.'

The figure didn't move. 'Sorry sir, there's been some trouble down the road and we're having to check everyone. It's just routine.' There was a firmness in his voice. Kevin felt a slight unease but he couldn't put his finger on why.

'All right lads, quicker we do it, the quicker we'll be on our way.'

'I don't fucking like this,' Sean muttered quietly as they got out of the car.

'Stand this side of the vehicle please, sir,' the voice asked. They did as they were told.

As Kevin and Seamus walked round, Seamus muttered to Kevin. 'Would you mind telling me what fucking accent that is?' Kevin realised too late the source of his unease. Under the Irish lilt was the occasional unmistakable West Country vowel. Not an Irish vowel from West Cork or Galway but the extended, lazy open vowel of the English West Country. As they lined up by the vehicle, Kevin felt a knot of fear form in the pit of his stomach. 'Easy lads,' he said gently, cleaning his glasses. 'Let the men do their work.'

Those were his last words. He never replaced his glasses. Kevin Dillon and his two lads were cut down in a series of long bursts from three silenced machine guns. They fell where they stood in a hail of bullets, which peppered them and their Sierra. The noise was surreal, a demented popping like a bunch of crazed woodpeckers. Wearing gloves, the five soldiers in black fatigues then produced two Kalashnikovs and a pistol and fired several more thunderous bursts from them into the darkness above the bodies so that the cartridge cases scattered around the bodies. This time the noise was deafening, a blasphemous assault against the silent calm of the night so that when it stopped, the shock seemed to hang in the air. Having made sure that the dead men's fingerprints were on these weapons, the assassins dropped them by the bodies, walked to their vehicles and drove north, into the night. They didn't speak again. After a while, the sounds of the night returned. From start to finish, the whole incident had taken barely three and half minutes.

FORTY-EIGHT

John, Jess and Uccello waited nervously in the foyer of the Albany Hotel. In the flesh, Pete Uccello had a habit of leaning in very close, invading personal space and speaking into your ear like a plumber with a knotty problem when he wanted to say something. While John paced nervously back and forth and Jess scanned the street, Uccello sat quietly, sweating and chain-smoking Embassy Regal.

'Something's up,' he said when Kevin didn't show at the agreed time.

Jess looked at him. 'Maybe the traffic's bad?'

John waited a couple of minutes then made a decision. 'I'm going to make a couple of calls.' Jess nodded and Uccello just shrugged. John walked into the lobby and rang a Dublin journalist he'd known at college. After the niceties, he got to it.

'Yeah I'm here following up a story, yeah. I just wondered if there'd been any incidents on the wire overnight.' As he listened to the reply, the knuckles holding the phone whitened with the pressure. 'No that's fine Hugh, thanks.' He listened again. 'Yeah, we should get together over a pint. I'll give you a bell.' John walked back to where Jess and Pete Uccello were waiting.

'What's happened?'

'He's dead.'

'What?' Jess started. Pete Uccello went very pale. The cigarette he was about to inhale stopped, marooned in mid-air.

'The official line is that three heavily armed members of the Provisional IRA were killed in a firefight with British forces inside Northern Ireland.'

'But Kevin said they would be unarmed.'

'They were. Unofficially, the SAS assassinated them inside

the Republic. It's caused a huge stink in Dublin. The British are having to offer the crown jewels to calm things down.'

John walked round the room. In the distance, the sound of crockery and shouting from the hotel kitchen on the floor below could be dimly heard. He turned to Jess but she was suddenly remote.

'They've won,' she said flatly.

'Not necessarily.'

'What can we do?'

'Tell Kevin's part of the story for him. The three of us, I mean.'

She looked at Uccello who was still smoking. He hadn't said a word. 'What do you think?'

'What about your evidence? Will your people give it up?' Jess frowned. She was thinking ahead, about the future, the next move; her next move.

'The tapes would seal it,' Uccello whispered.

Jess shook her head doubtfully. 'I don't know.'

John went over to Jess. 'At least give it a go. Pete's right.'

'All right.'

'We'll have to reorganise the press conference for tomorrow. Is that OK with you, Pete?'

Uccello shrugged. 'Haven't got much bleeding choice, have I?'

While Jess met someone from the embassy, Uccello went back to his seminary and John walked round Dublin, doing battle with his anger and a growing sense of futility.

John and Jess met in the hotel bar at five pm. She had been gone all day and he had prepared himself for the worst but she beamed when she saw him and ran over and kissed him.

'They said yes?'

She smiled. 'They said maybe, if we deliver everything else.'

He felt his hope twitching back into life. 'Do you want a drink?'

'No, thanks John.' Afterwards, they lay on the bed with the lights off, watching as the darkness enveloped the city.

'I'll miss him.' John said quietly.

'Who?'

'Kevin. I know he was a terrorist but I liked him.'

'You're right,' she said coolly. He looked at her. 'He was a terrorist.' They kissed but John couldn't shake the feeling he had broken the spell. Jess closed her eyes but he lay awake listening to the hotel heating roaring away in the distance. Just after two am he finally fell asleep, but by then it was too late.

There would be no press release or press conference, no exposé plastered across every front page and news bulletin. No one was interested. The media circus had shifted to another, much bigger story, which zapped everything else off the airwaves and front pages for days.

A little before three am on the night of the 12th October 1984, the IRA blew up the Imperial Hotel, Brighton, in an attempt to assassinate Thatcher and most of her cabinet. In the event, they blew a huge hole in the building, injured and killed a number of people and saved Gladio from exposure. The prime minister of the Republic, Garret Fitzgerald, condemned the outrage and worried over a new bombing campaign in the North.

For John, Jess and Uccello, the enormity of what had happened took time to sink in. John stayed focused on his goal, driven by his need for revenge and refusing to see the bigger picture. Plans for a new press conference were put back twenty-four hours. After that, there was nothing to do but wait. At dusk, the looming darkness seemed to echo something in him and he headed for the bar. Jess joined him and they drank quietly together.

In bed they made love but they were both preoccupied. Afterwards, Jess clung to him like a child. He enjoyed holding her even if he couldn't quite fathom her sudden vulnerability. He gave up trying and drifted into oblivion.

Pete Uccello appeared in the dining room while he was eating breakfast. He hovered impatiently, sweating in a heavy overcoat. John had woken early with a hangover and left Jess in the room while he ate breakfast and reviewed his plans for the assault on the media. It was still early and the hotel dining room was sparsely populated. Uccello declined his invitation to sit down but stood in front of him like a builder with bad news. 'I'm off.'

'What about the press conference?'

'It's not the right time,' he said, turning to go.

'At least talk this over with Jess?'

Pete Uccello turned back. A look of regret passed across his face like a windblown cloud. 'I already have.'

'What? When?'

Uccello put a hand on his forearm . 'Take care of yourself, John.' He walked slowly out of the hotel. John watched him go, then hurried to the lift. He found Jess in the hotel room, packing. She didn't stop when he entered.

'What are you doing?'

'The Americans are rethinking their policy on Northern Ireland,' she said without looking up. 'It's over,' she said, zipping her case with practised finality.

'What've the Americans got to do with us?'

She stood up straight and looked at him.

'Any peace process is dead in the water.'

'They won't release the tapes?'

'The IRA tried to kill the British government.'

John fought to remain calm. 'We can't let them win.'

'They have won, for now.' Wearing jeans, leather jacket and T-shirt, Jess looked fantastic, radiating energy and determination. It was impossible to mistake the moment but he shook his head in denial. She was right, and the strange confluence of the practical and emotional moment was not lost on him. It was over, this was over; they were over. Picking up her case she came to the door and stopped by him. Still holding the bag, she kissed him gently. 'Take care of yourself.'

John stared back at her. Later he would think of a hundred things he could and should have said but then, at the time, he said nothing. Instead he managed a wry smile. Jess smiled back, took a deep breath and then she was gone.

PART THREE

France and the Low
Countries 2004

ONE

As befits a major European city, Amsterdam is vibrant, cosmopolitan and busy, yet unlike London, Paris or Rome, what strikes the newcomer is the essential reserve of the inhabitants, part modesty, part privacy. A working port, the city retains a port's appetite for money and sex but like the canals running just below street level, there are powerful undercurrents. The people who claimed the city from the sea understood their insignificance in the face of nature and built on a human scale. Old Amsterdam is shaped like a heart. The left ventricle contains the red light district; the right ventricle contains the banks and the diamond merchants. The sprawling concrete mess of the modern city dwarfs the original but for the determined explorer, the old scale can still be discovered. The multinational banks may have migrated to glass and steel palaces close to the orbital motorways but the old merchant banks and diamond houses remain in their sixteenth century mansions, a stone's throw from the seething centre. In cobbled streets by dark, tree-lined canals, only the discreet name plaques and windowless ground floors with their heavy oak doors give a clue to the unseen vaults and numberless secrets within.

At thirty-four, Jules Swemmer was clever, witty, impatient, well-heeled and popular, a natural entertainer. People gravitated to the big man who was the life and soul of every party. Over two metres tall, Jules was not exactly fat but like his personality, his belly was always in danger of bursting its bounds. Shirt buttons popped open releasing crumpled shirt corners and tails to flap in silent appreciation of his exertions. Jules was well-versed in the habits of old Amsterdam. By night, he loved the clubs and brothels, the sex shows and bars, but lately, ambition and insecurity had been added to his natural bonhomie for by day, he was a banker. His great-uncle Jan had created the huge wealth of the RNF merchant bank where Jules worked under his father, Pieter, who was now the chief executive. Despite carrying the family name, Jules sensed the cautious reserve of his colleagues towards him. As his father remarked to another board member in the ugly management shorthand they employed, Jules wasn't a 'completer-finisher'. It wasn't that he was lazy; far from it, he brought energy and invention to his work as to everything in his life. He had bright ideas by the dozen but when confronted by the repetitive tedium of implementation, he tired easily, preferring the excitement of a new challenge to the slog of old routine.

It was the same in his personal life. Women were attracted to his energy and wit so when he fell in love, which was often, his generosity was legendary. The downside was the increasingly messy 'exits,' culminating in a spectacularly expensive divorce which had left him broke and in debt. Since his divorce, Jules had been more circumspect, avoiding commitment but this just reinforced the impression that he lacked the natural reserve and equilibrium of a banker, especially a Dutch one. By inclination and temperament, Jules was an optimist and until his thirty-fifth birthday, he had effortlessly ignored his own defects. Until then, he had seen himself as the crown prince of the bank. Whatever happened, his succession was his due.

That his nocturnal habits might count more heavily against him was brought brutally home on his birthday. Objectively, being thirty-five was the same as being thirty-four but to Jules on that day it felt uncomfortably like the border between youth and middle age. He had just signed the last of his divorce papers but instead of freeing him, the act had apparently sentenced him to an existence of permanent penury. As a result, he was feeling bruised and unusually vulnerable, which might account for the impact of what happened next.

One of the secretaries was struggling with a crossword and asked a colleague what 'Rabelaisian' meant. Despite his preoccupation with work, Jules was about to explain when the young, clever, newly-arrived legal director quipped, 'Jules', as he passed by. Everyone laughed, which in the hushed atmosphere of the reception area was a rare event in itself. At the time, Jules had joined in but underneath he wasn't laughing. In that moment, he'd understood that, far from being seen as the fun-loving brilliant individual of his imaginings, he was in fact a figure of fun, more clown prince than crown prince. Of course, he understood that his life hadn't changed in an instant and that in fact, he'd been moving towards this inevitability for years but, in that moment, he felt his life shift and maybe his instinct was correct. It was as if his previous excesses that he had always managed to excuse and forget were abruptly, and without warning, weighed against him. In that moment of painful self-awareness, his life did indeed change forever and the deep reservoir of seriousness on which his humour floated began to assert itself.

Jules still frequented his old haunts but the fun-loving Jules had passed on. He smiled and joked but a part of him was always serious, watching, waiting, planning and people sensed this. At least they did in the clubs and bars because his old friends gradually fell away and he became isolated. He took to visiting live sex shows where he sat alone in the dark with the other voyeurs impassively watching the noisy contortions. He was the same at the bank but in the timeless atmosphere of security and wealth where any change was glacial in its progress, few noticed the difference in him. He was still the jovial big man who struggled to keep his desk tidy, but he was planning. That's why he enjoyed the red light district; sex and money were different sides of the same coin and he had known this a long time. When he was six, his great-uncle Jan had taken him downstairs into the old cellar below the street and opened the huge door of one of the vaults. On the other side of the wall, Jules imagined the black waters of the canal sluicing by. It smelt dank and musty in the vault but as the old man led him inside, Jules forgot everything. The dull gleam of gold bars piled to the ceiling possessed him. The old man had picked one up and thrust it into the hands of the startled child. As he struggled to hold onto the heavy bar, his great-uncle had leaned in close to him; Jules remembered his stale breath and the forest of hairs growing from his nose.

'Money, Jules.' The old man had growled softly, 'Everybody wants it, everybody needs it; we can supply it.' Then he'd laughed unpleasantly for a long time but even at six, Jules had understood something. Although he didn't know exactly what his uncle meant, Jules knew that Jan had been talking about the 'other' side, about the people and the dirt where all the gold came from. Jules understood that better than his father or the other board members. He remembered the weight of the bar and the way it gleamed even in the half-light of the gloomy vault, as if it was lit from within. That image had stayed with him. More than any other, that memory had led him to believe that the bank was his birthright.

Jules also understood that all good business involves risk, that's why it's exciting. Every morning at eight-thirty the bank executives gathered round the great oval boardroom table behind the high windows where the only sound was the sedate ticking of the antique silver clock, and held their 'prayer meeting'. Although it had the flavour and reverence of a religious ceremony, the meeting was more concerned with mammon than God. There, they decided how to invest the twenty per cent of the bank's liquid assets on the global wholesale money markets, some short-term, some longer term but always the mix was cautious because they did not have to take risks. For every institution like theirs that was 'long' on cash and able to lend, there was another institution that was 'short' and needed to borrow. Some multinational banks had balance sheets the size of small countries. Discreet but very large trades were the bank's speciality, and very large trades meant very large commissions even if one was measuring commissions in one hundredth of one per cent or 'bips' as they were known.

When Jules had first attended the prayer meetings, he'd made many suggestions, largely ignored, but now he was content to watch and listen silently. If the others didn't think he was worthy of the succession, then he would have to prove it to them and he had an idea. It was not fully worked out, but an important part of business acumen is being able to recognise opportunity when it arises and then having the initiative to exploit it. Jules had a plan and a determination to prove everyone else wrong. He just had to be patient and wait.

TWO

Leaving Ventimiglia and the Mediterranean behind, John and Jess drove in silence. The rhythm of the journey allowed them time to reflect and digest something of what had happened. He had so many questions and he fought a running battle with the urge to turn the car round and drive back to his rustico and stay there no matter what. Then there was the fear that both exhausted him and filled him with energy while in his head, a Jeremiah voice told him they had no chance. And yet, being with her again rekindled something.

On the tortuous climb up the switchback road, the old 2CV groaned ominously, belching black fumes every time he changed gear. As the absurdity of the old banger as a getaway car became more and more pronounced, John affected a calm nonchalance, but every few seconds his eyes checked the engine temperature gauge edging dangerously towards the red zone. Jess didn't notice, apparently enjoying the magnificent view of the valley falling away below them but in reality, she was scanning the road behind. Once they reached the plateau, the going was easier and they relaxed a little, but conversation remained elusive. Sixty kilometres later, they stopped at a fork in the road. An ancient stone chapel, its walls peeling stucco, its roof crowned by a tiny bell tower stood guard like a lopsided sentry on a promontory above the fork. She needed to pee and he pulled over.

She hurried up a bank while he strolled up the grass to investigate a chapel. The front was dominated by a solid oak door, flanked on either side by two small windows each decorated with a plastic vase of dead flowers. He went to a window, moved the dead flowers to one side and leaned forward, peering into the ecclesiastical gloom beyond. Wire grilles had been placed over the openings but it was possible to make out the dusty interior. Wooden chairs crowded one another as if the occupants had left hurriedly in the middle of a party. In the half-dark at the rear, he could just make out the frescoes. In pale blue and gold, figures writhed and twisted, reaching out for hope and salvation. He loved these places, it was one of the things he liked about Italy. Beneath the deluge of the modern information age, these chapels bore witness to the enduring certainty of pain, doubt and regret, the corollaries of mortality and consciousness.

'John?' Jess reappeared and pulled at his sleeve. 'I think we should make for the mountains.' She nodded towards a small road.

'Why don't we carry on?' John suggested.

'To Turin?'

'The big city's anonymous, we can get lost there.' John said.

'It's empty and easier to hide in the mountains,' she replied fanning herself with the sweatshirt.

'And easier to be spotted.'

'Look, we can't sleep in the bloody car in the city can we?'

He wasn't sure why they were arguing. 'Sleep in the car?'

'We haven't got any papers remember? Up there,' she said pointing to the distant high peaks in the west, 'we'll be able to find somewhere to hide.' She was right. He nodded and walked back down to the car.

They drove along the narrowing, steadily steepening valley without speaking. As they climbed through a series of corkscrew bends, the land on either side of the road fell away sharply. Then, as they breasted the saddle point at the top of the pass, he saw the small ski shop and pulled over in front of it. She looked at him quizzically and he smiled back. 'I've got an idea.'

The ski shop was a one-storey concrete refuge on the high, wind-swept plateau sparsely populated with ski lodges and chairlifts. A persistent cool breeze set up a high-pitched whistle in the winding gear of the lifts clustered around the small road. Despite being churned bare by battalions of winter skiers, the disfigured slopes were covered in bluebells and alpine primroses. Ahead, the view down the steep valley was inviting, a, green patchwork Eden disappearing into the distance.

She followed John into the shop past the racks of skis and snowboards. 'John?' she asked impatiently, 'What the hell is going on?'

He pointed towards the back of the shop with a theatrical flourish. 'Camping.'

'Camping?'

'There's lots of tiny sites all over France,' John explained, checking the fabric of a tent on display. 'We'll arrive late and leave early, cash in hand. They won't care about passports.'

'I hate camping.' He caught sight of their reflection in a mirror at the end of the small shop. They looked as if they'd been married for years. He giggled which enraged her even more. After a moment, she flew at him, raining blows around his head. She stopped finally, her anger turning to laughter until they were both roaring. In a lull, they both became aware of the greying shop manager frowning at them by the racks of skis. A ski boot in one hand and a screwdriver in the other, he peered at them curiously over his reading glasses.

'Il y a un problème?' he asked tentatively. Outside the shop, a sudden gust rattled the empty, metal ski racks and the window shuddered. The wind was getting stronger; not a good omen for campers. She shook her head apologetically and explained something rapidly in French, nodding animatedly and smiling towards John as she did so. The greying manager examined John with renewed interest, shrugged and slowly walked away. Later, Jess explained that she'd told him that John was having an affair with a woman whom he always took camping. That's why she'd lost her temper.

Afterwards they drove down the mountain through steep, empty valleys populated with lonely chalets and distant brooding woods. Away from the tops, the wind eased and the sun broke through the clouds. A truce had been declared.

'Back there: not very clever.' Jess observed.

He nodded. Despite his lack of formal field craft, paranoia had turned him into a cautious, unobtrusive traveller. Drawing attention to themselves was the last thing they should have done but they were exhausted. They hardly knew each other, and he still didn't know who was after them or why.

THREE

They crossed the Italian frontier and found a campsite outside a tiny alpine resort in a high valley on the French side of the border. The village huddled beside the main road running through the steep-sided, narrow valley flanked by high peaks. It was early in the season and the place was populated with a few middle-aged walkers and some serious outdoor types who marched purposefully back and forth carrying ropes and climbing gear. A couple of elderly coach parties descended on the few shops and restaurants like a swarm of garrulous locusts.

Twenty pitches, surrounded by fields and shielded by poplar trees, the campsite was occupied by one ancient caravan and a couple of faded frame tents. In an impenetrable accent, a rheumy peasant demanded five euros and gestured towards the back of the site. They parked, unloaded the gear and set about erecting the tent. John enjoyed the physical activity; it reminded him of his rustico and made him feel sane again. Later they showered and walked into the town as the last of the sun's rays disappeared behind the distant, jagged peaks, overlooking the valley. Hues of ruby light played over the serrated summits to the west.

They passed by a small lake next to a meadow full of alpine wild flowers. Overhead, a red kite lazily adjusted the ragged vee of its tail feathers and steered silently across the valley towards its roost. For a moment, the world and all its associated unpleasantness seemed far away. A small red helicopter buzzed busily around the peaks before it disappeared and the sound faded.

'What happened to us?' Jess said as they strolled towards the town. It was a throw-away remark about when they were together in the 80s but it touched a nerve.

'You walked out on me.'

'I'm sorry.'

'I could never work out why you just left like that, without a word, anything.'

'You're still angry?'

'I thought you might get in touch.'

She looked at him tenderly. 'I did phone.'

'When?'

'Several times but each time you'd moved. Once, a woman answered.'

'When was that?' but he knew when it was.

'She wanted to know who I was. I could tell from her tone that she cared about you. I said I'd ring back later.'

'Anna,' he said. 'I met her when I was teaching journalism in Bristol.' Clever, sparky, working-class, she was one of John's students and she'd fallen for him. They'd talked about children, almost got hitched, but one day there'd been a phone call, a female Irish accent and the paranoia had come rushing back. He'd never told Anna about what had happened because he didn't want to place her in jeopardy and he'd feigned ignorance about the strange woman on the end of the phone, but they'd both known he was lying. It poisoned the relationship. Finally, they'd split up and he'd moved on again. There'd been others but nothing serious and as time passed, he'd stopped trying. He didn't explain about Anna, and Jess seemed content not to ask. He looked at Jess. 'What about you? There must have been someone in your life?'

Jess rubbed her forehead and looked away, momentarily unsettled. Then she looked back at him. 'I was always too focused. There were a few liaisons but when I finally worked out that I might want,' she paused struggling for the right word before giving up. 'Anyway, it was too late. I'd spent my life...' she trailed off, a sob caught in her throat. 'I'd spent my life going to bed with men instead of getting to know them.' John reached out a hand, took hers in his and squeezed it but Jess shook herself and grinned. 'Don't feel sorry for me. I had a great time but one morning, I woke up and realised I was lonely as hell.' John could see that she was upset but he didn't try to comfort her. 'I was damaged goods after Dublin.' He nodded. Afterwards, they walked on. That was all the talking they managed.

It wasn't surprising. They weren't the same people anymore. The passage of time had left them so used to secrecy that the ability to be honest and open had atrophied. Despite the ever-present dread, John felt his spirits lifting. Objectively, he knew that that there was too much to discuss and too many secrets to unburden. Objectively his brain advised caution, but his feelings weren't listening especially when, apropos of nothing, Jess stopped abruptly, turned and kissed him.

'What was that for?' he asked but she smiled, shook her head and they walked on.

They ate dinner slowly in a gloomy wood-panelled restaurant. The food and drink revived them. Jess was funny and warm. They giggled like naughty teenagers over Madame's haughty disdain when serving. John couldn't remember the last time he'd smiled so much but it was only temporary. Finally he could stand it no longer.

'What do they want, Jess?'

Her face twisted with difficulty. 'Not tonight, please?' She placed a hand on his arm. Ambushed by the caress, the hairs on the back of his neck stood up.

'I have to know,' he said gently.

'We can't talk here.' They walked back to the tent in moonlight. The air was heavy, punctuated by distant rolling thunder that seemed to inhibit discussion. Insects swarmed in excited numbers in the night air as if aware that violence was approaching. He was used to the dark but Jess was nervous. A screech owl flew out of the hedge causing them both to scream at the same time. She clung to him, trembling.

'So?' he asked quietly.

She replied with a kiss. 'Tomorrow,' she whispered.

They undressed and lay in their sleeping bags smelling the newness of the tent, listening to the strange wild sounds of the night. The darkness enfolded them and made them safe for now.

A storm woke him. A flash of lightning lit up the inside of the tent followed almost immediately by a gigantic thunderclap. Then came the rain, a cataract of astonishing intensity which threatened to wash them away. Jess woke with a start, then climbed into his sleeping bag and held onto him, quivering at each new explosion. He loved it all, especially her clinging to him against the wild excess of nature. He had brought a bottle of whisky and they both had a couple of shots. Then they were kissing and making love, slithering back and forth on the sleeping bags and giggling about it while the storm raged around them. It seemed perfectly natural. They felt like children, as if they were getting away with something. Maybe they were, because next morning, everything was different.

FOUR

He woke with a pounding headache and a mouth like a cat tray.

'Whisky and red wine; ridiculous. What the hell was I thinking of?' Jess echoed his thoughts.

He tried to be sympathetic but he felt like shit. She struggled out of the tent, pulling on some clothes and stomped back and forth, blowing and snorting angrily. He followed her out, but his knees were painful and getting to his feet was awkward and ungainly. 'Why didn't you stop me?'

'You ordered the second bottle of wine!' He said when he saw the car. Silver top, nosing into the lane to the campsite; something about it was familiar. She saw the look on his face and half-turned. It didn't have to be the same car but it was a silver Mercedes with tinted windows and it was coming down the lane. Even if it was a different car, it didn't look like the kind of vehicle a camper would use. Jess grabbed his hand and started to drag him to wards the fence.

'Come on!'

He refused to budge. She stopped and looked at him, her eyes wide with alarm. The car was halfway down the lane now. It would be with them at any moment. 'Who are they, Jess?'

'We haven't got time now.'

'I'm not going with you until you tell me.' He'd had enough evasion and difficulty. He wanted to be in the picture, to know who was after them and why. He wanted the truth. She stared wide-eyed at the car. It was a hundred yards away but had to stop for a tractor turning into a field. She looked back at him; this was the worst place, the wrong time.

'Is it Gladio?'

'I'm not sure,' she said glancing back and forth like a frightened

229

animal. The tractor had gone and the Mercedes continued on its way. How did they find them so quickly?

'Who else can it be?'

'British Intelligence; the CIA maybe.' The Mercedes appeared at the campsite gate. As the car doors opened, John and Jess were through the poplars, scrambling awkwardly over the wire fence, half-running, half-stumbling across the meadow towards the town.

'Why would the British or the Americans be after you?' John asked as he jogged at high speed through the meadow grass.

'It won't be them, it'll be some local freelancers they've hired.'

'Fucking great.' John stopped briefly to catch his breath. He looked back. A big man in sunglasses peered at them from the fence before climbing over it and beginning to jog after them at a leisurely pace. The Mercedes reversed at speed into the campsite entrance and with a squeal of tyre noise sped back down the lane towards the town.

John and Jess took off again, this time as fast as they could manage. The heavy rain had left the field wet and boggy in places. At one point she tripped and nearly fell but managed to continue without stopping. He looked back. Their jogging pursuer was gaining on them but he was still sixty metres distant. John couldn't see the car. As he ran, his mind cleared only to fill with questions. They were making for the town but he hadn't the foggiest idea what they could or would do when or if they got there.

The meadow was roughly rectangular in shape, about two hundred metres by four hundred of rough meadow grass clumps interspersed with bog into which they sank and which sucked at their legs as they hurried to extricate themselves. The campsite was near the base of one of the short sides. Diagonally opposite, the apex abutted the fast flowing mountain stream as it left the small town. The two long sides of the meadow were bordered by the main road to the north and the small farm road which led to the campsite, to the south.

They reached the opposite corner and the river exhausted, breathing like old harmoniums, their chests heaving for breath.

A precipitous earthen path made by local kids led up a steep bank to the bridge and the road into the town. John went up the bank first and caught sight of the silver top of the Mercedes before he got there and came slithering back down the bank.

Their muscular sunburned follower was now only twenty metres away; they were cornered. John pulled out the gun he had shoved into his trousers when he'd dressed. The man stopped, alarm animating his features. John pointed the gun but didn't fire. In that moment, he was back in his old platoon in Belfast, hearing the firefight and the lads shouting. The man smiled and took a step forward and still John did nothing. He didn't know the man or why he was following them. Jess grabbed the gun from his hand and fired in one quick movement. The muscular pursuer stopped and stood for a moment as if puzzling over something. His swarthy features took on a terrible, pale hue and he looked back at them before pitching falling backward. Jess ran forward with the gun aimed at the prone figure but John followed and knocked her hand as she fired again, catapulting the automatic into the long grass. At that moment, a second younger figure appeared on the road by the bridge and began to slither down towards them.

Jess stared at John, a wild, scared look on her face. 'What the fuck do we do now?'

John grabbed her hand and led her down to the river. After the storm, the water boiled and foamed angrily over sharp rocks but they had no alternative. He jumped onto a flattish rock in midstream, swayed precariously but managed to cling on. Jess followed but her foot slipped and she slid into the icy torrent with a shriek. John grabbed her hand and hauled her shivering onto the rock. They jumped onto the opposite bank and made their way upstream away from the bridge. Below the bridge on the town side, the bank was sheer rock; there was no way down and the younger jogging pursuer did not attempt the crossing. Instead he hurried up to the bridge and the car as John and Jess scrambled up onto a small road. They scanned up and down the road before hurrying across to the inviting cover of an alleyway opposite. They scurried into the shadowy hole like animals into a burrow. Halfway up the alleyway, they stopped, panting, and considered their situation.

It was an old part of town; the alley walls were made of irregular, stone blocks rough-hewn from local rock. It was still early, the morning air cool and still. Jess shivered and held herself; her leg badly grazed from her fall in the river, her clothes soaked. Exhausted, confused, with a pounding headache, John didn't feel great either. To warm Jess, he put his arms round her but she pushed him away. 'What the hell did you think you were doing back there?' A squeal of brakes behind them made them start and look back. He caught sight of the Mercedes and watched as two men leapt from the car and began to hurry down the alley towards them.

They were both young and fit looking. John took off after Jess only to be struck by an excruciating cramp in his right calf. He yelled and staggered clasping the ball of the muscle, trying to ease the spasm while still trying to keep moving. She halted but he waved her on, hobbling after her, half hopping, half running, the echo of his footsteps a discordant descant to those of his pursuers. They burst out of the alley into the bright, bustling normality of the main street busy with trippers, shoppers and draymen unloading. Jess went left and John followed, catching her just as the Mercedes turned into the road in front of them. When they turned back, their pursuers blocked their way. They were cut off. The two followers were young, with short black hair, well dressed in identical white shirts, black trousers and shoes with apparently matching sunglasses. As they slackened their pace and strolled confidently towards them, unsmiling, John couldn't help thinking about the man she'd shot. John supposed he was a friend of these two. He turned to her. 'I'm sorry, Jess.'

She didn't speak but there was a strange, glazed, distant look in her eyes. As the two men closed in, she turned, took one step into the main road and collapsed in front of an oncoming vegetable truck. There was a squeal of brakes as the vehicle skidded, slewing to one side and shedding boxes of vegetables onto the road and pavement as it attempted to miss her. It came to stop inches from her head but she lay still on the asphalt.

John stared, unable to take it in. In retrospect, he remembered a hand gripping his arm before he shook himself free, dashed into the road and knelt beside her. Her breathing was shallow and she was terribly pale. He cradled her head and whispered her name gently. He took hold of her wrist and tried to detect a pulse but all he could feel was his own blood roaring in his ears. Exhaustion, heart attack, whatever; the run across the field and the icy dip must have been the last straw.

A crowd gathered round her gabbling excitedly in French. Breathing heavily, the stranger took Jess's hand from John's. John watched still holding her head.

'Is she all right?' he blurted out without thinking. 'Er, elle est OK?'

The man looked at him. 'I do not know,' he replied in heavily accented English. 'Your wife?'

John didn't answer, his attention taken instead by his two pursuers standing a few feet away, watching sharply. A brief siren wail heralded the arrival of two gendarmes. Apparently chatting amiably, the pursuers began to move away. The fat Frenchman spoke again. 'Monsieur?'

'What? Oh yes... she's, er, my wife. Are you a doctor?' The man nodded then spoke to the gendarmes. After a brief animated exchange, he turned to John.

'They want the road cleared,' he said. John looked at the two policemen who shrugged and pointed to the growing tailback of traffic. Behind them, the truck driver was cursing the lost produce scattered across the road while resetting his load. The gendarmes helped John carry Jess from the road into a hotel nearby. They laid her on a tiny bed in a downstairs room. It wasn't a bedroom, more a rest room for hotel staff. She moaned, reminding John uncomfortably of his mother in her last days. It occurred to him that if Jess pegged out, he still didn't know why he was here or where they were headed. He was broke and alone, unable to reveal anything of value to police or British surrogates. The gendarmes were not, however, remotely interested in John or Jess. With traffic flowing freely again on the main road, they nodded perfunctorily and disappeared.

John accompanied the gendarmes to the front door and watched them go, anxiously scanning the street for their pursuers from behind the window. There was no sign of the assailants or the Mercedes and he sighed with relief but then saw one of the men opposite. White shirt, black slacks, sunglasses, he couldn't be certain but he instinctively ducked back into the shadows, his heart pumping again. Now the gendarmes had gone, what was to stop them walking right in, there and then?

Right from the start, the truth had always been just out of reach. At times, he'd glimpsed pieces of it; fragments had appeared from the shadows before disappearing again. Who was the man Jess had shot? Was he all right? The Mercedes looked the same as the previous car but when it had pulled up at the gates, John had seen that the number plate had been French, not Italian. They could have changed the plates, but why? Could two different groups of people be after them? Anger vied with exhaustion and fear as he contemplated the futility of his situation.

He returned to the small room, to discover the doctor listening to Jess's heart and lungs before taking her pulse. Her breathing was deeper and she had a better colour but she was still unconscious.

'Is she all right?'

The doctor shrugged and eased himself off the bed. A white shirt covered the vast expanse of his belly, which he thrust in front of him. To balance himself, the doctor stood with his feet splayed wide and his head thrown back as if about to launch into an operatic aria.

'She needs tests, in hospital.' The next questions would be about passports, insurance and money. He was wrong. 'Has anything like this 'appen before?'

Surprised, John blurted out, 'I don't know.' The doctor looked at him. John tried to recover. 'Erm, not as far as I know.'

The doctor looked at Jess again, then back at John, his eyes narrowing. 'She has a wound on her leg and she is wet.'

Despite his accent, it was impossible to mistake the accusing note in his voice.

'She fell in the river,' John explained lamely, adding, 'we're camping; we were walking into town. She likes to walk, it helps with her hot flushes.' This final invention clinched it because the doctor pursed his lips and nodded. Who could understand the English?

'Is a hospital absolutely necessary? Can it wait till we get home to England?'

The doctor shook his head. 'I would not advise that. Of course Monsieur it is up to you but...' he trailed off. John smiled weakly. A distant shout in the hotel made him jump. 'Unfortunately, there is not one nearby.'

'What?' John asked, only half-listening, his mind still on the shout.

'A hospital,' the doctor replied, the note of suspicion back in his voice.

'Where's the nearest one?'

'Gap. I will go and phone.'

The room looked out onto a walled terrace which had once been an orchard but was now overgrown with brambles. Beyond the back wall were a few houses before the land began to rise steeply towards the looming mountains. Getting out of the village might be feasible but getting over the mountains would be all but impossible. Even so, John tried the small double glazed window, which opened easily. A familiar voice interrupted. 'Running out on me?'

He turned round to see Jess sitting up on one elbow, smiling, if a little unsteadily. Relieved, he went over to her. 'How do you feel?'

'Fine, I just blacked out.'

'You did it deliberately?'

Jess shrugged. 'Not exactly, I fainted but when I came round I saw the gendarmes and decided to stay unconscious.' She swung her legs off the bed and tried to stand. He offered his arm in support and helped her to the window.

'What are we doing?'

'Getting the hell out of here. They're still out front.' Jess looked pale and shaken. 'Do you think you can manage it?'

235

Jess nodded then perched on the ledge, she was about to swing a leg out when the doctor returned. His face lit up at the sight of her on her feet only to be replaced by a frown. She explained quickly in French that she was having trouble breathing and needed some air. She added that she had passed out once or twice but she'd always felt fine afterwards.

The doctor took her pulse. 'How do you feel now?'

'Fine, back to my old self.'

'Any luck with the hospital?' John asked, changing the subject. The doctor nodded.

'Oui, you can go to Gap. I have an appointment there myself today. Perhaps you can follow me? I have explained,' he ended. John nodded, smiling in gratitude.

'Can you give us a lift?' she asked, swaying and leaning wanly on John. The doctor looked puzzled. 'Our car needs a new fan belt. I'd hate for it to break down on the way.'

Objectively, John understood that the car was a liability and it was best to leave it behind with the tent. There was a chance their pursuers would wait for them to return and give them a breathing space. John didn't feel remotely objective. He hated the idea of leaving the car and the tent. In spite of everything that had happened, he still harboured the hope of a return to his olive grove. While they were camping, it had been possible to persuade himself that all this was temporary, a holiday from which he would return to his tiny house.

'We can get a bus back later or John can if I have to stay there. If that's all right?' she smiled brightly. With a Gallic shrug, the doctor nodded agreement.

The doctor's car was parked in a small street behind the hotel. John and Jess hung back in the doorway until the last minute then scuttled to the vehicle and dived in. John made a play of dropping something on the floor and he and Jess pretended to look for it as they drove from the village so it would look as if the doctor was alone. What the doctor made of it, he didn't say. He'd given up on the strange couple. He worked in Gap as a GP but had a weekend place in the village. Jess and the doctor talked while John lay on the back seat and pretended to sleep but in reality he was looking for silver cars coming up behind. Each time he saw one, his stomach clenched until it passed and he calmed a little. He wondered how ill Jess really was and what else she hadn't told him. If she'd killed their pursuer, the police would be after them too. He tried not to think about that.

FIVE

The doctor left them in the hospital reception. He wrote a short note in illegible French to be given to the hospital doctor, then after wishing them good luck, he left. The receptionist gave Jess a large form to fill in and bade them wait on the seats provided. When the receptionist wasn't looking, they hurried away into the hospital. They avoided the front door in case they'd been followed and scurried towards a fire exit. John struggled with the mechanism but it wouldn't budge.

'For Christ's sake, John!' Jess hissed.

'It's fucking stuck!'

'Monsieur!' a voice called. John fiddled with the handle furiously but the voice came again. 'Monsieur!' John turned to see a security guard lumbering towards them.

'Fucking great, John,' Jess whispered.

'My wife,' John began to the guard, 'we're English and she needed some air,' he added lamely, looking at the door. 'It's locked.'

The guard regarded them without expression for a moment. Then he leant past John and pressed a switch above the handle. The door clicked open. John smiled. 'Ah, easy when you know how. Thanks.' The guard raised an eyebrow, turned and walked away.

They watched the security guard go, then ducked out and made their way down the stairs, past a series of concrete blockhouses and out into a small side road. They scanned the street then Jess hurried towards the centre of the town with John struggling to keep up. She headed towards the cathedral spire keeping to the back streets where possible. John tried to talk to her.

'Jess, for fuck's sake will you slow down?' She stopped, looked round then dragged him into a baker's shop. 'What?' he began.

'Silver BMW.' She scanned the street through the window while John struggled with the delicious smell. They had no money so they couldn't buy any bread despite the fact that they were both hungry. Outside, they hurried on again.

'Who's after us, Jess?'

She shook her head. 'Later.' She dived across the road with John behind, dodging traffic heading for an ATM. She turned round. 'Fuck.'

'What?'

'My credit card. I left it in the tent.' John shook his head, then delved under his shirt and produced a wad of euros.

'Will that help?'

She smiled then stopped. 'Where did that come from?'

'Same place as the gun; my insurance policy.'

'When were you going to tell me about them, John?'

'When you told me what was going on.' He'd hidden the money belt in his clothes but out of habit, he'd put it under his shirt when he dressed. He'd lost the gun but he wasn't about to start shooting people unless he had no choice and even then, he might think twice.

Jess smiled, took the wad and then they were off again to the station for two tickets on the first train to Lyon but they didn't hang about. In the twenty-five minutes before the train, they went to a department store near the station and bought new outfits. They changed in the station toilets and caught the train just as it was pulling out. The carriage was crowded and they sat near the doors, Jess glancing about like a frightened cat. John was fed up.

'Who's after us, Jess?' She shrugged but didn't answer. 'The car at the campsite had different plates. Are we being chased by two groups of people?'

'It's possible. If they're using local freelancers.'

'They being the CIA or the British?' She nodded. 'And why are they after you?'

'Not here.'

'Yes, here.' He was exhausted, hungry and he wanted some answers. She sensed his resolve and dipped her head in acknowledgement. They spoke in whispers.

'For the last two years I've been working in a small bank in Monte Carlo. Monaco and Andorra are on the EU banking black list. Bank accounts in their countries remain secret and are not available for scrutiny by the authorities. Since 9/11, the pressure has been on and they'll have to open up to inspection sooner or later.'

'And what have you been doing at this small bank in Monte Carlo?'

'Gladio's main holdings are there. They moved them out of Switzerland a few years back.'

'It still doesn't explain the CIA or the British. I thought you worked for them?'

Jess nodded. 'They didn't approve of my plan.' The door of the carriage flew open with a bang causing John and Jess to start as a group of schoolkids charged in shouting excitedly, followed by a couple of harassed-looking adults who herded them down the compartment.

John looked at Jess again. 'The plan?

'I'm going to steal Gladio's money.' John shook his head. 'All those years I kept tracking them and they kept getting away with murder and I couldn't lay a glove on them. I got mugged walking down Piccadilly. Two kids took my purse, my mobile, everything. They were tiny, about thirteen with attitude. They did it in thirty seconds flat and I was outraged. I stomped around St James Park trying to decide whether to report it and it came to me. Why not mug them?' She looked up, flushed and excited. 'I had the bank account numbers; they hadn't changed them because they didn't want to attract attention. Then they moved the holding company's account to Monte Carlo.'

'How much are we talking about?'

'Fifty.'

'Fifty thousand?

'Million.'

'Fifty million!' he began but she put a finger to his mouth and shushed him, but she couldn't suppress a smile.

'I've spent two years setting this up.'

'That still doesn't explain the British and the Americans.'

'After 9/11, it's about the war on terror. They don't want to be reminded that their own hands might have been dirty in the past,' Jess said slowly.

'Why should the Americans care?'

'They set up Gladio in the first place and a lot of the neo-cons in the Bush administration have some far right friends. Some of them were money trading with the Nazis before the start of World War Two via a merchant bank in Amsterdam. The bank's still there. They don't want any of this stuff coming out.'

'So why did you come looking for me?'

'I'd heard you'd moved to the area. I mean, San Remo and Monte Carlo are practically next door. It was fate don't you think?' Now he knew the truth. Not the whole truth, there was always something else.

'Where do I come in?'

'Later.' She yawned and shivered. It wasn't cold.

'How ill are you, Jess?'

'I'm fine, really I am. I was checked a couple of months ago. I fainted, that's all.' He sighed. 'What?'

'The man you shot, I wonder if he's OK?'

'We can't afford to think like that,' Jess whispered. 'And knocking the gun out of my hand was pretty silly.'

'There was no need to kill him.' The train was beginning to slow. Jess thought for a moment, then she was up pulling him after her back down the train. 'What are we doing?'

'Getting off.' They hurried out of the station into a small market town. Jess split the wad in half, told John to go back and buy a single to Grenoble and come back. He did as he was told. After a couple of minutes, Jess did the same. Two people got off the train but no couples bought tickets, only individuals. The endless tradecraft was wearing. They were tired, hungry and thirsty. They had ten minutes before the train and risked a hurried sandwich and coffee at a nearby cafe.

On the train, they sat apart, near the doors but pretending to be strangers. In Grenoble, they bought more individual tickets to Luxembourg and boarded yet another train. It was crowded and they sat on adjacent aisle seats. As they headed through the rolling wheat fields of the Vosges, John leaned towards her and whispered,

'So Gladio doesn't know about you at the bank?'

'I don't think so,' she replied.

'Where are we going?'

'Amsterdam.'

'They'll be looking for us,' John whispered.

'I've got an apartment there.'

He settled back and watched the golden fields rolling past.

'Why did they let us go when you fainted?'

She shrugged. 'Too many people. A murder in a tourist spot, a high profile killing is the last thing they need, especially if there's even a chance it could be traced back. They'll wait until they can get me alone.'

'Us,' he muttered. 'It's both of us they want rid of.'

She sighed and took his hand in hers across the aisle. 'I'm sorry, John.' Despite himself, he couldn't help smiling back. Was it the truth? Maybe.

Their train took them to Luxembourg where Jess planned to buy new tickets to Amsterdam, using cash again. John didn't ask why they kept changing trains; he knew. They were covering their tracks, trying to leave no trace of themselves. The train passed from France into Luxembourg without incident. They bought yet more tickets, turned to leave and found their way blocked. Two uniformed policemen were checking documents as passengers left the booking office. John felt his mouth go dry. He looked round casually but the only other doors were marked 'Staff only' and were locked. Right then, the police were busy with a young 'Rasta'. One examined his documents with practised slowness while the other one asked a series of complex questions. The young man had two minutes to catch his train and became increasingly impatient and vocal, pointing to his watch and gesticulating. No one helped him. Like everyone else, Jess and John pretended it wasn't happening and looked elsewhere.

The officers ignored the young man's protests, finally allowing him on his way a minute after his train had left. He walked off, muttering oaths and shaking his head but he knew better than to complain. Jess and John stepped forward apprehensively. She smiled and held out the tickets as John tried to appear preoccupied but the police chuckled to each other and waved them through without looking. They weren't interested in a white, middle-aged couple. They also let two young white female students through behind them and the three or four travellers after them but they stopped the elderly Arab couple at the rear and began to interrogate them. John turned and watched angrily before Jess pulled him away.

It was well after midnight when they arrived in Amsterdam. The city was hot and airless and the streets crowded. Jess adopted her routine of dodging down side streets and alleyways, endlessly checking behind for pursuers. Someone tried to sell them drugs, another offered sex as routinely as if he were selling lottery tickets but they hurried on without speaking. In an empty street, they passed a burnt out shop in an old tenement. Someone had spray-painted 'Fight the rich, not their wars' on the wall next door. It seemed an impossibly long time since the morning when they had fled from their tent in the mountains. The city was surreal, a hologram projected around them. Only the fear in their innards was left.

SIX

Without knowing, John and Jess passed within a hundred metres of Jules Swemmer sweating uncomfortably in a strip club in the summer heat. Jules mopped his brow and panted; his body poured sweat on nights like this. He preferred the city in winter when the canals froze and the snow blew, when Amsterdam became a warren of warm secret bulwarks against the cold. Jules enjoyed the winter, skating, snowballing, sledging – brief energetic excursions into the freezing blasts before returning to welcoming fires and cups of hot wine full of fruit. And there were other advantages. The heavy suits and overcoats looked well on his frame, unlike the summer when even the most exclusive lightweight fabric seemed merely to emphasise his bulk and ungainliness. But on this hot summer night, his sweat did not come from the heat. Jules was worried and he feared that his plans might come to nothing.

Jules had discovered his niche by accident. One Friday afternoon before a bank holiday the other partners had left early, apparently en masse for a weekend break, leaving him to hold the fort. Most were family men and the bank holiday heralded a short school holiday. They were keen to make an early start and trading was always quiet on the last day of the week before a holiday. Divorced and isolated, Jules had no one to hurry home to and preferred to stay at the bank. That's when the trade had occurred. Late in the afternoon, about half past four, there was a transfer of a million euros authorised by a holding company in Monaco from the bank to a holding company in the British Virgin Islands. It was all in order but the checking clerk had left at four so Jules authorised the transfer himself and gratefully pocketed the commission. By the bank's standards, it was not a large transaction and when they reopened on the Tuesday, no one remarked on it. Short-staffed because of the holiday, the staff that were in work were preoccupied with a Swiss chemical giant manoeuvring some very large funds for a takeover. As people chattered about their weekend, Jules wondered about the Friday transfer.

The holding company directing the funds and the destination accounts were all in jurisdictions that were not covered by international banking regulations. As a banker, Jules was required by law to ascertain the probity of such transfers, to ensure that the bank was not laundering drug money or moving terrorist funds. Because the transfer was authorised by a legitimate bank and checked by a legitimate receiving bank, Jules was sticking to the letter of the law, but he wasn't a fool. Like all bankers, he knew well enough that some of the money that passed through their hands was tainted; there was nothing new in that. By inclination and habit, bankers knew better than to ask too many questions. Their business was money; the rest was detail and Jules knew something of the bank's 'interesting' history. As a child, he'd heard snippets of conversation between Uncle Jan and his father, which stopped when they became aware of him. As a family member he'd absorbed the shibboleths of look and glance that talked of a dark and important secret. Looks and glances that occurred at certain times of the year when his father packed and disappeared to unspecified destinations. Looks and glances that related to what was stored in the old vault which he had glimpsed thirty years before. And what Jules craved above all else was to see the gold in the vault again but he had begun to despair of receiving another invitation. Despite their wealth, the Swemmers were not blessed with fecundity and Jules was an only child. Reserved and fastidious, his father had not enjoyed child-rearing and had left the activity to his wife who spoiled the boy. At thirty-five, Jules had finally attained a perspective on himself, who he was and why. He knew he was a disappointment to his father and even though he had tried to restrain his nature in recent months, he despaired of further advancement. That's why he was surprised and apprehensive to be summoned to his office on his father's return from holiday.

Behind Pictor Swemmer's back, the bank's lowliest employees called the boss's office the 'throne room'. The huge room, directly above the boardroom, looked out at tree height to other unassuming mansions across the canal. The walls were plain white, the carpet modest and grey. At one end, behind a large antique mahogany desk, Pieter Swemmer sat in a wing-backed armchair mounted on a small plinth so that anyone sitting on the other side of his desk was always a little below him. It was extremely rare for Jules to enter the throne room. These days, his father preferred to talk to him at family gatherings, away from work, as if emphasising Jules' lack of favour. Unlike Jules' desk, which was crowded with scraps of paper and balance sheets, his father's desk was always pristine and tidy.

Visitors to the bank were escorted through the silent, tastefully renovated old building without ever seeing a calculator or a computer. If figures were required, an executive would speak softly into a phone and the requisite piece of paper would appear, brought silently by some soberly clad functionary. When Jules had first worked there, the building had reminded him of a 'show' house where no real people lived or worked but as time passed he had come to appreciate the significance of this austerity. It was their brand, the air of timeless, effortless certainty combined with the mystique of wealth that permeated the place and gave comfort to the wealthy and insecure.

Jules lumbered across the room to his father's desk and sat down apprehensively. He wondered what he had done wrong. Pieter stared at his son evenly for a moment before speaking. 'Last Friday, you authorised a trade.' It wasn't a question or an accusation just a statement of fact but Jules felt a need to explain.

'There was no one else here because of the holiday,' he began but his father held up a hand.

'It was our friends.' Pieter's gaze fixed on a point somewhere beyond Jules' left shoulder. Jules felt himself growing excited. He knew not to ask anything but he also knew that he was being initiated in some way. These 'friends' had been spoken of before; they were the bank's guarantors, the bank's great secret. Jules had some notion of who they were but he had always detested politics. His father spoke again. 'It may happen again.'

Jules nodded. That was all they said about the transaction but Jules had understood that his father had sanctioned his authorisation of the movement and, he assumed, given him licence to repeat the activity. Afterwards, he felt as if a burden had been lifted; redemption was possible, his efforts had not been in vain. The meeting was a nod of approval. He still craved access to the musty cellar and the vault but that was surely possible now so long as he didn't do anything foolish. He made a point of staying late on Fridays and several more transfers took place, often before a bank holiday but always late on a Friday. As the commissions began to mount up, Jules regained some of his self-confidence. Signing off each time, he made friendly remarks to the initiator in Monaco, thanking them for the trade and suggesting light-heartedly a larger sum next time. The response was encouraging and he allowed the possibility of success to revive his optimism.

The reason he was sweating in the bar was that he had started gambling excessively again but unfortunately, he had started losing. He needed to make a lot of money and soon and the transfers appeared to have stopped. He fervently hoped the interruption was temporary.

SEVEN

The flat was a tiny one bedroom bolt-hole on the fifth floor of a modern block about half an hour's walk from the centre of Amsterdam. Well-appointed, the only access point was the front door which had been reinforced with several vertical and horizontal steel bolts. The main room opened onto a small balcony no bigger than a ledge. It overlooked a grove of plane trees in a small square. John threw open the balcony doors and breathed in the hot night air. Apart from the hotel in Ventimiglia, it was the first time he had spent indoors in a city for months and he didn't like it. The flat was too small and the height unnerved him. If trouble came to the front door, there would be no quick getaway. Sitting on the tiny balcony, he felt like a flightless bird on a perch waiting to be despatched.

Jess busied herself in the flat producing bedding and towels. They were exhausted, and they said little as they sipped a beer on the balcony. Later in bed, with Jess curled in his embrace, the unanswered questions returned. When he finally fell asleep, his dreams were haunted by tormented faces of people he knew but who didn't recognise him and then recoiled in horror when they did. Jess woke him with coffee and doughnuts. She looked younger, her hair still wet from a shower and she'd thrown on a loose-fitting, pale summer dress that suggested comfort and a lack of urgency. Domesticity softened her somehow. She kissed John gently but he didn't respond. The time to think had allowed the anger he'd bottled up to resurface except that now he thought he might have worked something out.

John had more coffee on the balcony. It was a hot, overcast day. In the distance, the sound of a Hendrix album wafted from an open window, sounds of another life from another time. He stopped eating and pushed his coffee away, his jaw set. Jess didn't speak.

'I've been thinking about something Kevin Dillon asked you in Glasgow,' he said quietly.

Her face clouded. 'What made you think of that?'

'Brian.'

'That was a bad business,' she said.

'I still have dreams about it.'

'Survivor guilt is inevitable,' she said softly.

'Ever watched sheepdog trials?' John asked. 'The sheep are all terrified of the dog. The fear enables the dog to drive them where the shepherd wants.'

'What's that got to do with Brian?'

'Maybe it wasn't me they were after.' A shadow appeared in her eyes. 'Maybe they killed Brian to keep me angry?'

She shook her head. 'Sorry, you've lost me.'

'I was the bait,' he said quietly. 'It was Kevin Dillon they wanted.'

'That's ridiculous. They killed Maria because she knew too much.'

'Yes, but maybe once I got involved and Dillon made contact, maybe things changed?' John explained.

'And maybe you're wrong, John. Maybe it was just as it seemed. Brian was killed by accident and Kevin because he was a terrorist.'

'They wanted Uccello and Kevin out of the way. Kevin because he represented a threat to the status quo and Uccello because of what he knew, like Maria.'

'Why didn't they kill us, then?' she asked.

He shrugged. 'That's what I can't work out.'

She leaned forward. 'What was it you used to say? If it's a choice between conspiracy and cock-up, always go for the latter.'

He nodded. 'You heard about Pete Uccello?'

'He drowned.'

The day the miners went back to work. His body was found at the bottom of cliffs near his sanctuary in the Republic. John nodded. 'That was the inquest verdict. There were reports of bruises on his body as if he'd fallen from the cliff-top.'

'It was a long time ago. Gladio are bad people, end of story.'

'You shot someone yesterday, Jess. Doesn't sound like end of story.'

'Last time Gladio won but now we have a chance of really doing them some damage. So, do you want to hear my plan?'

John lit a cigarette. 'When did you start working for the British?' The question winded her. 'That was the question Kevin asked.' He paused. 'You didn't answer it then either.'

'Leave it, John.'

'Over the years, I thought a lot about what happened. I kept coming back to Dublin and you walking out like that. I just couldn't work out why.'

'I was upset. We all were.'

'We were a team and we were...'

She sighed. 'I know.'

'Which group killed your father, Jess?' She shook her head. 'It was Kevin's, wasn't it?'

'Look, you don't understand...' she began but he overrode her.

'I was the bait?' She shook her head but a tear detached itself from the corner of her eye and began to roll down her cheek. 'I thought so.'

'He killed my Dad.'

'So you killed Brian and Maria to get to him?'

'No!'

'Someone did.'

'I swear it wasn't me!' Jess protested. 'Maria was my friend and Brian was yours.'

'And I was your lover. Brilliant diversion tactic.'

'It wasn't like that!' she said.

'How was it then? Tell me! I'm interested.' He was angry but he stayed in control. 'For fuck's sake, Jess, how much more of this is there?'

'I didn't know I'd meet him in Glasgow but when I did, it all came back. I wanted revenge.'

'And I was a pawn?' he asked.

'No!'

'Because if I was then, there's a good chance I am now, isn't there?'

'You aren't, I promise,' Jess said quietly.

He wanted to believe her. 'I still don't understand. I mean, yes he was a bad guy but we were going to get Gladio.'

'It was my fault,' she said.

'What was?'

'I had this friend when I was sixteen, a girl who was a Protestant. We went horse-riding together; then we started to see each other after school, secretly. We were just bloody friends, two kids interested in books, music and politics and boys.'

'What happened?'

'Her father found out and suddenly she wasn't allowed to talk to me. I told my Mum and she said it was for the best and I was so angry at the stupidity of it all.'

'You went to the British?' John said, incredulous

'They came to me. The house was raided at dawn. The usual nonsense, herd everyone into a room and check for missing men. They took me into another room. A man spoke to me. They'd heard I was dissatisfied.'

'That's when it started?'

'I was idealistic. They said I'd help to create a future without sectarianism. I told them things. Small things at first.'

'And the IRA?' he asked.

'They suspected there was an informer.'

'They thought it was your father?'

'Someone told them.'

'Who?'

'Who do you think?'

'The British? To protect you?'

'Some protection.' She laughed mirthlessly. 'They gave my Dad a death sentence and locked me in forever.'

'That's why you wanted Kevin dead?'

'Mum and my brother never got over it.'

'Did she know about you?'

Jess shrugged. 'I don't know. Whenever I tried to talk to Mum about it, she'd change the subject and have a drink. I stopped trying after a while.' She looked at the ceiling and shook her head. 'Time's a great healer, that's what they say isn't it? It's bollocks. Some pain goes on happening every day, for ever.'

'How did you feel when you heard Kevin Dillon was dead?' he asked.

'That's just it. I didn't feel anything. I thought I'd feel better but I just felt empty. That's why I ran away. I liked you. I'd messed things up again and I felt bad.'

'We let Gladio off the hook.'

'They did that themselves.'

'They were involved in the Brighton bombing?'

She shrugged. 'What do you think? I've paid for it, John, and I'm not going to let them off the hook again. All right?!' She was angry now.

He looked across the rooftops. In the streets and houses, people were living their lives.

'Well?' she said, 'Do you want to hear the plan?'

'No,' John said firmly, 'I want to get drunk.'

John hurried from the flat and Jess didn't go after him. Three hours later, she found him slumped against the bar in a noisy working-class cafe full of lunchtime punters shouting and calling to each other. Jess went over to John.

'Come on,' she said gently.

'I want to finish my drink,' he slurred.

She leaned in close and whispered, 'This is dangerous, John. Come back to the flat.'

'So you can tell me some new lies? Or rehash the old favourites?'

'Please,' she squeezed his arm. 'Come back.'

John looked at her, then drank the rest of his beer down in one go and turned to go. Outside, the light was blinding and he shielded his eyes as she led him, weaving from side to side back to the apartment. Once there, he collapsed on the sofa and fell asleep.

John woke late afternoon and had a shower. Then he sought her out. 'I'm ready,' he said. 'You can tell me the plan.'

'I've changed my mind,' she said busying herself with something.

'What are you so angry about? It was me who was fucked over,' he hissed.

'Getting drunk was a really stupid thing to do.'

'Oh right, sorry. Forgot I'd been press-ganged into your war.'

Jess took a deep breath. 'I was scared.' He didn't speak. After a moment, she added, 'I'm sorry about Dublin.'

'All right.' He looked at her expectantly. 'Go on then, tell me.'

'Gladio's deposits are in a vault in the RNF merchant bank close by. At four-fifteen on Friday afternoon, you will enter the bank and empty Gladio's account.'

'How much are we talking about?'

'One billion euros.'

John spluttered in disbelief. 'One billion euros!?' Jess nodded. 'Why will they give them to me?'

'They won't give them to you but they will to Sir Jeremy Gimlet.'

'This is crazy, Jess!'

'There aren't any photographs of Gimlet and the only person who can identify him is the bank's chief executive Pieter Swemmer who's in London with him for the second week of Wimbledon. They're both big fans.'

'Why will they give the money to me?' John asked. 'Even if they think I'm Gimlet, I'll need proof that I'm who I say I am.'

She nodded. 'A letter of authorisation on bank notepaper signed by Pieter Swemmer. I've got one.'

'How?' John asked, incredulous.

'I've been planning this a long time. You're about the same age and height and you know what he's like.'

'I met him a couple of times twenty years ago. Christ.' John protested.

'It'll work, John.' Her eyes were shining. Talking about the plan buoyed her up.

'What about you? What will you be doing, Jess?'

'Throwing them off-balance.' He frowned. 'I'll be in Monaco transferring the current account. The holding company has been transferring money in million pound lots into untraceable accounts in the old Soviet Union and the Far East. I'm going to transfer the rest of it. I've taken two weeks' holiday from the bank in Monaco but I'm going back for a last shift. I'm going to transfer the final fifty million euros.'

'Jess, won't our friends be waiting for you?'

She shrugged. 'I'll slip into the bank for two hours at the end of the week then I'm gone forever. I've been working there for two years. I know the account numbers and the access codes and I'll find out the passwords for that day when I go in.'

'It's that simple?'

'Authorisation comes from Amsterdam but it's the lowly bank employees who actually do the work. Even though it's a large sum, it's still chickenfeed in bank terms and if it's legit at my end and okayed at the destination, it should go like clockwork. It happens all the time.'

'What will actually happen to the money?'

'It'll be sent to a holding company I set up five years ago in the Cayman Islands. They're five hours behind so the receiving bank will have time to process it and send it on.'

'Where to?'

'Jakarta. Saturday's a working day in Indonesia. I will arrive around midday and authorise dispersal to several disreputable banking jurisdictions in the Pacific Rim and we'll be home free.'

'What if it goes wrong?'

'Best case scenario, you'll be arrested and able to tell the world.'

'Otherwise I'll be fished out of the Amstel with a boat hook.'

'If it works, we'll destroy Gladio and if it doesn't, you'll do them a great deal of damage anyway.'

'It's mad.'

'Will you do it?' He retreated from the balcony, seeking solace in the shadows but she came after him. She put her arms round his neck and he let her kiss him. In the distance, Hendrix had been replaced by a Dylan track from John Wesley Hardin. Christ, when was the last time he'd heard that? The DJ was probably another rock and roll casualty marooned in middle age. 'So?' she asked again. 'What do you say?'

He smiled grimly. 'Couldn't we just...?'

'What?'

'Go to the authorities and tell them our story.' Jess shook her head emphatically but he persisted, 'We haven't done anything wrong and we could stop running.'

'No.'

'Why not?' he asked.

'We need evidence before they'll listen and we haven't got any.'

'This is what happens if you live in the shadows. You end up running and hiding and shooting people you don't know. You end up like them.' He went back to the balcony. She followed him.

'You're wrong, John.'

'Fight the rich, not their wars,' he said slowly.

'What?'

'The planet's dying. There's an Aids pandemic, three-quarters of the world's children don't get enough of anything. What difference does it make if we steal Gladio's money?'

'We can hurt them.' Jess stated.

'I spent the last twenty years looking over my shoulder until I bought the rustica. Even then, I was still running but working on the land. Tending the olives struck a chord. Growing things, it's important for its own sake. When it comes down to it, most of the things we think are indispensable are either superfluous or destructive or both.'

'Justice isn't superfluous,' she replied quietly.

'No, but revenge and money and all the things that go with them – hubris, ego, hate – they are.'

'All right,' Jess said. 'We'll go to the press and tell our story.' John began to smile until she added, 'Afterwards. We'll have all the evidence we need then.' He started to protest but the look in her eye stopped him. 'I'm going to do this, John. I need your help but if I have to, I'll steal the fifty million and manage alone.'

That was it. They retrieved some food from the freezer and made something to eat. The normality of the activity was calming and being with Jess again had re-energised John. He yearned for his life in Italy but it had always felt transient, as if he was waiting for the unpaid debt to be called in. John liked Jess a lot; being with her again made sense of his life. Freed from the pressure for a few hours, Jess relaxed. Absurdly they played Scrabble, arguing over words like kids. They had fun. Just as before, they fitted one another.

'Where shall we go afterwards?' she asked after their last game. 'Where would you like to live?'

John shrugged. 'I don't know. I'm still getting over Liguria.'

She smiled apologetically and squeezed his hand. 'Sorry.'

'Don't be.'

Something occurred to her. 'What about Indonesia? There's a thousand islands to get lost in or we could head north into Malaysia, try the hill country there. It's not unlike Italy.'

Until that moment, he hadn't really considered 'afterwards'. He'd suppressed his disappointment for so long that he was unused to optimism. If the plan worked, they might have a future together and he couldn't help liking the picture in his mind's eye. He began to imagine what their lives might be like. A new life, a new beginning at his age. It was intoxicating.

EIGHT

The next day, the weather broke. A series of depressions began to drench western Europe. The forecast for the rest of the week was no better. In Britain, would-be sunbathers cursed their luck and Wimbledon officials glanced anxiously at the sky and their match schedules.

In Holland, John was glad of the rain. Cars ploughed through large puddles clearing pedestrians from the kerb and the few who remained hurried along, heads down. No one noticed the erect, immaculately clad Englishman, briefcase in hand, walking along under his umbrella. It was a dummy run, John's first try-out as Sir Jeremy Gimlet. John walked up the street on the other side of the canal, past the RCN door. He had a brief look but carried on walking past the diamond houses and merchant banks. He wasn't worried; the hard part would be on Friday, in two days' time when he did it for real. Then someone called his name, 'John?' He felt a shiver run down his spine. The voice came again, 'John, is that you?' John froze.

The day before, Jess and John had gone shopping in the most exclusive gentlemen's outfitters. John was kitted out with a wardrobe appropriate to a member of the British establishment. Jess knew a great deal about Gimlet's personal habits, his preference in shirts, what he liked for breakfast and she supervised John's transformation, monitoring his diction, the way he stood, sat and moved and the cutting of his hair. She gave him tips.

'You're a powerful man. Never run, always walk, the slower the better. Never smile or apologise. It suggests weakness.' John practised speaking in the clipped tones of an officer and a gentleman. The strange thing was that it influenced the way he stood so that he found himself standing erect. Jess arranged two new passports for him, one in the name of James Braddock, which was to be his new identity when he left Holland, the second in the name of Sir Jeremy Gimlet. She took photographs of him with a digital camera, one in casual dress with his hair mussed and one dressed in his new uniform of blazer, white shirt and regimental tie, which she supplied. He was impressed but when he asked how she'd got it, she made a mess of tying the knot in his tie and had to start again. Obtaining a regimental tie was a relatively simple matter but something about the way she averted her eyes alerted him.

'Now tomorrow, we'll have a try-out.'

'So soon?'

'Don't worry, it's just a walk in the financial district to get you used to being outside.'

So next morning, he showered, shaved and dressed as an important diplomat and set out, glad of the rain until the voice.

'John Bradley?' It was weirdly familiar but he couldn't place it. It had to be Gladio or some spook. He'd only get one chance. He tightened his grip on the umbrella handle and tensed, ready to strike and turned round slowly. In front of him was a squat, balding Asian man in khaki who grinned amiably.

'It is you! I thought so.' John gawped like an idiot. 'You don't know me, do you?'

All he knew was that he needed to be away from there, now. 'Look, I'm er...' he stumbled.

'It's me, Naz!' John examined the rotund face and as he did, his old friend gradually emerged. Encased by the middle-aged countenance was the face he remembered. It was as if the Naz he'd known was wearing a inflated pneumatic suit. Fat, middle-aged and bald, it was him.

'Naz!' he said trying to smile.

Naz stood back and looked at John in his Gimlet outfit admiringly. 'Bloody smart, John, bloody smart.' Then he noticed the case John was holding. 'Business?'

'Yes, actually, and I'm er late,' John said gratefully and began to walk. Naz hurried along beside him, chatting cheerfully.

'I was going to ask what you've been doing all these years, but you've obviously done all right for yourself.' John couldn't think how to get rid of him so he strode purposefully towards the city centre. He didn't want Naz to be seen with him and implicated in some way. Naz prattled on happily. 'I'm still doing camera, got a partner, university lecturer, a house with a garden, you must come and stay.' Despite himself, John smiled at the invitation as he looked for an escape route. If he bolted now, Naz would be upset and surprised but at least he would be safe. They passed an alley that led towards river. John tensed himself ready to run when he glimpsed a tall, muscular figure with a suntanned face leaning against a wall watching them. John's pulse went through the roof. It didn't have to be him; it didn't have to be the man that Jess shot. How could it be? It could be anyone, except that it looked like him and his right arm was in a sling.

Naz took hold of John's arm and steered him towards a café. 'Come on, you've got time for a coffee' he said lightly enough but the grip on John's arm was firm and John didn't want any trouble; he just wanted to get away.

The cafe was an old-fashioned, wood-panelled place with a plate glass panoramic window onto the street. It smelt of coffee and cigarettes. They ordered a couple of coffees. John chose a seat in the corner away from the window but with a good view of the place.

Naz looked at him and smiled. 'Bit of a coincidence, eh, John?'

John smiled queasily, scanning the street for the suntanned man, but he seemed to have disappeared. 'Bet you're wondering what I'm doing here, eh?'

'Er yes.'

Naz laughed. 'Boozy works outing. Caught the ferry from Hull last night, going back in a couple of days. We're all staying at the King George Hotel.' John nodded. Naz's face lit up as an idea occurred to him. 'Fancy meeting up later?'

Grateful for a way out, John nodded. 'Fine. How about eight?'

'Lot of changes since your day; not many of the old faces left, just me and Clemmy.'

'Clemmy? She isn't here?'

Naz shook his head. 'Booze cruises aren't her thing.'

'Arthur?' John asked

'They split up years ago. I'll tell Clemmy you were asking after her,' Naz said with a wink. 'We're good mates these days.'

It was strange to think of Naz and Clemmy as friends after so long. Clemmy, the scar from his old life before Gladio that he still felt bad about. Naz leant forward, about to vouchsafe something else but a sudden, violent gust of wind blew the door open. It swung back and hit the wooden panelling with a bang like a pistol shot causing John to flinch and crouch. The barman shrugged apologetically before shutting the door again.

Naz looked at John. 'What happened when you left, we all felt really bad about that.'

'It was a long time ago.'

There was a beat and through the window he saw the lumbering figure of the man Jess had shot approaching the cafe. He got up to go but Naz put a hand on his arm. 'So what is it, John? A bet or a joke?' The man with his arm in a sling stopped outside the café and examined the menu. 'Well?'

John looked at Naz. 'What?'

Naz grinned. 'The blazer and the regimental tie. Not exactly your style is it? It wasn't anyway.' John looked at the man outside, felt the weight of his old friend's hand on his arm and sat down again.

When John got back to the flat, Jess was agitated. So was he. She didn't ask how he'd got on but kept looking at the door as if she was expecting someone.

'Anything wrong?' he asked. She shook her head without conviction. 'Don't you want to know how it went?'

'How did it go?'

'Fine.' He went into the bedroom. A suitcase was open on the bed, full of clothes. 'What's this? Running out on me again?'

'We've got to get out, John.'

'Why, Jess?'

'It won't work. It can't.' They stared at each other for a moment.

He took off his blazer and tie and laid them carefully down on the bed.

'There's something you need to know,' she said, the lilt of her accent returning in the rhythm of the sentence. 'Something I haven't told you. The plan to steal the money, it's Gimlet's plan; his escape route.'

He stared at a fine crack on the ceiling and heard the lift doors opening somewhere in the building. Silence returned but it seemed to acquire a low hiss. She sat on the bed and looked down at her hands open on her knees and began to speak in a low monotone.

'I had an affair with Gimlet. It's not something I'm proud of but...' she paused. 'I met him again at a party in London about six years ago. I could see he was interested. It seemed too good an opportunity to pass up so I let him think I reciprocated.' She broke off for a moment as if stumbling over something, then went on. 'It was a difficult time in my life. I was lonely and he was charming, confident.' She stopped again before adding in a tiny voice, 'It was confusing.' She lifted a hand and examined it absently. John said nothing. 'At first I thought, I'll target him. Everyone else had lost interest in Gladio and I still had this idea. After Dublin, I lost it for a bit, you know. I was upset about you, my dad, Maria. Took me a while to sort myself out. I taught English here and there, a bit of Tai Chi. Worked for the British as a freelancer. That's how I got into banking. Then I met Gimlet again.' Again he didn't respond. She sighed. 'He was my handler in Northern Ireland, in the beginning. It was his idea to use you, and me. I went along with it. I thought if it went well, I might at least have a comfortable old age. I thought I might finally get back at them but I was lost. Being undercover was all I knew. He and I had that in common. He was the only one who knew what I'd been through.' She looked up at him. 'I lied to you, John. Right from the start. All lies.'

'And now?' he responded.

'I met you again,' she replied simply. 'Dublin was great but it was a long time ago and I didn't think I'd feel like this again.' She stood and played with her hair.

'How do I know you're telling the truth?'

'You don't.'

'Were you going to tell me, Jess?'

'I thought you'd be so angry that you'd just walk away. I didn't want that on my conscience and...'

'What?'

'I'd put so much effort into the plan, I didn't want to give up on it, John.'

'So?'

'I thought we could go through with Gimlet's plan but take the money for ourselves.'

A ship hooted on the river, a distant mournful sound.

'Why can't we do that?' His voice was quieter now.

'Pieter Swemmer's coming back,' she answered.

'When? When's he coming back?'

'Tomorrow, Friday maybe.'

He went and sat on the balcony. The rain had stopped and blackbirds hailed one another energetically. At last, the story had the stench of truth. Right from the start, he'd been the target. He hadn't asked how she knew Swemmer was coming back; Gimlet had told her. He wondered if there was anything else. On the other hand, he hadn't mentioned his meeting with Naz. For once he had a card up his sleeve, if you could call it that. She came and joined him.

'Are you angry, John?'

'No.' He wasn't. He was churned up and annoyed but now, finally, he felt a kind of completion. All the parts of his story came back together and made sense.

She brushed his arm with her hand. 'Thanks.'

'When you were at Menwith Hill? Was Gimlet your handler then?'

'Yes.'

'So you were working for him when he was with Gladio?' he asked.

'He told me he was infiltrating Gladio. He's clever, very persuasive. After Dublin, I realised I'd been played.'

'Yet you had an affair with him?

'I thought I could play him for a change.'

'So what now, Jess? Any ideas?'

'We run.'

'Where to?'

'We'll find somewhere to hide. I'm good at that.'

He looked at the tiny apartment. The idea of living in a procession of temporary bolt-holes for the rest of his life didn't appeal, not after he'd worked so hard at putting it behind him. 'Let's do it anyway. Let's rob the bank like you planned.'

'Swemmer's coming back!' she protested.

'We'll do it exactly as planned except a day early.'

'Tomorrow? That's much more dangerous.'

'Of course it's fucking dangerous but we might have a chance at laying a glove on them and surviving. If we do nothing, we've no chance, Jess.'

'What if Swemmer comes tomorrow?'

'You'll have to make sure he doesn't, won't you?' She stared at him. 'Contact Gimlet – you must have a way?' She nodded. 'Tell him it's my idea, I've insisted. Blame it on my idealism. That's what the whole scheme was based on anyway, that and my gullibility.' She came over and kissed his cheek. 'It's all right Jess. I'm OK.'

'I thought you didn't believe in the plan, it's the old way of doing things?'

'That was before. Anyway, you're right, it makes sense of our lives.'

'Gimlet will be waiting for us, John.'

'We aren't going to Indonesia.' Her mouth began to form the inevitable question. 'We're going back to Liguria, to my place.'

'They'll find us.'

'What difference does it make? It's mine and I want to go back there. If they come after us, at least it'll be on my patch.'

The payphone was round the corner. At ten pm UK time,

Jess dialled Gimlet while John waited. She had a brief animated conversation, then turned and shrugged.

'Well?' John asked.

'He wasn't pleased.'

'He wouldn't be.'

They walked back to the apartment. Later they sat on the balcony for the last time and listened to the city. They knew what they were going to do and it was clear. The odds were against them and they didn't contemplate the future aloud but both of them engaged in private speculation. In bed, Jess wanted to talk.

'I'm sorry,' she whispered again.

'If you hadn't had the plan, I wouldn't have had this chance to sort things out.'

She smiled and kissed him. ' And we would have seen each other again.' Surrendering to his feelings for her felt like redemption.

'If it doesn't work out,' she began.

'Don't think about it.' And then they were embracing. Afterwards, Jess fell asleep but John lay awake into the small hours, his mind running and re-running over the plans.

CHAPTER NINE

At seven next morning John walked Jess to the railway station to catch the train to Schiphol Airport. He was dressed casually for once but she was wearing an expensive linen suit, reminiscent of the one she'd worn when she appeared in San Romolo. He stood by while she bought her ticket. They walked down the crowded platform and waited for her train together. They chatted but he couldn't help checking the other people waiting. Nearby, three excited students from somewhere in south-east Asia stood guard over their huge suitcases. A businessman, overdressed and sweating in the summer heat, stood on the other side. A man in a leather jacket smoked impatiently, like a nervous assassin. John found himself inventing convoluted back-stories for everyone nearby until the arrival of the train put him out of his misery.

'Good luck,' he said and held her tight. 'I'll see you the day after tomorrow.'

She kissed him gently on the lips and climbed onto the train. 'I'll be there,' and then she was gone. He waited until the train began to move, then turned and walked away without looking back.

As John was escorting Jess to the station, Jules switched off his alarm, dragged himself into the shower and regretted the last few beers he'd swilled the night before. He'd got drunk because he was broke. He'd earned a lot of commission in the last few months but the money had reawakened his optimism and with it the habits of largesse and excess. Now he was broke again and a month behind in his payments to his ex-wife. He caught sight of himself in the mirror and grimaced. He was putting on weight again; he always did when he was worried. He made a mental

265

note to begin a new regime at the gym as he shaved hurriedly, worried about being late. Then he remembered: the old man was away and the bank always had a more relaxed atmosphere in his absence. On the other hand, if the rain continued, he might come back early and turn up unannounced. He'd done so before. It had the effect of keeping the staff on their toes. Jules sighed and began to hurry again.

Four and half hours after leaving John, Jess landed in Nice and showed a Canadian passport to the immigration police. It was in the name of Claire Roberts, the identity she'd adopted while working for the bank in Monte Carlo. While at the airport, she purchased one-way tickets from Nice to Paris and from Paris to Jakarta using an American passport in the name of Kate Delaney. Then she went outside and caught the shuttle bus to Monte Carlo. By one fifteen, she was having a light lunch in a harbour restaurant crammed with tourists. Nobody paid her any attention.

John spent the morning in the apartment waiting for the drama to begin and trying to contain the crippling doubt and apprehension that threatened to overwhelm him. Supposing it was a trap, that Jess had lied right to the end? It didn't seem reasonable but he couldn't be certain. His hand was shaking so much that he cut himself shaving and spent what seemed like an age cursing and staunching the flow. It was after two when he began to dress in his Gimlet uniform. As he knotted the regimental tie around his brilliant white collar, Jess slipped from the restaurant and climbed up from the harbour keeping to back streets and alleys. The heat of the mid-afternoon left the old part of town quiet and empty. The older buildings, their ancient green shutters closed against the heat of the day, crowded together creating an oasis of shade and, for those that wanted it, anonymity. The door of the bank where Jess had worked for the previous four months was considerably less ostentatious than the Dutch merchant bank. The BBK Credit Mutuel craved anonymity and only the smallest nameplate advertised its presence. After a final check, Jess darted into a side door and stood in the security cage while the door behind locked. She punched in her personal code and the light by the electronic door in front flashed green as the lock clicked open. It was two-thirty; so far so good.

At the exact same time, John regarded the clothes and documents of Jack Braddock, which he would use later. Then he stood to attention and checked his appearance in the mirror. The sight of his brilliantined hair still took him by surprise. The shaving cut was subsiding. Outside the sky was leaden and grey, the clouds moving east with a relentless energy heralding more rain. He cursed to himself. He'd planned to calm his nerves by walking but he didn't want to arrive at the bank looking like a drowned rat. In the end, he watched TV for an hour, standing behind the chair so as not to crease his trousers. At three forty-five, he put on his blazer, rechecked his appearance, collected his documents and let himself out of the flat.

Jules was in the throne room trying his father's chair for size when one of the secretaries walked in. Embarrassed, Jules blushed and blustered some excuse but the look of concern on the young woman's face alerted him.

'The same account?' She nodded and he blurted out, 'but it's Thursday!' The secretary shrugged and he regretted drawing attention to the transaction and himself. Jules followed her downstairs. Sitting at his computer he saw the reason for her concern: they were transferring fifty-one million euros, and on a Thursday. Jules' pulse raced as he calculated that his commission might be one and a half million euros. The dealing room was quiet but there were a couple of senior executives working at their consoles. Jules typed the acknowledgement and checked his watch: twelve minutes past four. A bead of sweat formed on his brow as the details printed off and he took them over to the checker. The destination was different, the Cayman Islands instead of the British Virgin Islands but the authorisation was in order. The change in destination didn't bother him. Given what he knew about the account holders, it was a sensible strategy to use several destinations. What did concern him was that by rights, he should check the transaction with his father but that meant risking the commission. On the other hand, not checking could mean risking his future at the bank. He agonised over the decision. It was up to him. His father had given him carte blanche but this was a larger sum and it was a Thursday. Fishing his mobile from his pocket, he stared at the computer screen trying to divine the truth as he selected his father's number. He was about to call when a secretary from reception buzzed him.

'Yes?'

'Sir Jeremy Gimlet in reception.'

'Impossible,' he replied without thinking. The receptionist was highly experienced and didn't make mistakes, and within the micro-world of the bank she wielded enormous power. She saw who came and went and on occasion, overheard conversations. In the enduring struggle for supremacy among the younger executives, this information could be very useful. It was not a good idea to upset her. Jules tried to recover himself. 'Are you sure?'

'Quite,' she replied tartly.

'I'll come down.' Leaving the checker and the transaction on hold, he hurried down to the reception area where a tall, well-dressed man with a military bearing was waiting.

The rain, which had threatened all day, had held off allowing John to walk to the bank. The result was that he was feeling in control of himself as he marched along the quiet cobbled street by the canal. He stopped outside the bank, then walked up the four steps to the understated but massive front door and pushed it open. The receptionist looked him up and down, then released the security door into the small, silent lobby. Two original Dutch masters hung on opposite walls, one showing 'The Massacre of the Innocents', the other, rather wittily for a bank John thought, 'Jesus throwing the moneychangers out of the temple'. The door opened and Jules Swemmer appeared. John handed him his passport.

'Sorry to barge in unannounced, but needs must,' he blustered in his establishment accent, immediately regretting his apology. He hoped his flat northern vowels didn't slip into his speech under the radar but maybe the Dutch wouldn't notice such subtlety. Jules examined his passport and handed it back with a frown.

'I thought you were in London with my father?'

'I'll be back there tonight.'

'Why have you come here?' Jules was worried about losing his commission on the trade upstairs.

'Security.' This time John sounded more clipped and authoritative. Beneath his beautifully cut trousers, his legs were shaking. 'I'm making a withdrawal.'

'How much?'

'All of it.' He handed the letter of entitlement to Jules with a flourish. Jules examined the letter with a mixture of incredulity and excitement. It was an authorisation on bank notepaper signed by his father, which informed bank employees that the bearer of the letter was to be given the contents of vault number one, the old vault. Puzzled and excited, Jules looked up. 'You wish to enter the vault?'

'To collect what's mine, that's all.' John fixed a neutral, unemotional look on his face, an expression born of authority and expectation. Sweating profusely, a corner of his shirt adrift from his trousers, Jules looked back at John nervously, excited at being accepted into the inner circle but unsure what to do.

'Why now?'

John didn't like this questioning. 'Look, you know who I am. I want my money,' he snapped like an officer giving an order.

'I must phone my father.'

'Not a good idea.' Jules glanced at John, his eyes narrowing. 'Call him if you must but I don't think he'll be too pleased. It's bad form for mobile phones to ring during a match on Centre Court.' Outside, it had started to rain again. John prayed it was fine in London.

Jules considered. His father hated being disturbed at any time but more than that, he hated being the centre of attention. Then again, he had given Jules free reign in his absence. At that moment the checker, a neurotic young man, appeared looking harassed and worried. He hovered animatedly until Jules turned to him. The checker spoke quickly in Dutch. 'The transfer to the Cayman Islands, they're waiting for confirmation.'

Jules looked at John and back at the checker and tried to think. His old mantra came into his head. All business is a risk. The trick is seeing an opportunity and exploiting it when it appears. He nodded. 'OK,' he replied in Dutch. 'Accept the trade.'

'You're sure?' the checker asked.

Angry at the implied criticism, Jules snapped, 'I'm sure!' The checker recoiled, turned and hurried away. Jules tucked his shirt back into his trousers, stood up straight and nodded. Then he led John to the back of the building.

The door to the cellar was accessed by a security code, which Jules punched in. He pulled open the heavy oak door and a draft of cold dank air hit him just as it had thirty years earlier when his uncle Jan had led him down here. A light came on automatically, illuminating the seventeenth century lattice of irregular small red bricks that glistened with age and mildew. Years before, when Jules first joined the bank and his father had high hopes of his son, Pieter had explained that access to the vault itself required two passwords. In the intervening years, as disappointment increased the distance between father and son, Pieter had not seen fit to mention it again. They approached the great steel bulk of the vault and, just as he had as a boy, Jules imagined the black ooze of the canal centimetres away on the other side. The thought still disturbed him. His pulse was racing at the thought of seeing the gold again. With a start, he wondered how on earth Sir Jeremy would carry it away. The memory of the weight of one small bar had stayed with him and although he was bigger and stronger, it was obvious that without proper transportation, it would be impossible to move more than a few of the bars.

They stopped in front of the vault. On the right of the door was an electronic keypad. Jules punched in the bank's first password, his grandmother's birthday. He stood back and gestured to John. 'Now you.'

John's mouth emptied of moisture as if touched by a wand. He didn't know any codes. Nervous he smiled grimly, and then stopped himself. 'You enter both codes,' he ordered.

Jules looked at him for a moment, then smiled unpleasantly. 'Of course.' He punched in the second code, adding, 'if it's been changed, you'll have to come back tomorrow.' His Dutch accent gave the words a harsh and unsympathetic tone, but the code was accepted. After an interminable pause, the display flashed green and the multiple locks of the great door opened with a bang. Jules beamed, swinging the great door open. In the gloom, the vault appeared empty until he switched on the light but the sight, which assailed his eyes, was unreal. Instead of gleaming gold bars piled to the ceiling, the vault was empty apart from an airport suitcase, standing on its wheels, the handle extended and sticking up like a trombone. Jules gulped in surprise as John marched in and wheeled the suitcase out, hurrying towards the steps. His instinct was to grab the case and run from the bank but he forced himself to walk. Astonished, Jules examined the vault again and watched John as he picked up the case and began to manhandle it up the stairs. The case was heavy but not unduly so. Jules watched for a moment, then hurried after him.

'There is no gold?' Jules asked as they left the damp, cool air of the cellar. John didn't bother to answer. He wanted to be out of there. He walked towards the front door wheeling the case behind him but Jules caught him up and barred his way. 'Where is the gold?'

'Too bulky. It was converted some years ago for ease of transportation,' John replied and hurried past.

Jess had explained that the money was now in unnumbered blue chip share certificates and high value bearer bonds. John was surprised that a few pieces of paper that were worth so much and virtually untraceable, could be concealed in a piece of luggage.

Jules wasn't placated. 'Why wasn't I told?'

Now it was John's turn to sweat. Jules had bought the subterfuge, his impersonation, the documents and not phoning his father but now he was getting upset because his father hadn't told him about the gold. 'You'd better take that up with Pieter. Now if that's everything, I've got a plane to catch back to London.' It was his last card. If Jules cut up rough now, all bets were off. Jules thought about it for a moment, then nodded and stepped aside, opening the security door and the front door for him. Outside it had started to rain heavily, the raindrops bouncing high off the pavement. Jules looked at him.

'Wait inside, I'll call you a cab,' but John's nerve had gone. He grabbed the door from Jules and pulled it open, saying,

'It's OK, I've got one waiting at the end of the street.' A look of concern appeared on Jules face as John pushed past and leapt down the four steps to the cobbles. John hurried up the street, the wheels of his case rumbling ominously behind him like an omen. He didn't look back but after thirty yards, he dodged into a doorway and stood there cursing the rain and trying to recover his composure. His hand grasped the handle of the case so tightly that his knuckles were white. So far so good. He'd got away with it. He left the doorway and hurried towards the main road that crossed the canal. It was four forty-seven.

CHAPTER TEN

In Monaco, Jess completed her trade and logged off her computer. Then she quietly left her desk, leaving her jacket over her chair as if she were just going to the loo and slipped down the fire stairs and out of the emergency door into the street. The heat of the day was starting to ease, giving way to the languorous Mediterranean evening. It had gone like clockwork but now she worried about John. A wave of light-headedness overtook her and she had to stop for a moment, leaning against a wall. She took hold of herself, glanced casually around to check that she wasn't being followed and began to make her way upwards away from the harbour.

In Amsterdam, the rain was easing which was a good sign. John walked towards the station then turned towards the red-light district. He found the side street he was looking for and walked down it until he came to the burnt-out shop with the slogan on the wall next door. He checked no one was looking, pushed open the charred door and pulled the case inside. The room was charred and stank of burning and decay. The floor was covered in ashes. He moved some debris to one side with his foot to clear a space and opened the case. One billion euros didn't look like much: a few bundles of papers held together with elastic bands. He transferred some into the lid, took out his cigarette lighter then thought better of it. Turning round, he took a plastic jerry can from the corner and began to pour petrol over the paper bundles. He didn't hear or see anything.

'That's a damn stupid idea.' The voice stopped him dead. It was clipped, authoritative and familiar somehow. John saw the gun first, the black nozzle of the automatic pointing at him and cursed his stupidity. He hadn't heard any footsteps but then he hadn't checked and double-checked. The relief of getting away from the bank with the case had made him careless. What a bloody fool he was. The voice came again.

'Put the container down. Slowly.'

John did as he was told and stood up straight. Unlike Naz, Gimlet had lost weight over the years. There was grey around the temples and his nose was pinched as if he'd spent too much time squinting in bright light, but it was him. He was wearing a light summer suit, cream shirt fashionably open at the neck.

'Wimbledon rained off?' John asked lightly.

'Shut up and give me the case.'

John had no room for manoeuvre. If he did nothing, he'd be very dead very soon. He nodded toward the case at his feet and gambled. 'Petrol dissolves the watermarks, you know. All those bundles, worthless now.'

Gimlet couldn't help himself. The paper bundles were what he had risked so much for. Even if just for a moment, he had to look down at the case and that was when John flicked his lighter that he still held in the palm of his right hand. He held the flame ostentatiously above the suitcase. Gimlet stared, his face twisted and intense. John smiled. 'It's a Zippo, petrol, bought it this morning,' he explained. 'It'll burn for as long as the fuel holds out. If you shoot me, I'll drop it.'

'You stupid fool.'

His mouth dry, his heart racing as he stared at the nozzle pointed at his midriff, John found himself rambling. He had the idea that as long as he talked, he would stay alive. 'Burning the money, I got the idea from the slogan on the wall outside: 'Fight the rich, not their wars'.'

'Still the sentimentalist.'

'It's more realistic that that. When you think about it, it's rather a good solution. I mean it fucks you doesn't it? Totally.' Gimlet said nothing. John took a breath and carried on. 'These bonds and certificates aren't plants or food or people or anything of real value. They're just bits of paper.'

'That you're going to die for,' Gimlet replied smoothly.

'What makes you think I won't drop the lighter?'

'You'll be dead as soon as you do.' Gimlet had called his bluff. He was prepared to wait until the lighter fuel ran out and the Zippo was starting to get hot. John carried on.

'Actually, we're in the same boat here. I mean, both on the run, desperate, playing the last card but there is one big difference between us.'

'I've got the gun,' Gimlet smiled.

John shook his head. 'You're still running. I've stopped.'

'That's ridiculous.'

'It isn't actually. When you stop, you realise that it doesn't matter where you go or how fast. You can run away from everything except yourself.' Gimlet's eyes paled for a moment then the focus snapped back.

'Sentimental rubbish.'

'Jess and I planned the whole thing.'

'That girl has a real gift for duplicity,' Gimlet murmured. 'Still, so have I.'

The Zippo was burning John's fingers and he didn't know how long the fuel would last. He had to keep going. 'What are you talking about?'

'Insurance, John.'

'You're at the end of your rope, Gimlet. You haven't got any insurance.'

Gimlet responded, 'When we located you in Italy, Jess was convinced she could persuade you to go with her. I wasn't so sure.'

A finger of fear stabbed inside as John struggled with the implications. 'You sent those thugs after us?'

Gimlet smiled. 'I thought you might need some encouragement.'

'What if they'd caught us?' John spluttered.

'Jess is very good at what she does,' Gimlet looked down at the suitcase. 'And here we are; you, me and the money.' Gimlet pointed the gun at John's head.

John braced himself for the inevitable. 'Yes, but this is our plan. Jess is with me now.'

'Jess is history.' The response was offhand and brutal but neither of them had time to consider it. Without warning the door was forcefully pushed open behind Gimlet, causing him to pitch forward and drop the gun as he fired it. John ducked, dropping the lighter in the process.

The report echoed and filled the small room so that afterwards, it seemed there was a moment when nothing happened. Then there was a whoosh as the petrol soaked bundles ignited in a column of flame and Gimlet was running out the back of the small room away up the stairs. John went after him. He heard someone call his name but it was too late.

All the pent-up anger of the last month and the last twenty years drove him on. It was his turn and he wanted his revenge. He went up the stairs two at a time. Above he could hear Gimlet's flying footsteps as he climbed up through the incinerated building. The banisters had burned away in places and there were gaps in the some of the charred stair treads but Gimlet's footsteps didn't stop until John arrived at the final floor.

From the last landing, he could see the open roof door and the sky beyond. Flattening himself against the wall John climbed the last few stairs and checked the roof space. He cursed himself for not picking up Gimlet's gun; there was a good chance he had another. John kicked the door back then eased himself out. The roof gave onto a small flat area that appeared deserted. On one side there was a sheer drop to the narrow street below but to the other, the landscape was of canted roofs, chimney pots and the occasional washing line. Beyond that he could just make out the glint of the river.

John heard a roar and half-turned to see Gimlet launch himself from a small ledge above the door. Something painful raked his shoulder and then he saw the blade in Gimlet's hand. John grabbed at the wrist holding the knife and missed, giving Gimlet the opportunity to stab him again, this time in his side. In desperation, John kicked as hard as he could and caught Gimlet a glancing blow on the left knee, jarring his dodgy hip. Gimlet swore and fell backwards. He was up in a moment, the knife in his hand. There was a popping noise and Gimlet fell backwards.

He struggled to his feet, looked at John with a mixture of anger and puzzlement, then he turned and holding his side, hobbled away across the rooftops. John went to follow but a hand took him by the shoulder and spun him round. John found himself looking into the face of the big man with his arm in a sling. Naz appeared at his side.

'Leave it, John,' Naz said gently, 'Yossi will take care of Gimlet.' John allowed himself to relax as Yossi took off across the rooftops. At his side, in his free hand, he had a gun with a silencer and, just as he had with John and Jess in the Alpine resort, Yossi took his time.

'Couldn't save the money,' Naz said. 'Fire took hold so quickly.' John remembered something Gimlet had said.

'Give me your mobile! Hurry!'

Naz fished in his pockets and handed over the phone. 'Did you hear me? The money's gone.' John dialled a number, made a mistake and dialled again.

'Come on. Answer, damn you,' he pleaded. As he listened, Yossi reappeared alone, shaking his head.

'What happened?' John asked.

'Jumped,' Yossi replied in a guttural accent John couldn't place.

'Into the street?' John asked.

'River.'

'That's it, then,' Naz replied. John nodded but he didn't take it in. Ear clamped to the mobile, he was desperately listening to the distant insistent ringing tone.

Jess had been walking for about five minutes when she became aware of the man following her. Around thirty, tanned with thick black hair, he walked purposefully behind her as if he was going somewhere. Without appearing to, she quickened her pace. The road ran along a contour of the hill but unlike other streets, it was not bisected by alleyways and walkways running up and down the hillside. She searched the street ahead and cursed her foolishness. Why had she come this way? It was empty of people, shops and escape routes. She hastened along but the man stayed resolutely behind her. Thirty metres ahead was an opening on the other side of the road. She crossed over and hurried towards it, but the man came after her. She darted into the opening intending to flee up the steps, only to find the alley blocked by scaffolding and a rubbish chute running down to a skip from the third floor. Cursing her luck, she turned round only to find the man smiling at her. She thought about trying to run past him but it was hopeless. As he came towards her, she consoled herself with the thought that at least she had stolen the money.

'Madame?' the young man began, but instead of attacking her, he asked the way to the casino. She stared at him, wondering if it was a trick. Tourist maps were plentiful after all but he repeated the question. She watched as he walked away her nerves still jangling. Normally she would have checked for a second follower but she was too preoccupied with the bank transfer. It was rank bad fieldcraft. The first she knew about the second man was when the knife entered her back. She never saw him or the glint of steel in his hand as he plunged it into her, expertly piercing her heart. She gasped, realising too late what had happened. The assassin held her for a moment as she folded, then laid her gently down on the steps before walking quickly away. As he walked away, the quiet of the afternoon was punctuated by the muffled ringing of a mobile phone coming from Jess's handbag. As the phone rang, the handbag was surrounded by a thick ribbon of blood which flowed past to mingle and congeal with the dust in the gutter.

John listened to the ringing tone for a long time until Naz took the phone from him and helped him back down the stairs. The pain from John's stab wounds mingled with the anguish he felt. Naz summoned an ambulance and went with him to a hospital where the young, articulate south Asian doctor explained in perfect English that he'd been very lucky. The blade had missed organs and arteries by a whisker. He would be kept in for a couple of days. They put him in a clean, quiet room with a vase full of carnations. Naz stayed with him until he fell asleep. There were no police and no questions and John wasn't surprised.

Naz's bumping into him hadn't been a coincidence. In the café, Naz had leant close and asked, 'Where is she?' John shook his head. 'Is she still calling herself Jess?'

'What do you want, Naz?'

'She's dangerous, John. People have habit of dying around her.' John got up to leave but the muscular guy with his arm in a sling was still out front and he sat down again. 'Gimlet's up to something, isn't he?' Naz asked quietly.

'Is he?'

Naz became animated. 'The wolves are circling. He's been under suspicion for a while. It's just a matter of time.'

John changed the subject. 'You were waiting for me?'

'When we heard you'd gone missing and she'd disappeared, we put two and two together.'

'The booze cruise?'

Naz nodded. 'Cover. There was one happening this week so I joined in.'

John's heart began a tango. His mouth was dry and he felt sick but he had to ask. 'And Jess?'

Naz sighed. 'She and Gimlet, they're an item, have been for a while.'

'You could be lying,' John said.

'But I'm not and you know I'm not.' John felt sick. At last, he had the truth in his nostrils. He'd worked it out; he just hadn't wanted to accept it.

'Was she with him twenty years ago?'

Naz shrugged. 'She was a British agent sent to infiltrate Gladio. They may have turned her.'

'Don't you know?'

'It makes sense. She survived when everyone else didn't,' Naz said.

'So did I.'

Naz nodded sadly. 'Maybe she had a soft spot for you.'

John struggled to stay in control. 'How do you know all this, Naz?'

'Jess told you she used to work for the British?' John nodded. 'Well, I used to work freelance myself,' Naz said quietly.

'For the British?'

'Israelis.'

'What?'

'They like to keep tabs on fascists, John.'

'When did you begin? When were you recruited?'

'Uganda, my Dad had a job at the airport in Kampala when the Entebbe raid took place. I helped them, told them stuff about the layout and they made sure Dad was OK. I was just a kid but being Asian, I was useful.'

'For Christ's sake. Were you working during the strike?'

Naz shook his head. 'I stopped being active when I went to the UK. I wanted to leave all that behind.'

'So what changed?'

'Brian.'

'And now?'

'I was sent here, to help.'

John looked at his old friend, the fat, balding middle-aged Asian who worked for a foreign government.

'You're working with him?' John asked, indicating the guy out front.' Naz nodded. 'I'm glad he's OK.'

Naz grinned. 'Not as much as he is.'

Naz leant forward again. 'So do you know what Gimlet's plan is?'

'I do now,' John said slowly. He told Naz about the headlong flight from Italy, the perilous journey north and the plan to steal the money.

Naz wasn't immediately convinced. 'He's taking a hell of a risk. What's to stop you walking away with the loot?'

'Jess,' John said simply, 'and me. He's gambling that I'll fall under her spell again; that and my ego. It worked before. Even if the big job fails, it'll create a diversion and he'll have fifty million in loose change.'

Naz looked round the café. It was empty apart from the bartender carefully drying glasses. 'What do you want to do, John?'

'I don't know.' He paused, then added, 'there's a complication. I like her... ' Naz began to object, 'I think she feels the same.'

'How can you be sure?'

'I can't.'

'That's shit, John.'

'Isn't it?'

John was released from hospital a couple of days later. Naz brought him some clothes from the flat. Doctors and nurses repeated their assertion that he'd been very lucky but he didn't feel it. He kept asking for news about Jess. Naz had stalled before but this time he told John the truth.

'A party of Japanese tourists found her,' he explained. 'Police think it's a mugging gone wrong. Local media's in overdrive, you know.'

'Did she suffer?' John asked.

Naz shook his head. 'It was quick.' John wondered why Naz was still agitated and avoiding his gaze.

'What? Is there something else?' Naz looked at his feet and shook his head but John insisted. 'Tell me, I have a right to know.'

'She was running out on you.'

'How d'you know?'

'They found two airline tickets in her bag. Singles to Paris and Jakarta.'

'OK,' John replied struggling to keep his face impassive. Afterwards, they took a cab to the station. Like Jess previously, he was taking the train to Schiphol and then a flight to Nice. After they paid the cabby, they turned and faced one another.

'Any news of Gimlet?' John asked.

Naz shook his head. 'Nothing found in the river. Mind, the currents are lethal. People can disappear for months. Sometimes they're never found.' They said nothing for a moment, each alone with their thoughts. Naz put his hand on John's arm. 'Are you sure about going back to Liguria?'

'Italy is my home now,' John said placing his own hand on top of Naz's.

They smiled at each other, friends again. After a moment, Naz fished out a business card and handed it to John. 'Good luck then. If you're ever in Leeds, look me up. I mean it.'

'Same to you, Naz, if you're ever in Liguria.' Naz nodded. They shook hands. John watched Naz walk away before turning and walking into the station.

EPILOGUE – Italy 2005

It was all there, as if he'd just been away for a couple of days. John didn't know what to expect. He'd thought his little house might be damaged, ransacked, looted, but it was fine. A couple of roof tiles had fallen off in a storm, mice had eaten most of his stores and the terraces were in dire need of weeding but the olives were fattening and the water tank was full. Even his Land Rover was still parked in the bend where he'd left it. The tyres were slashed but it hadn't been vandalised. No one was waiting for him, no one arrested him; there were no police sirens careering up the hill. It was quiet, calm and beautiful, just as he remembered. He walked his land, pulling up the occasional weed by hand, smelling the wild herbs, not quite believing it was real. The apricot tree was covered with fruit and he tried a fig. It wasn't ripe but it still tasted delicious. That evening, he opened a bottle, put on a Dylan tape and sprawled in his sun-lounger again.

Had it only have been a month? It felt like a million years. In that brief time, his former life had been decanted, sieved, distilled, refracted, bottled, emptied and shaken up again. He was different; everything was different except these familiar hills, this hidden Eden. He'd used the Jack Braddock passport Jess had made to travel back. Then he destroyed it. It felt good being back but he missed Jess and he agonised over what had happened, wondering if it could have been any different. Being back on his land helped. The steep green hills were where he belonged. When he'd bought the place, he'd still been looking over his shoulder but that had changed. He'd stopped running. It wasn't that he didn't fear the future; he knew someone might come for him and probably would at some point, but he'd made his stand and at some deep level he was content to let the cards fall. If they came, so be it. Until then he would enjoy what he had.

In the days that followed, he strimmed his terraces, fixed the roof tiles, bought new tyres for the Land Rover and acquired a small generator. Guiseppe's terraces were overgrown and he ran the strimmer over them but was puzzled by the lack of an investigation. When John went to his local bar, Silvano explained that Guiseppe had died under his olive trees, a stroke apparently but he'd been in the place he loved most. He'd been lonely since his wife died but John's arrival had changed things. The respect he'd shown towards the old man and his renovation of the oliveta had made Guiseppe very happy.

'E la Vespa?' John asked lightly, remembering his wobbly flight to Ventimiglia on Guiseppe's ageing scooter.

Silvano shrugged. 'Bambini della città ,' he said. 'Kids from the city.' John nodded. And that was that. He was back.

After a month, he'd received a parcel from the UK. There was no acknowledgement but Jess's handbag and a few other things were inside including a photograph he hadn't seen before. It was summer, taken in Monaco judging by the background, and she looked happy. It must have been taken just before she reappeared. He stared at the photograph for a long time before he examined the rest of the bag. There wasn't much, her phone, a lipstick, purse and the two plane tickets. He picked them up and something detached itself and fell on the floor. He picked it up and peered at it. It was a railway ticket from Monte Carlo to Ventimiglia. The date stamp was the day she'd arrived back in Monte Carlo, the day she was killed. Once more his insides gyrated as he plundered the implications. She wasn't running out on him, she was going to join him just as they planned. Why else buy the train ticket? Buying the airline tickets was always part of the plan. If anyone were shadowing her, buying the plane tickets would throw them off the scent. That was the only possible explanation and yet he couldn't be certain. Sometimes, he'd feel sure and happy because he'd been right and at others, the doubt would return to torment him. Even if he and Jess had

284

got away together, Maria would always have been between them. He put Jess's documents in the same plastic bag that he kept the single share certificate he'd liberated from the suitcase in Amsterdam. It had been her idea, an investment for the future and he'd agreed but now he was back, he wasn't sure he'd ever redeem it. The plastic bag contained all his tangible memories of her. He put it back in its hiding place, behind a loose stone in a hole in the wall

As the weeks passed into months, he had good days and bad days. He slept fitfully, haunted by flashbacks. Sometimes he would wake with a start in the darkness of the night, sweating and gripped with terror. Then he would lie back staring at the ceiling and wait for the solace of dawn. Winter, when the nights were long and the days damp and gloomy, got to him. The site of the stab wound in his side ached and his mind turned to Jess. There had been something important between them and it hadn't all been an act. She had cared for him but she'd been under Gimlet's spell just as John was under hers and for the same reasons. Gimlet was the only one who understood what she'd been through, just as Jess was the only one who knew what John had suffered. She'd had this incredible talent for deep cover work and it had nearly taken her over. When she tried to escape, it was too late.

Deception always leads back to darkness and the past. There's always one more treachery before paradise can be regained. He and Jess had so nearly succeeded, and sometimes he crucified himself fantasising about the life they would have had if they'd run away as she'd suggested. On wet, gloomy days, the past always reclaimed him. Then he would lounge about ruminating unhealthily while Dylan wailed in the background but there was always something to be done and activity usually brought him out of it. The dog helped.

John bought the dog from a peddler in Ventimiglia, a floppy, brown Labrador puppy who fussed over him ridiculously and followed him round as he worked. Guard dog and friend, he'd called him Dillon after Kevin, a macabre private joke. In his quiet moments, John couldn't shake the feeling that there were still a couple of columns that hadn't been totted up but the first new growth and early flowers marking the beginning of spring lifted his spirits. Occasional warm days anticipated the searing heat to come and he began to allow himself to think it might finally be over.

Silvano told him first. It was a glorious day and John was enjoying a quiet beer, Dillon and his shopping at his feet, when the innkeeper came over. He looked round furtively, then said, 'Signor John, someone has been asking for you.'

John's pulse quickened as the familiar clenching in his innards began. 'Who?'

Silvano shrugged. 'A man.'

'How many? Uno, due?'

'One, I think,' he said and nodded. 'Sì.' John frowned. So it was starting again. It was a shock. He knew it could happen at any time but he'd allowed himself the luxury of hope. Silvano didn't know what had happened to John after the woman had appeared but he sensed he was troubled and had a need for isolation. Like the rest of the village, he respected the careful work John had done on the oliveta, taking the time to learn the old ways of doing things from Guiseppe. Even if he hadn't said so out loud, Silvano's instinct was protective. So was John's. The last thing he wanted was for anyone else to be hurt because of him.

He turned and looked at Silvano head on. 'If he asks where I am, tell him,' he said deliberately in Italian and then again in English. Silvano looked concerned. 'Non è problema,' John added slowly. 'Tell him.'

Silvano sighed and nodded, then turned back. 'Is strange,' he said quietly.

John looked. 'What?'

'He walk into the village. He has no car.'

John shrugged. It made no difference. He shook Silvano's hand warmly. 'Grazie Silvano, grazie tanto.' Silvano looked at John's hand in his and frowned. He patted John on the shoulder and walked back into the bar. John sipped his beer thoughtfully.

It was dusk when Dillon started barking. John was just washing up after dinner when he heard the commotion. At first he thought it was cinghiali again. If there were any wild boar within half a mile, the dog went mad, growling and barking, baring its teeth. Then the noise stopped. John came out of the kitchen to find Dillon playing with a stranger. John was nettled by the dog's behaviour; fat lot of good he was as a guard dog. John watched for a moment, his heart racing then scuffed his boot against a rock. The man looked up. He was tall and angular, early twenties, with a mop of unkempt hair and a rucksack. There was something familiar about him but John couldn't say what.

'Dillon, come here,' John said firmly. The puppy looked at him reproachfully but moved away.

'After Bob?' the young man looked round. He was English. 'I heard you were a fan.'

John shook his head, 'No. What do you want?'

The newcomer was suddenly unconfident. He cleared his throat nervously. 'You are John Bradley?' John nodded but didn't speak. 'I'm Nick,' he said uncertainly. 'My mother said I should look you up.'

John was confused. 'Your mother?' he repeated stupidly.

The boy nodded. 'Nick Clements. My mother was... well I think you knew her?'

'Er yes,' John muttered, his mind in turmoil.

'The thing is, I've got some questions.'

'Right... erm... you'd better have a seat. I'll put the kettle on.'

The boy nodded. Dillon wagged his tail hopefully.

THE END

APPENDIX

In 1982, a part-time builder called Barry Prudhom killed a policeman near the American secret listening-base at Menwith Hill, Yorkshire. Prudhom fled until he was cornered in the village of Malton where he killed two more policemen and a number of other individuals. For nine days he held the small town hostage.

Much was made in the press of his membership of a territorial SAS unit – his ruthlessness and his ability to find cover and live off the land.

News was strictly controlled. After nine days, an unmarked helicopter landed carrying three men in balaclavas and black fatigues. The press speculated that one was the man who trained Prudhom and/or the other three members of his SAS unit. Whoever it was, Prudhom was discovered lying under a tarpaulin and dispatched with a number of shots to the head. The unmarked helicopter and the men in black left, leaving many questions behind.

What was Prudhom doing at Menwith Hill? Why did he kill the policeman? What was the importance of his SAS unit? Later, witnesses said that the masked men all had Ulster accents. What was the connection with Northern Ireland?

Two years later, during the miners' strike, another member of Prudhom's territorial SAS unit killed two policemen in Leeds, was cornered and shot himself. On finding his body, the police discovered hi-tech radio equipment and state-of-the-art weaponry.

No satisfactory explanation has ever been given for these events.